Angela felt her ears burning and her blood boiling. How dare Harry accuse her of infidelity when he had acted in so outrageous a manner with the stunning Matilda?

"You forget, tradesmen's daughters have honor, too, strange as that may seem to you," she said. "I have every right to expect you to believe me when I deny any impropriety."

"And if I don't?" Harry demanded harshly.

"Then I dare you to find out for yourself, my lord," she said, her voice clear and cool despite her wildly pounding heart. Her hands dropped, as if of their own accord, to the knot of her sash and rested there in mute invitation.

"Here and now?" Harry asked.

"Yes, my lord," she replied, stepping into the abyss from which there was no return. "Here and now."

Lord Harry's Angel

by
Patricia Oliver

Ⓞ
A SIGNET BOOK

SIGNET
Published by the Penguin Group
Penguin Books USA Inc., 375 Hudson Street,
New York, New York 10014, U.S.A.
Penguin Books Ltd, 27 Wrights Lane,
London W8 5TZ, England
Penguin Books Australia Ltd, Ringwood,
Victoria, Australia
Penguin Books Canada Ltd, 10 Alcorn Avenue,
Toronto, Ontario, Canada M4V 3B2
Penguin Books (N.Z.) Ltd, 182-190 Wairau Road,
Auckland 10, New Zealand

Penguin Books Ltd, Registered Offices:
Harmondsworth, Middlesex, England

First published by Signet,
an imprint of New American Library,
a division of Penguin Books USA Inc.

First Printing, April, 1993
10 9 8 7 6 5 4 3 2 1

 REGISTERED TRADEMARK—MARCA REGISTRADA

Printed in the United States of America

BOOKS ARE AVAILABLE AT QUANTITY DISCOUNTS WHEN USED TO PROMOTE PRODUCTS OR
SERVICES. FOR INFORMATION PLEASE WRITE TO PREMIUM MARKETING DIVISION, PENGUIN
BOOKS USA INC., 375 HUDSON STREET, NEW YORK, NEW YORK 10014.

Prologue

Mr. John Hamilton, solicitor and man of business to the earls of Castleton for the past forty-odd years—as his father had been before him—glanced across his cluttered oaken desk at the harsh, sunburned face of the present earl and sighed.

"It is a sad day indeed in the history of your illustrious family, my lord, when the Davenports are brought this low. To be struck down, as your esteemed brother was, in the prime of manhood, so soon after your poor father went to his reward, was a stroke of the direst misfortune."

"Not nearly soon enough for either of them, it would seem," came the curt reply.

The austere solicitor blinked, not quite sure he had heard aright. "You surely do not mean that, my lord," he said gently.

The sixth earl of Castleton gave a harsh laugh which had not a shred of humor in it. "Do you really expect me to mourn for a drunken fool who had no more sense than to gamble away his entire inheritance?" The contempt in his voice was icy. "What was left of it, I should say. From what you have told me, Hamilton, my father was no better, and left the estate so heavily mortgaged that there is no hope of raising another penny on it, I presume?"

"Unfortunately, that is true, my lord." Hamilton laced his thick-jointed fingers together under his chin, and gazed mournfully at the young man sitting opposite him. The sixth earl had been a rather pleasant surprise to the old man. If circumstances had been different, he would have rejoiced at the sight of this almost eerie likeness Major Harry Davenport bore to the third earl, his grandfather.

He had been a very young man at the time, of course, but Hamilton still remembered vividly the striking presence of

Black Harry, as the third earl had been called. The square jaw in an otherwise lean, aristocratic face; the unexpectedly deep blue eyes contrasting with the unruly shock of black curls that had taken their toll of hearts at the *ton* gatherings Black Harry had graced with his presence. Or so the rumors went, which had filtered down to the City offices of Hamilton and Hamilton, Solicitors. Even in those early days, the third earl had refused to wear a powdered wig and had flaunted his black head defiantly. His grandson showed every sign of possessing that same defiance and strength of character.

For a moment it seemed to Hamilton that those days were back again, with old Black Harry sitting opposite him, demanding to know what the deuce was being done to improve his holdings in the Funds.

Hamilton sighed again. There was nothing left of those Funds, of course, as he had just explained to the major. Nothing left at all, in fact. Old Black Harry must be twisting in his grave.

"What about the income from the estate?" the major inquired. "I know my brother was no farmer, but there must be rents still coming in."

"Nothing worth mentioning, my lord. A couple of hundred, no more." Under his client's stony stare, Hamilton felt obliged to offer an explanation. "His late lordship was not an easy man to get along with, my lord."

"That is an understatement if ever I heard one." The craggy brows lightened, and a suspicion of a smile flickered across the dark face.

"Most of the tenant farmers have left or were driven off by his lordship's repeated attempts to raise the rents," the solicitor continued.

"What was Lockhart thinking of to allow things to come to such a sorry pass?"

"Your father's agent is getting on in years, my lord. And besides, Lord Castleton threatened to turn him off without a pension if he didn't follow orders. I have it from old Lockhart himself. Came to me almost in tears he did once, but there was nothing I could do, of course. Nobody dared to gainsay his lordship. Real nasty he could be when he wanted, could your brother. Begging your pardon for being so frank, my lord. But there you have it."

"When he was in his cups, you mean, don't you?" the major growled. "Which, if I know anything about Nigel, was most of the time." He stared moodily out of the grimy window, his eyes bleak.

"My mother's portion is safe, I gather?"

"Aye, my lord. But it is not as generous as it was when your grandfather set up the trust for her. Your father persuaded her ladyship to put some of her principal into the estate. As a loan, of course," he added hastily, as the major's face set in a scowl.

"So?"

"It was never repaid, my lord. I reminded his lordship regularly of this obligation, but he was so seldom in funds. And Lord Castleton refused to acknowledge the debt at all, I am sorry to say. A bad business it was, to be sure."

The major only grunted. "Then all that remains intact is my sister's portion, I assume. Thank God that Black Harry set up that ten-thousand-pound dowry so it could not be tampered with. At least his granddaughter will not be another penniless debutante when the time comes."

Hamilton looked askance at the major and cleared his throat nervously. "I regret to inform you that—well, that Lord Castleton found a way to overset your grandfather's instructions in that respect."

"What are you telling me?" the major said, his voice ominously quiet.

Hamilton cleared his throat again. "There is no dowry, my lord."

The muscles in his lordship's jaw rippled dangerously, and his mouth set in a grim line. "How did you let this happen, Hamilton?" The words were spoken softly, but after a brief glance into the murderous depths of his client's eyes, Mr. Hamilton felt a frisson of fear run through his old bones.

"Your brother did not come to me, my lord. He sought the advice of one of the most nefarious members of my profession, a man with a reputation for upsetting inconvenient wills, marriage contracts, and other agreements between gentlemen. He is much patronized by rogues and—"

"What's done is past mending," Davenport interrupted brusquely. "Tell me what is to be done now, Hamilton, in order to save Castleton Abbey for the future. Tell me what debts must be paid off immediately and which may be drawn out a little longer. We must prevent this ultimate humiliation of having our possessions auctioned off to the highest bidder. I will not have every curious fop and brigand within traveling distance strolling through my home, ogling everything we own."

Mr. Hamilton sighed for the third time during the interview, which had been much more painful that he had imagined. It would have been easier for him had the major been a man like his late brother, concerned only with obtaining immediate cash for his own personal expenses and let the devil take everything else, including the estate. But the major was another Black Harry, a man whose loyalty to his name would, under the present dire circumstances, bring him nothing but heartache. For, in Mr. Hamilton's opinion, there was no saving the Davenports this time.

"There are debts long outstanding for over thirty thousand pounds, my lord. From your father's time, that is. Lord Castleton made no attempt to pay any of them, as far as I know. Then there are the mortgages on the London house and on all unencumbered lands in Kent. Two of them, amounting to nearly forty thousand, including interest. There are undoubtedly other, small debts run up by your brother, but I have yet to get a full accounting of them, my lord.

"My lord?"

During the solicitor's recital, the major's face had gone gray and his eyes, first an angry, icy blue, had become clouded with pain and despair. At Hamilton's sharp exclamation, however, he pulled himself together with a visible effort.

"You paint a distressing picture, sir," he said briefly.

Mr. Hamilton was again struck by the quiet dignity in his client's ravaged face, so like his grandfather's that the solicitor felt himself again slipping into the past.

He shook his head. "I am truly sorry that you should come home from the Peninsula to this, my lord."

As if wishing to forestall any further commiseration, the major stood up abruptly and paced over to a small window

overlooking a cobbled courtyard below. His step was noticeably uneven since he favored his left leg as he walked. Sitting
so long had stiffened the recent wound in his thigh and made
him wince with each step he took.

When he turned back to face the comfortably round figure
at the desk, there was naked appeal in his eyes.

"Advise me, sir, if you please. You and your father before
you have handled our affairs for generations. All I know is
soldiering." A painful smile crossed his ravaged countenance.
"If this were a battle, I would not hesitate. But in affairs of
business, I am a rank novice, as you well know, still wet behind the ears." He stared out the window for several moments
before returning his gaze to the old man, who sat regarding
him patiently. "As you may have guessed, I am nothing like
Nigel, sir. I am willing to fight for my heritage and am prepared to do anything to pull the family out of this hole. Only
tell me what I must do to save the Abbey, Hamilton, and I
promise you, on my grandfather's bones, that I will do it."

Hamilton met the unflinching stare and saw determination
there; but he also caught a glimpse of the bitter, hard, angry
man the young major had become, and knew that—unlike his
sire and late brother—the new Earl of Castleton was as good
as his word.

He motioned to the empty chair. "Sit down, my boy," he
said kindly. "I must be perfectly frank with you. The
prospects are dim indeed that you will be able to put the
Abbey back in the tip-top condition it enjoyed when your
grandfather was master there. It would require a massive in-
flux of capital, which—unless your own fortunes have improved monstrously since we last met—we have no way of
obtaining."

The major's shoulders, comfortably clad in a bottle green
hunting jacket that had seen better days, sagged wearily.

"You are saying that it is impossible, I take it?"

"Perhaps not entirely impossible, but exceedingly difficult,
certainly. I do not wish to raise false hopes, my lord. But
without some capital there is no way to build the estate up to
where it can support itself again. The London house must go,
of course."

"I am surprised Nigel has not already sold it," the major said bitterly.

"There would have been no point to it, my lord. Any monies obtained from the sale would have gone to buy up the mortgage, and your late brother preferred London living to the relative quiet of Kent. The bank has been most accommodating, I must say, to accept an occasional interest payment when the late earl was faced with losing his London residence."

"Then sell it, by all means," came the brusque reply. "I do not plan to stay in London at all if I can help it. And I certainly cannot afford to give my sister her come-out."

"You should also consider selling the various unentailed farms attached to the estate—"

"No," came the sharp reply. "I will sell nothing that belonged to my grandfather." The major paused, his blue eyes filled with frustration. "That is, unless there is absolutely no other way, sir."

The older man returned his lordship's stare speculatively. "In a general way, I would say that no, there is no other way. Your creditors are far too numerous for anyone to advance you a large enough loan. Besides which, you have no means of repaying it. There are, however,"—he paused briefly to scrutinize his client sharply—"other ways of coming about in a case such as yours." He eyed the young man closely, an apologetic smile on his round face. "If you are not too squeamish, my lord."

The major let out a crack of mirthless laughter. "After all these months on campaign, sir, I can assure you that squeamishness is not one of my sins. What would you have me do, Hamilton, take to the High Toby? I doubt that would answer, or I would do so tomorrow."

"No, my lord," the solicitor chuckled. "I would not recommend that life at all. Too little return for the effort, I would say."

When he did not continue, the major raised an impatient eyebrow.

"I was speaking of marriage, my lord," Hamilton said quietly.

This unexpected announcement was greeted with astonished silence. After a moment, the major regained his voice.

"I have been back in London for only two days, sir. I am in no position to know of any eligible heiresses and have no means of meeting any since the Season is long over. Most of the *ton* has removed to the country or to Brighton for the summer. In mid-July, London is very thin of company."

"I was not talking of eligible heiresses of the *ton*, my lord," Hamilton said dryly.

"A wealthy widow of dubious reputation, perhaps?" The major grinned. "I rather think not, Hamilton. Not my style at all, you know."

The old man shook his head. "Not talking about dubious widows either."

"What then?" The major's face was suddenly serious, his eyes wary. "Come on, man. Say what's on your mind."

The solicitor took a deep breath. "There are a growing number of very wealthy families in the City who have derived their fortunes from trade," he began delicately.

"You are not suggesting an alliance between a Davenport and a Cit's daughter by any chance, are you, Hamilton?" The tone was dangerously quiet, and the major's gaze contemptuous as he glared at the solicitor.

Mr. Hamilton wiped his brow and sighed yet again.

"You spoke of being prepared to do anything to save the Abbey, my lord. I naturally assumed you meant what you said." His patience was wearing thin, and he spoke more bluntly than was his wont.

The major had the grace to blush. "I did mean it, sir. But marriage to a Cit does appear rather extreme." In point of fact, the idea horrified him, but he was in no position to discard the proposition out of hand.

"I warned you not to be squeamish, boy," Hamilton said gruffly. "Your case calls for drastic measures. And I can make no promise that such an alliance would even be possible at present. But unless you agree to consider it, of course, there is no use making any inquiries."

The major got to his feet again and began to pace the length of the small office. His brows were drawn together in a black fury, and his face, hardly inviting at the best of times, was now frozen in such harsh lines that Mr. Hamilton had no difficulty in recognizing that his proposal had thrown his client into an emotional upheaval.

After Mr. Hamilton had begun to think that the major's tigerish pacing would wear away what little was left of his father's favorite carpet, the young man came to an abrupt halt before the solicitor's desk.

"Is there truly no other way, Hamilton?" he demanded wearily.

The old man shook his head. "None that I can see, my lord," he replied.

"Then do it, man. Make your inquiries. And by God, if I have to marry a Cit to come about, damned if I won't do it."

1

A Civilized Understanding

"How many times must I say this, Papa? I have no desire at all for a husband, titled or otherwise."

"And how many times do I have to tell *you*, my dear Angela, that you are being excessively caper-witted about this whole matter. And unnatural, too, I might add." George Walters regarded his only daughter with genuine concern, which gave the lie to the severe scold he was giving her. "I daresay your dear mother would agree with me if only she were here to listen to you make a ninnyhammer of yourself."

"Mama would have warned me not to trust a Greek Adonis bearing gifts he had no intention of bestowing, Papa. And well you know it." Angela regretted her words instantly when she saw her father wince at the implied criticism.

"So, it's that Medford fellow that's made you fly into high fidgets again, is it not, my love? I might have guessed it. Although it's been all of three years now if I remember rightly." He smiled gently at the angry moue that crossed his daughter's lovely face. "I had hoped you would have put that nasty business behind you by now, dearest."

"I shall never forget, much less forgive," Angela declared heatedly. "In point of fact, it will be three years exactly next week on my birthday, Papa. What a monstrously flattering birthday gift that was, indeed." She took a sip of tea and found it to be cold.

They were seated in the breakfast room together, as was their wont at this hour, and the summer sun shone brightly in the wide bay window overlooking the enclosed garden at the back of the Walters' town house. Angela wondered, not for the first time, why she still remembered so vividly that horrendous scene three years ago which had shattered her innocence and her dreams of happiness forever. The pain was as fresh today as it had been then, and her anger flared again at the humiliating proposal she had been forced to listen to.

"He would never have dared if I had been a real lady," she said, pouring herself another cup of tea in a fresh cup.

"You are a real lady, my pet. And don't you ever forget it. For your dear mama's sake, if not for mine. It was her dearest wish that—"

"Oh, Papa," Angela interrupted with unaccustomed curtness. "You have told me often enough that Mama wished me to marry someone of her own background. But don't you see? It's impossible now. I refuse to expose myself to such treatment ever again, Papa. So please don't ask me." Besides, she thought to herself with a small sigh, her heart had been crippled for life by that blond Adonis with the false smile. She could not imagine falling in love again.

"You should not judge all gentlemen by one bad apple, my love."

"That wretch was certainly no gentleman, Papa," she replied. "I only regret I did not realize it sooner."

"That is precisely what I mean, Angela. You made a wrong choice, that is true. And the blame is mostly mine for not scrutinizing his lordship's reputation more carefully."

Angela reached out to clasp her father's hand affectionately. "That I will never accept, Papa. I am not precisely witless, you know, and should have seen the warning signs. It's just that he was so very handsome," she sighed. "He quite obscured my judgment, I'm afraid."

"There, there, my pet," her father murmured. "You know how I dislike seeing you out of humor. Only promise me you will forget this unhappy episode and be merry again, my dear, and I will accompany you to Brighton next month. It promises to be full of entertainment since I hear the Regent will be in residence. What do you say, Angela?"

"The Regent? And why should I care a jot about him, Papa? It's not as though I will ever be invited to visit his Chinese Pavilion or anything so exalted."

"You never know, my dear. You never know. And if you are not there, how will you ever find out?"

Angela laughed. "You are a romantic, Papa. Shame on you

at your age. Whatever am I to think? Perhaps you have set up a flirt that you have not told me about. Is that it?" She regarded her smiling parent with affection.

"No, my dear. That is out of the question. However, I see no reason why you should not meet any number of eligible gentlemen down there. I hear it is a favorite summer place for the *ton*."

He was regarding her so artlessly and his eyes were so full of love that Angela hadn't the heart to scold him again. "That would be wonderful, Papa, if I were nineteen again and on the catch for a husband. But I am nearly twenty-three and will soon be comfortably on the shelf. So I must regretfully decline your kind offer. I simply could not face playing the simpering miss again to some heartless rogue who would be but trifling with me." Her smile took some of the sting out of her words, but nevertheless she knew she had hurt her father's feelings.

"Well, my love," Mr. Walters answered after a long pause, during which he polished off two thick slices of York ham and a heap of scrambled eggs. "I will not plague you any further. I hate to think what your mother would say to me, however. I seem to have bungled your education badly indeed if you regard matrimony with such distaste."

Angela could see that her father's feathers were truly ruffled and set about making her peace with him. "It is not marriage I dislike so much, Papa. I have seen how good it was for you and Mama," she explained. "But rather the absurd lengths to which one must go in order to bring a gentlemen up to scratch. I refuse to put myself out in that way ever again, sir. I tried it once, you know, and look where it got me."

"So," Mr. Walters mused, regarding his daughter speculatively. "Am I to understand, my dear, that you are not opposed to matrimony at all, but only to the process of obtaining a willing victim?"

Angela laughed, her spirits somewhat restored by her father's sense of humor. "Yes, you could say that." She smiled. "Except there are always two victims, you know."

"Hmm. And following this same line of reasoning, my dear, could we not also say that if you were offered an eligible *parti*, served up on a platter, without the conventional courting procedure you seem to find so tedious, you would accept an offer?"

Angela started to laugh, but then she saw that her parent was serious. She regarded him curiously for a moment, considering her reply. "I can find no fault in your reasoning, Papa," she said carefully. "Except, of course, for the obvious fact that one cannot shop for a husband as one would for a gown or a pair of gloves, for example." A sudden giggle escaped her. "I can just see myself, Papa," she said, mimicking a fastidious shopper. "Not this one, I fear he is too skinny. And this one is already growing bald. This poor creature walks with a stoop. Hmm. This one might do, except that his nose is too long. I think it might be rather amusing. Terribly embarrassing for the gentlemen, of course, but at least you would get what you really wanted without roundaboutation."

"Would you, my love?" her father said softly. "I wonder."

"It hardly signifies, does it? Since husbands cannot be bought so easily, I shall remain single, Papa."

"Which only goes to show, my love, how little you know of the world," Mr. Walters remarked, stirring a lump of sugar into his second cup of tea.

"Whatever do you mean, Papa?" A slight frown marred the smoothness of Angela's brow.

"Husbands certainly can be bought, my love, as can wives. Titled ones, too, if that's your fancy." He paused to butter a piece of toast and spread it thickly with strawberry jam. "In fact, if you have a mind to go shopping, I learned of an excellent specimen just yesterday who might be worth considering. No need to commit yourself, of course," he hastened to add as he saw his daughter's eyes widen in shock.

"I should hope not," she spluttered indignantly. "Father, how could you even suggest it?" Angela did not know whether to laugh or be offended at this preposterous notion.

"No need to fly into a pelter, my love," Walters said calmly. "To tell the truth, I felt sorry for the fellow. One of our brave soldiers he is, a Major Davenport, just come back from fighting Boney. Wounded, too, I understood. Recently came into his title and finds himself without a feather to fly with. Has an estate somewhere in Kent, but it ain't going to do him a bit of good unless he can come up with the blunt to run it. But never you mind, my love. If you dislike the idea of looking him over, forget I mentioned it."

Having said all he intended to say on the subject, Mr. Walters retreated behind his morning paper, content in the knowledge that he had piqued his daughter's interest.

Little did he guess that Angela's sympathy was also aroused, so he was both surprised and pleased when, an hour later, she bearded him in his study with a demand to hear the whole story of the destitute Major Davenport.

The following morning promised to be another warm, lovely day, but Angela rose at her usual early hour with a vague sense of foreboding. Her father's proposal had initially shocked her. Naturally she had heard of arranged marriages, but had always assumed—apparently quite erroneously—that such contracts were limited to those unfortunate ladies of the *ton* who had more fortune than beauty. Never had it occurred to her to consider herself in that category.

Fortune she certainly had, she thought, watching as her French dresser, Clothilde, tucked a particularly rebellious dark curl into the knot at the top of her head. Thanks to her grandfather, who had built this comfortable house in the most fashionable part of London, in defiance of his aristocratic neighbors, none of whom had acknowledged his presence. Angela smiled at the thought of her Grandfather Walters. Irascible, impulsive, independent, he had certainly been, but also astute and indefatigable in his business dealings, and soft as putty in the hands of his only granddaughter.

"I think I'll wear the new green silk this morning, Clothilde," she said, determined to throw off the dismals and face the day with her usual cheerfulness. The green dress was just the thing to raise her spirits, she thought, critically examining her face in the ornate mirror. She was one of the few women she knew who could wear green without looking bilious. As a child, she had always lamented her unruly mass of dark curls and prayed every night that she might wake up with a head of fashionable golden blond tresses. It had never happened, of course, and Angela had come to take pride in her coloring, which allowed her to wear shades that other females would never dare to.

As Angela descended to the breakfast parlor twenty minutes later, she thought of the pampered, carefree life she had led, thanks again to Grandfather Walters, who had called her his little Princess and left her the tidy sum of a hundred thousand pounds in trust when he died. The only sorrow to touch her had been the passing of her dear grandfather and, two years later, during her fifteenth year, the sudden death of her mother from a severe inflammation of the lungs.

And then, three years ago, she had fallen under the spell of blond, Greek-profiled Roger Hyland, Earl of Medford, and felt that all her romantic dreams were about to come true. Oh, but what an innocent widgeon she had been in those days, Angela mused, her generous mouth tightening at the memory of that heart-shattering scene which had replayed itself with distressing frequency in her mind ever since.

Angela fixed a smile on her face to greet the butler as he held the door of the breakfast parlor open for her.

"Good morning, Higgins," she said, casting a glance around the deserted table. "Is my father gone already? I fear I am a little late this morning."

"Yes, miss. He was called down to the harbor before dawn. It appears one of the Walters' vessels has arrived from the Orient. Mr. Julian has gone with him, miss."

Angela was disappointed to have missed her father's company at breakfast. She had counted on his comforting presence and calm good sense to allay some of the misgivings which had assailed her during the night. Her father could have provided the reassurance she needed that in agreeing to meet Major Davenport, she was not committing herself to marry him.

Things were proceeding far too quickly for her taste, she thought, as Higgins served her a plate of coddled eggs and poured a cup of strong tea into the delicate Wedgwood cup. During their interview yesterday, Papa had revealed enough details about the major's circumstances, gleaned—he had told her—from that gentleman's man of business, to arouse not merely her curiosity but her sympathy as well. And it was based on these feelings, which had quite obscured her natural reluctance to risk an encounter with another lord, that Angela had agreed to allow her dear Papa to set up a meeting with the major.

That he had done so with such precipitation had both surprised and alarmed her. What must the major think of her, she wondered, for seeming to jump so anxiously to take the dangled bait? He would put her down as a vulgar title-hunter, or an ape-leader and antidote who could not attract an eligible suitor on her own merits. The thought comforted her. He must certainly be disabused of that notion when he sees me, she thought, not without a flicker of amusement at her missishness. And besides, why should she care a fig what the major thought?

She asked herself the same question repeatedly during the course of the morning as she moved about the big house, attending to her household duties. She had been her father's hostess for eight years now, and took special delight in the role. Although their circle of close friends was small, consisting mainly of her father's business associates and a scattering of distant relatives on her mother's side who had—for one reason or another—chosen to acknowledge the connection, Angela's reputation as a hostess was firmly established.

As the morning slipped away, however, Angela began to doubt the major would come. Perhaps he has decided he cannot possibly tolerate an alliance with a Cit, she thought, annoyed at herself for caring what this stranger chose to do. She could not help but feel, however, that it was ill-bred of him to keep her waiting around like this.

As the luncheon hour approached, Angela became more restless. Her father had not returned, and she was on the point of going up to her room to change into her riding habit for a canter in the Park when Higgins knocked on her sitting room door to announce that a Major Davenport was downstairs.

"Show him into the small morning room, please, Higgins. And tell the major I shall be down directly."

"Very well, miss," the butler replied. "Will the major be taking luncheon with us, ma'am?"

"I shouldn't think so, Higgins," Angela said, certain that she, at least, had no intention of inviting him to do so.

*   *   *

The small morning room at the Walters' London residence was one of the most pleasant in the house. Facing east, it received the morning sun in abundance from two large bow windows overlooking the garden. The gentleman who stood gazing out of one of them, however, did not seem to notice either the bright sunlight or the inviting atmosphere of the room.

Major Harry Davenport was preoccupied with a host of less pleasant thoughts. What the deuce was he about? he asked himself for the umpteenth time since receiving Hamilton's note yesterday evening advising him that he was expected to present himself at the St. James's Square address the following morning. He had postponed it until the last moment, inventing excuses for not leaving the lodgings on Jermyn Street where he had been quartered since arriving back in London three days previously. Finding Castleton House shuttered and with the knocker removed, he had been glad of Captain George Woodall's invitation to rack up with him until he could finish his London business.

Not that George knew the exact nature of the business his friend and fellow officer was contemplating, Harry thought disgustedly. He vividly recalled every word of Hamilton's neatly penned note, a missive the major regarded as merely another link in the chain of events which seemed to be compelling him toward a decision he was extremely reluctant to make.

It had been Jimmy Dunn, his army batman, who had finally pushed him out the door with the admonition that shilly-shallying around was not going to put bread in their bellies. Although the major would not have phrased it in quite those terms, the result was the same. He had to admit that this proposed connection with Miss Angela Walters, whose father was—according to a jubilant Hamilton—a veritable Croesus, seemed to be the only way out of his straitened circumstances.

His lip curled instinctively at the thought of what awaited him. The wench must be an eyesore, he thought, if she cannot land a husband without resorting to the cold, calculated arrangement Hamilton had placed before him only yesterday. The Cit was fully prepared to lay out his blunt, Hamilton had told him, his old eyes sparkling at the prospect of putting his client in the way of receiving such a windfall. And that alone must be his sole consideration, Harry told himself cynically. There was no room for fastidiousness in this connection. If the girl was an antidote, so be it. If she was quiet and modest, and did not expect him to play the beau, he would muddle through. There would be more than enough to keep him occupied at the Abbey; if he played his cards right, he need see very little of her at all, much less listen to her prattle.

The major was distracted from these morbid thoughts by the sound of a door opening and closing behind him, and a cool, cultivated voice addressing him politely.

"Good morning, Major Davenport. I trust I have not kept you waiting."

Harry swung around and stared open-mouthed at the elegant young lady in green who approached him across the Oriental carpet, her smoky eyes veiled in spite of the welcoming smile on her lovely mouth.

"Good morning, Miss Walters," he managed to say, furious with himself for standing there with his mouth hanging open like some country gapeseed. He sketched a stiff little bow over the hand she extended him, taking care to hold it as briefly as possible.

Then he stood, ramrod straight, his hands clasped behind his back, and glowered at his hostess from beneath lowered brows. He had been unprepared for anything like this, and he wondered irrationally if he had mistaken the address. But no, she had addressed him by name, and had certainly been expecting him. By no means loquacious by nature, the major now found himself completely at a loss for words.

Miss Walters returned his gaze unflinchingly. Her eyes were a dark gray, almost like charcoal, the major noted, and her hair was as dark as his own. Involuntarily, the thought crossed his mind that Black Harry might yet have a grandson in his own image. He felt the heat rise to his neck at the wayward notion, which he repressed immediately.

Miss Walters seemed unembarrassed by the silence between them. After a moment, she seated herself gracefully on a yellow brocade settee and motioned him toward a nearby wing chair.

"Please sit down, Major. May I offer you some refreshment? A glass of sherry, perhaps?"

"No, thank you."

Miss Walters regarded him quizzically, then smiled. "I gather you prefer to get right to the point, sir? I like that. I do not favor shilly-shallying around myself either. Although I can see that this whole notion is highly distasteful to you."

The major stared at her, startled at this forthright approach. "Nothing of the kind, ma'am, I assure you," he murmured stiffly. She had perceived the truth about his feelings immediately, he realized, and furthermore, her choice of words reminded him forcefully of Jimmy Dunn's warning that their future depended on his making a favorable impression on the Walters. It was a bitter pill to swallow, but swallow it he must.

"Fustian, sir!" Miss Walters exclaimed with a cheerfulness that made him want to grind his teeth. "Why else would you be scowling at me in that odious way? It stands to reason that you must dislike the idea excessively. To tell the truth, I don't care much for it myself."

Harry swallowed hard. There was something definitely havey-cavey about this business, he thought. He had expected to find an appropriately modest female of questionable origin eager to puff herself up with a titled husband. Instead, this pretentious hoyden had the temerity to inform him that she did not much care for the connection. No, he corrected himself. If he were honest, he would never call Miss Walters hoydenish. She exuded the quiet grace and self-possession one might expect to find in the most highly starched leaders of the *ton*. For some reason this admission only intensified his dislike of the arrangement he had come to discuss.

"I beg your pardon, ma'am?" he said, putting every ounce of cold disdain he could muster into the words. "I must have been misinformed. I was led to believe that you wished for this interview."

Miss Walters smiled at him kindly, apparently insensitive to the snub. "The truth of the matter is that my dear Papa is anxious to fulfill my mother's particular wish that I marry a gentleman of her own class. A misguided ambition, if you want my frank opinion, sir, but there you have it. So, in a sense, it is my Papa who desires the alliance. I am merely willing to consider the arrangement to oblige my Papa."

The major glared at her frostily. Hamilton had not prepared him to be treated with such confounded condescension, he fumed. This encroaching wench had as good as informed him that he had been summoned to present himself for her approval. Major Harry Davenport on parade inspection, he thought bitterly.

He started to tell Miss Walters what she could do with her Papa's aspirations when he remembered the unbelievable sum purported—according to Hamilton—to have been settled on Miss Walters. He bit off the curt retort that trembled on his lips.

"Am I to understand that your father has left the decision up to you, Miss Walters?" he inquired brusquely. The notion that his fate hung on the impressionable, capricious reaction of a female made his blood boil. He had been determined not to play the gallant, he reminded himself, and he would be damned if he would pretend to be anything other than what he was, a soldier, not a lady's man.

"Yes, entirely." She smiled. "And to you, too, Major. Obviously you have some say in the matter, don't you? Papa would not countenance this connection if either of us thought we would not suit."

Harry was suddenly conscious that his wound was throbbing, and he wished fervently that he had not come. Miss Walters was nothing like the docile, gauche female he had expected, and, quite frankly, he found her alarmingly forward and too self-possessed by half.

"And what do you think, Miss Walters?" Harry fixed his eyes on his hostess's face. And a very lovely face it was, he admitted reluctantly. Widely spaced eyes set in a smooth brow, a small, elegantly shaped nose, and a mouth that was obviously begging to be kissed. Harry drew his own mouth into a hard line and pushed such rebellious thoughts firmly aside. He watched, fascinated in spite of himself, as Miss Walters's lips relaxed into a genuine smile.

"That is hard to say, Major. First impressions can be so misleading, wouldn't you agree?" She made another gesture toward the wing chair. "Please sit down for a moment, Major, and let me offer you a glass of sherry."

With a sigh, Harry capitulated. His thigh was giving him a devil of a time this morning, and it felt good to settle into the comfortable wing chair and stretch his legs out. Miss Walters had risen and, moving gracefully to the sideboard, carefully poured him a glass of sherry which she then placed on a table beside his chair.

"Thank you, ma'am." He raised an inquiring eyebrow. "Aren't you going to join me"

With another smile, Miss Walters poured herself a glass of the amber liquid and returned to her seat on the settee. "There," she said, raising her glass to him. "Now we can be more civilized about this. Here's to a better understanding between us, Major."

Well, Harry thought cynically, raising his glass in return and taking a gulp of what he discovered to be excellent Jerez, he could certainly drink to that. So she thinks Harry Davenport is uncivilized, does she? He gazed reflectively into the pale yellow sherry and tried to assess his chances of bringing this highly unconventional maneuver off without too many losses. He had already thrown most of his pride to the winds in presenting himself here at all, he thought. Now he must endure the lady's censure for his uncouth address.

He glanced up and saw Miss Walters was regarding him calmly with those mysterious gray eyes of hers. Perhaps he had been rather curt with the wench, he admitted. It might be wise to deploy some diversionary tactics unless he was willing to engage the enemy directly. The option of making a strategic retreat to safer ground did not seem to be available to him under the present circumstances.

Unsure as to which way he wished to attack his present dilemma, Harry raised his glass again and locked Miss Walters's smoky gaze with his startling blue one. He felt his face relax into the glimmerings of the first amusement he had experienced since entering the house on St. James's Square.

"And here's to a *civilized* understanding between us, my dear Miss Walters," he amended, not without a disturbing sensation that he was proposing a truce unworthy of old Black Harry Davenport.

2

The Challenge

When Angela looked back on that first, inauspicious interview, there were two prevailing characteristics about Major Harry Davenport that stuck in her mind. The predominant impression which lingered with her long after the major had taken his leave was one of deep-seated aversion to the proposed alliance with a female of her class. Although he had stoutly denied it, Angela had immediately sensed his rejection and disapproval. He had been hard pressed to maintain even the barest of civilities, and on several occasions had come perilously close to being offensive.

"It appears to me that you showed admirable restraint, my love," her father remarked as Angela related the highlights of her encounter with the reluctant major at dinner that evening. "Perhaps Julian was right. I should not have allowed you to face the man alone, dear. He obviously took offense at having to discuss such a delicate arrangement with a mere female."

Angela knew her father well enough to realize he was teasing her, but the same thought had occurred to her. "That may be so, Papa," she agreed. "He seemed to be dreadfully uncomfortable, but that is to be expected, I suppose. For a man of the major's stamp, accustomed to command and control, it must be very awkward to find himself suddenly in the position of supplicant. I am not surprised that it has made him bitter and cynical."

"He has aroused your sympathy, I take it, dear?"

"Oh, yes." Angela confessed. "How could he not? It must be very distressing to find that the senseless extravagance of one's brother has reduced the family to such straits."

Mr. Walters regarded his daughter anxiously. "Do not let your tender feelings for the gentleman's plight influence your decision unduly, my dear Angela. A marriage based entirely on pity can only bring unhappiness to both parties. There must also be respect, loyalty, kindness, and a solid understanding between you before you embark on such a venture."

"I thoroughly agree, Papa. And there are several things that still need to be discussed before that happens." She smiled engagingly at her worried father. "For example, Major Davenport informed me that he is the guardian to his cousin's orphaned boy, Jeremy. His father was killed in action two years ago, and the child had been the major's sole responsibility since then. From what I could gather, the lad has led a ramshackle existence, first in Spain and then in Brussels."

"Has the child no mother?" Mr. Walters inquired, helping himself to another slice of raised pigeon pie.

"His mother died in Brussels when he was only four, so the boy has grown up in army quarters. I should think that his education has been sadly neglected." Angela motioned to Higgins to refill her father's glass.

"And how old is this Jeremy, if I may ask?"

"He is just ten. The major appears to have a strong affection for the child. He has Jeremy here in London with him, so I asked him to bring the boy tomorrow when he comes."

Mr. Walters glanced at his daughter in surprise. "From what you have told me about your interview with the major, my love, I had quite supposed you had sent him packing."

Angela laughed. "I confess I am seriously considering doing so, Papa. The major may have all the qualifications for an outstanding soldier, but these are not precisely the qualities one would wish for in a husband. He is autocratic and stern to a fault. Not once did he crack a smile during the hour he spent with me this morning. And you know how much I love to tease. I had the hardest time trying to say something to break down that icy reserve of his. The closest I came to overcoming his grim expression was when I implied he was uncivilized. That seemed to rattle his composure a little."

"Never say you did anything so uncivil, Angela," her father exclaimed in shocked tones.

"Oh, but I did, Papa. He quite tried my patience, I declare. And besides, he *was* uncivilized. I practically had to beg him to sit down and accept a glass of sherry. I suspect he thought we would offer him some inferior brand that would offend his superior palate. It was not what he feared, of course." Angela laughed at the memory of the major's surprised face when she had walked into the room. "But then, neither was I quite what he had expected, I suspect."

"Perhaps you should not see him again, my love, if you have so many reservations about his suitability. I can send a messenger round to his lodging this evening, if you wish, and cancel his visit."

Angela regarded her father, considering his offer to rid her of Major Davenport's presence forever. This morning, immediately after the major had taken his leave, she might have jumped at the chance to avoid a repetition of the uncomfortable interview. However, for reasons that were not entirely clear, she had herself proposed that the major return the following morning accompanied by his young ward. She owed him the courtesy of delivering her negative response to their proposed alliance in person, she thought. It will be hard enough for him to accept rejection from a mere Cit's daughter, in the best of cases. She had been too cowardly to deliver it this morning, especially after she had realized he was in physical pain. And she shrank from inflicting such a set-down to his self-esteem in the cold impersonality of a note. Though why she should care if the major's self-consequence received a blow, she could not say.

"I think not, Papa," she replied at last. "It would hardly be fair to reject a man based on such a short acquaintance. His wound was obviously bothering him, too, which may have put him out of sorts. I will reserve judgment until tomorrow morning. If I see that there is no hope of *rapprochement* between us, I will send him away, I promise."

What Angela had failed to mention to her father, and what she had deliberately pushed to the back of her mind, was the second characteristic about her visitor which had impressed her. For all his scowling, disapproving demeanor, his deliberate rudeness, his obvious contempt for her and everything she stood for, there was no denying the disturbing fact that Major Harry Davenport exuded an animal magnetism which had shaken Angela's inner tranquility more than she cared to admit.

*   *   *

The next morning, Angela was quite unprepared for the early arrival of her callers. She had enjoyed an early breakfast with her father and Julian, during which the latter had reiterated his opinion—loudly and repeatedly voiced since he had learned of the scheme—that Angela should refuse to consider a match with an impecunious earl.

"I cannot see that a title would add to your consequence in the least, Angela," he remarked when he learned that the major was expected to call again. "Heaven knows you could have any man you want. I much prefer Uncle George's notion of spending a month or two in Brighton. If you must have a title, my dear girl, at least choose one with a few pounds to his name. This Davenport fellow is only interested in lining his pockets at our expense."

Angela smiled at the stolid, square-jawed young man who sat opposite her at the breakfast table. Julian Scarborough was her brother in everything but name and had been her most loyal champion and companion for as long as she could remember. Son of her father's business partner, Julian had lost both parents in a shipwreck when he was six and had been adopted by Walters and his new bride as a matter of course. Two years later, when Angela was born, Julian had appointed himself her official guardian and protector. He still took that role very seriously.

"It seems to me, Julian, that you are making a piece of work about nothing. As I have already told Papa, I seriously doubt the major and I would suit. Furthermore, he is not one of those odious fortune-hunters you seem to feel are lurking in wait for me behind every tree. In fact, I would say he dislikes the idea of this connection as much as you do."

"Then why is he calling again today?" Julian wanted to know, and Angela did her best to explain, although her reasoning sounded even weaker than it had last night at dinner.

She was not given much time to dwell on the vagaries of her mind, however, for at nine o'clock, while she was penning a few notes in the library, Higgins appeared to announce the arrival of Major Davenport.

"Accompanied by a small person," Higgins added, meticulous as ever. "I have put them in the small morning room again, Miss Angela."

"Thank you, Higgins." Angela rose and went over to the mirror above the mantel. Clothilde had done her work well, as usual, and Angela's dark hair made an attractive frame of curls for her oval face. I wonder what the major will find to disapprove of today, she wondered as she made her way along the hall to the morning room.

The major stood where he had yesterday, gazing abstractedly out the window. The boy at his side was the first to turn away from the window as Angela approached, and greeted her with a spontaneous smile.

"Good morning," she said, returning his smile. "You must be Jeremy, are you not?" She extended her hand, which the boy shook politely.

"Good morning, Miss Walters," he replied, making his bow.

Angela was conscious of being observed, and when she raised her eyes, she found the major's deep blue gaze fixed on her.

"Good morning, Major. I trust you are in better spirits today."

Angela saw his mouth grow taut and his eyes frost over. There, she'd done it again, she thought ruefully. She had put his back up with her thoughtless chatter. Well, considering that she had to offend him still further with her rejection, perhaps it would help to have him angry with her.

"I am quite well, thank you, Miss Walters," he replied, holding her fingers only a fraction of a second longer than yesterday as he bowed over them.

"What a rapper," remarked Jeremy unexpectedly. "You know your leg hurts like the very devil today, Uncle Harry."

"Jeremy!" the major snapped. "Watch your language, boy."

"You said so yourself just now as we got out of the hackney, Uncle. I heard you." The boy seemed undaunted by the major's black scowl.

Angela looked at the boy with aroused interest. "I am glad you told me, Jeremy," she said, casting an amused glance at the grim-faced major. "Your uncle is too stiff-rumped for his own good, I can see." She turned with one of her most cordial smiles to the major. "Please sit down, sir." She indicated the leather wing chair he had occupied yesterday. "I believe this was to your liking."

He glared at her. "I am very well as I am, thank you," came the curt reply.

Angela looked at Jeremy and shrugged her shoulders eloquently. "Is he always this pig-headed?"

Jeremy glanced up at his uncle and giggled. "You are found out, sir," he remarked with disarming candor. "Perhaps it would be better if you did sit down. For your leg, I mean, sir." he added hastily as his uncle's expression became choleric.

"Hold your peace, you impertinent brat," the major blazed. "Or I shall send you home immediately."

Sensing that a full-scale quarrel was about to ensue between the major and his charge, Angela thought it time to intervene.

"I was under the impression that, only yesterday, we had agreed to be civilized about his matter, Major. Perhaps if you were to sit down, you might feel less inclined to brangle with poor Jeremy here, who only has your well-being at heart, I am sure."

The major turned his fulminating gaze on her, and Angela held her breath for several seconds, fearing that she was in for a blistering set-down. The moment passed, however, and she saw something flicker in the depths of his blue eyes before he relaxed and the scowl left his face.

"Jeremy is right," he said unexpectedly, seating himself in the wing chair. "I am deucedly blue-deviled this morning. I crave your indulgence, Miss Walters, for my uncivilized outburst."

"What is this matter you have to be civilized about, Miss Walters?" Jeremy asked with characteristic directness.

"Oh, it was just an agreement your uncle and I made yesterday, to be civil to each other, Jeremy. That's all."

The boy observed her closely. Angela saw that he was not taken in by her smooth explanation.

"Sounds like a hum to me," he said flatly. "Why would Uncle Harry not be civil to you?"

"That's a good question, Jeremy. I confess I wondered about it myself. But it no longer signifies."

No, she told herself, catching the major's penetrating glance over Jeremy's head. It no longer signifies if the gentleman is civil or not, since she was going to turn down his preposterous arrangement anyway, wasn't she? She would wash her hands of him and his uncouth outbursts. He obviously had no more desire for a connection with her than he had yesterday. If it had not been for her foolish scruples and her equally foolish desire to meet the major's ward, she would have been rid of him already. What had she expected, anyway? That he would suddenly develop an overnight *tendre* for her? How absolutely nonsensical to imagine that a man as hard and cynical as this one obviously was could develop tender feelings about anyone, much less a strange female whose station in life disgusted him. Besides which, she reminded herself quickly, nothing about the major recommended itself to her on any level.

"May I offer you some refreshment, Major? she asked, belatedly reminded of her duties as hostess."

"No, thank you, Miss Walters," came the curt reply she had come to expect from him.

"Oh, I would, if you please, ma'am," Jeremy responded eagerly, his sharp eyes shining expectantly in his thin face.

"You have just had your breakfast, Jeremy," his uncle pointed out.

"Oh, yes. But that was hours ago, Uncle Harry. Besides," he added, with a conspiratorial glance at Angela, "it's only civil to accept refreshment when one pays a morning call, wouldn't you agree, Miss Walters?"

"Yes, absolutely," Angela laughed. "And I, too, had my breakfast so long ago I no longer remember what I ate. So, why don't you jump up and ring that bellpull for me, and we will ask Higgins if he cannot persuade Cook to send up something to sustain us until luncheon?" Angela regarded the boy speculatively. "Just how hungry are you, Jeremy?"

"Actually, I could eat a horse, ma'am," came the frank reply.

Angela turned to Higgins, who had entered in time to hear

this last ingenuous remark. "I doubt we have any horses in the kitchen, do we, Higgins?"

"No, Miss Angela," the butler replied with a straight face. "I can't say that we do."

"Then we shall have to ask Cook to send up something equally filling, won't we?" Angela smiled. "Tell him we have a ten-year-old here, Higgins, who seems to have a prodigious appetite. He will know what to do, I'm sure."

"If you think to satisfy that rapscallion with a few pastries, ma'am, you are in for a surprise," the major commented dryly when the butler had departed on his errand. "He is constantly hungry. The breakfast he consumed an hour ago would have fed three grown men comfortably."

"He is a growing boy, Major." Angela laughed, surprised and pleased to hear her taciturn guest utter a comment free of rancor or disdain. She glanced at him as she spoke and was taken aback at the open affection in the major's eyes as he gazed at his ward. He is capable of tenderness after all, she mused, noticing how much the softened expression improved the major's looks. He is truly a fine-looking man when he is not scowling, she thought, her composure suddenly threatened by the lazy smile that had transformed his grim expression into an unexpectedly attractive one.

All at once, Angela was not quite so sure that she wanted to send the major packing, as she had expressed to her father only last night. She wondered what had brought about this subtle change in her attitude. Part of it was Jeremy, she decided, watching him demolish the last of the plateful of ham sandwiches provided by Higgins. There was a wistful air to the boy that had touched her heart. She suddenly realized that this elfin impression was caused by his clothes, which were neat and clean but too small for him. His thin wrists protruded an ungainly two inches beyond the sleeves of his jacket.

Angela glanced at the major and noticed again that the expertly cut riding coat he wore was well worn. She had known, of course, that the major was short of funds, but it had never occurred to her that he might actually be unable to replenish his own wardrobe, or buy new clothes for Jeremy. This realization gave her pause for serious thought. She began to understand the major's bitterness and frustration a little better. If he were as destitute as she was beginning to believe, no wonder he resented her, she thought. For a proud man, it must be intolerable to have to dance attendance on a Cit's daughter to salvage his ravaged estates.

As these thoughts passed through Angela's mind, she came to one of those sudden decisions which her Papa always said she had inherited from her mother.

"Jeremy," she said impulsively, determined to carry out her plan before her courage failed her, "how would you like to visit the stables and look at my new colt? Higgins will show you the way."

As soon as an excited Jeremy had disappeared with the butler and the door closed behind them, Angela went to her little escritoire between the two bow windows and quickly wrote out a draft on her bank for one hundred pounds. Her plan was a daring one which was bound to put the major's back up, but it would also test his willingness to enter into the kind of relationship that had been proposed between them.

The major had risen and was now standing with his back to the hearth, regarding her warily.

"Jeremy is a delight," she remarked, settling herself on the yellow brocade settee again. "I envy you his company; he seems to be bright beyond his years."

"He is indeed," the major replied dryly. "But I doubt you sent him out of the room in order to discuss his admirable qualities."

Angela regarded him, noting again the bitterness lying just below the surface of his curt civility. She would obviously have to take the initiative in bringing up the subject of their interview, and she considered her words carefully before she spoke.

"No, of course not," she replied. "There are certain things which must be discussed between us that are better done in private. I know how distressing this whole arrangement is for you, Major, but there are things I must know if we are to make a decision on whether to proceed or not."

"What do you wish to know?"

Angela had been unprepared for the harshness of his tone or the bleak despair in the dark blue eyes he fixed upon her face. A wave of pity washed over her as she stared back into those chilling blue depths. This man was hurting more than she had imagined, she thought, wondering how to say what she must without provoking his wrath.

"Well, the first question has to be whether you do, in fact, wish to continue this interview at all, sir."

"I would hardly be here if I did not, Miss Walters."

Angela regarded his bleak expression and chose to overlook the shortness of his reply. "Then why do I get the distinct impression that you would rather be anywhere else but here, Major? My impressions rarely mislead me in these matters, I should add."

Major Davenport's gaze did not waver from her face. "I had not thought to take a wife, Miss Walters. I am a soldier by choice and intended to make that my career. Jeremy is my heir, so I thought I had no need of a wife. Circumstances beyond my control have decreed otherwise. I now find my duty to my name outweighs my own wishes."

"Even though you find it personally distasteful?"

An unexpected gleam of amusement softened the major's expression as his eyes brushed lazily over Angela's person, causing a faint blush to rise to her cheeks. "I would have to be very hard to please indeed to find you distasteful, Miss Walters."

"That is not what I meant at all, sir," she replied, dismayed at the sudden tendency of her heart to jump into her throat.

"What exactly did you mean, then?"

"You find it distasteful to be obliged to marry a Cit's daughter, do you not?" There, she had said it, she thought. He could hardly avoid a direct answer to such a question.

"Yes," came the harsh reply. "Wouldn't you find it distasteful to be obliged to do anything?"

"Perhaps," Angela had to admit. "But then, I am not obliged to do so, therefore, if I do, it will be because I choose, not because I must."

"You are lucky." The major strode over to the window and stood staring out, his hands clasped tightly behind his rigid back. After a few moments, during which Angela had the opportunity to admire her prospective husband's broad back, tapered waist, and well-shaped legs in their tight-fitting gray breeches and polished Hessians, he turned to face his hostess.

"And you, Miss Walters? What do you wish to be the outcome of this interview?"

"I can tell you what I do not wish for, Major," she answered promptly. "I do not want a husband who will scorn my background or imagine for one moment that the Davenport title is a fair exchange for the Walters' fortune." She had spoken partly in defiance, partly in anger, and was surprised to see the arrested look on the major's face. "I would demand respect, loyalty, and, above all, friendship," she added, determined to speak her mind even if it meant giving the major a greater disgust for her than he already seemed to have. "And to be perfectly frank with you, Major, I do not think you have any of this to give me."

He regarded her in silence for a long time before transferring his gaze to the window. Angela felt herself relax and the color fade from her cheeks. She was glad she had finally said it. They would not suit. A feeling of regret invaded her heart, and she was conscious of a sense of loss that befuddled her. What had she to lose, after all? The major was nothing to her, and now he never would be. And she had fully expected to reject him in any case, hadn't she? For a fleeting moment, she wished she were her mother, the daughter of an earl and the major's social equal; but instantly she repressed this disloyalty to her beloved Papa. She was what she was, a Cit's daughter, and proud of it. And if the major felt this was beneath his dignity, so much the better. She would remain single as she had vowed to do three years ago when Roger had betrayed her.

"How can you be so sure?"

The question was spoken so softly that Angela wondered if she had imagined it until he turned from the window, his deep blue eyes quizzical.

"A foolish question, no doubt." He smiled faintly, as if amused at his own statement. "Your impressions do not mislead you, I gather. But have you considered that in this case they may be wrong, Miss Walters?"

Prepared as she had been for a surge of anger from her

guest or at the very least, a cutting rejoinder, Angela could only stare in surprise.

"Of course, I could be wrong," she admitted finally. "But you have given me no cause to believe that you could be comfortable with me."

"How could someone as elegant and accomplished as you obviously are, Miss Walters, make me uncomfortable?" That self-disparaging little smile hovered on his lips again.

Angela rose to her feet, the bank draft clutched in her nervous fingers. "I will show you exactly what I mean, Major," she said, a little breathless at her own audacity. She walked slowly over to stand before him, her eyes, wide with apprehension, fixed on his face.

"Here," she said, holding out the draft. "Do you recognize this?"

Davenport took the piece of paper and glanced at it casually. "Of course. It is a bank draft for one hundred pounds," he replied, raising his gaze to scan her face curiously.

"I wish you to take it and outfit Jeremy with a complete new set of clothes," she said. "He seems to have outgrown those he has on."

As she had expected, the major's face was instantly disfigured by a thunderous scowl. "I am fully capable of deciding when Jeremy needs new clothes, Miss Walters." He thrust the draft back at her. "I do not need any assistance in taking care of my ward, thank you." His voice was harsher than she had yet heard it, and she stepped back in alarm.

"Here," he growled. "Take your money; I do not want it." He advanced as Angela stepped back again, holding the offending paper out as though it would bite him.

Angela came to a halt before the hearth, her hands behind her. "There, you see. I was right. I have made you uncomfortable with a paltry one hundred pounds, Major." she smiled triumphantly up into his scowling face.

"I'm not uncomfortable, I'm insulted." He was so close to her that Angela could detect the faint smell of the Holland water he was using.

"That amounts to the same thing," she insisted. "The thought of taking money from me is something you find unacceptable, therefore it makes you uncomfortable."

"Call it what you will, Miss Walters. I will not accept it."

"Then I am right in thinking that you are wasting your time here, Major," Angela said, wishing for a wild moment that she was wrong. "If you find taking a mere hundred pounds from me so offensive, how can you possibly reconcile yourself to accepting the thousands I understand will be necessary to restore your estates?"

"That would be different."

Angela shook her head. "You are wrong, Major. The principle is exactly the same, and you cannot bring yourself to do it."

Davenport looked down at the paper in his hand as though he would crumple it and throw it into the empty hearth. When he raised his head, his eyes were so full of torment that Angela felt she was witnessing the struggles of a drowning man. She had an overwhelming urge to reach out to comfort him, but knew it was beyond her power to do so. She could not bear for her gesture to be misunderstood, so she did nothing, watching as the major's conflicting emotions flitted across his face.

Suddenly he turned and strode back to the window, limping a little with his left leg. Angela's heart was touched by the awakening he was undergoing, but she said nothing. This was something the major had to work out for himself.

He looked down at the draft in his hand, "Very well," he said slowly. "You may very well be right, my dear, but I shall endeavor to prove you wrong."

3

A Husband for Angela

By the time Harry Davenport got back to his lodgings, he felt sure the draft for a hundred pounds had burned a hole in his pocket. He was still torn by indecision. On one hand, he regretted his weakness in allowing Miss Walters to persuade him to keep the offensive thing in his possession; on the other, he felt a glimmering of relief that the first step toward saving the Abbey had been taken. It remained to be seen if he could indeed spend the money as Miss Walters had requested.

Harry grimaced as he regarded himself in his dressing room mirror. He could at least be thankful that the enterprising Miss Walters had not offered to frank a new coat for himself. The old green riding coat he had worn—the best in his meager wardrobe—was not exactly the *dernier cri* as far as fashionable gentlemen's wear was concerned. He should count himself lucky that Miss Walters had shown sufficient modesty to limit herself to refurbishing Jeremy's wardrobe.

Harry let out a crack of mirthless laughter, and his batman, who had been putting away a small stack of freshly washed shirts in the dresser drawer, looked up at his master curiously.

Jimmy Dunn had been with Major Davenport during most of the time he had spent on the Peninsula, and knew—better than his master could have guessed—the major's exact sentiments regarding the prospect of having to take a wife below his station. Mighty stiff-necked he could be where family honor was concerned, Jimmy knew. And the discovery that he now held the sole responsibility for that honor weighed heavily on him, as his foul temper over the past few days testified to. Of a more practical nature, and unhampered by such scruples, Jimmy had not hesitated to encourage the major to settle the matter with the Walters chit *tout de suite*, as the

Frenchies would say, so they could lope off to the country and be comfortable again.

"The mort ain't going to hedge off, is she, guv'nor?" he demanded, anxiety causing his homely face to pucker up more than usual. "We can't punt on tick much longer, ye know. Master Jeremy is already growing out of all his threads something awful. And ye could use a few new 'uns yourself, Major. If ye don't mind me saying so."

Harry turned away from the mirror and glanced at his batman with a faint smile of derision. "No such luck, Jimmy. It seems as though the redoubtable Miss Walters is ready to receive an offer from me. At least she shows no sign of outward revulsion in my presence. And she has given me this, so our troubles may soon be over."

He fished in his pocket and withdrew the offensive draft, by now showing definite signs of ill use, and tossed it onto the bed.

Jimmy took it up reverently and ineffectually tried to smooth out the crumpled slip of paper.

"Coo! 'Tain't often I seen so much mint sauce all at once, Major. A whole pony! It won't buy an Abbey, that's for sure, but at least we can flash the dibs a bit and not have to live at rack and manger for a while." He regarded his master speculatively. "And you can buy yerself a new coat at Weston's, Major. Ye could use one, too, if ye ask me."

"No!" The major's face had become stern, and a black scowl distorted his brow. "The lady has given specific instructions that the money be spent on Jeremy, my lad. So I want you to go to the bank immediately, Jimmy. Take a hackney," he added, fishing in his waistcoat pocket for a coin. "I don't want some pickpocket getting his hands on it."

Jimmy bristled at the implication that he could not take care of himself. "Look'ee here, Major. No peevy-cove is going to make a fool out of Jimmy Dunn. Yer blunt is safe as houses with me, and let nobody tell ye otherwise."

Harry looked at his henchman affectionately. He owed his life several times over to this thickset, stolid, dependable ex-soldier, whose only flaw—if it could be so called—was that he spoke his mind a mite too freely at times.

"I know, Jimmy. I know. But you will take a hackney all

the same, if you please. And don't dawdle. We have some shopping to do for Jeremy this afternoon. And then I think I'll take a canter in the Park with Duke. Both of us need the exercise."

Yes, Harry thought to himself, watching from the narrow window as Jimmy obediently hailed a hackney and drove off in the direction of the City, he needed something to take his mind off the inevitable. Much as he had resented the test which Miss Walters had imposed upon him, he had been inexplicably relieved that she had not rejected him out of hand, as he was sure she had every intention of doing when they met this morning. Why she had changed her mind was a mystery to him. He did not pretend to understand feminine logic. He had never been one for the ladies like his brother, Nigel, he thought without bitterness. As a second son, he had never expected to inherit the title and had jumped at his father's offer to buy him a pair of colors when he came down from Oxford that summer, seven years ago, when he was twenty-one.

The deuce take you, Nigel, he muttered—not for the first time—as he went downstairs to join George for a simple nuncheon. If his brother had done his duty instead of wasting both his life and what was left of the Davenport fortune on birds of paradise and high wagers, Harry might still be on the continent living the life he liked best. He sighed. Instead, here he was practically trapped in a marriage of convenience with a woman he would not have looked at twice if he had a choice.

No, he quickly corrected himself. He would definitely have looked more than once at Angela Walters. Any man not blind or in his dotage would have been drawn to her elegant form and enchanting face. Had she been of the *ton*, she would undoubtedly have been considered a Diamond of the First Water. No doubt about it. Her dark beauty was not really his style, of course. Personally, he preferred a female of ethereal fairness and the fragility which evoked a protective urge in his breast.

Harry grimaced at the thought, and before he could prevent it, the vision of one particular flaxen beauty flashed before his eyes: Miss Matilda Woodall. Harry groaned inwardly at the memory of her sweet face as he had seen it last, over two years ago at his father's funeral.

He had known the Woodalls forever, of course. Their small estate lay adjacent to the more extensive Davenport holdings in Kent, and George Woodall, two years his junior, had been his playmate and friend for as long as Harry could remember. He had become aware of Matilda during his nineteenth summer when she turned fifteen. Without warning, she ceased to be the tiresome schoolroom chit who followed him and George around like an adoring spaniel, and became—to his inexperienced and newly opened eyes—a fairy princess, whose heart-shaped face, framed with a halo of the palest gold curls, began to haunt his dreams every night.

By the end of that glorious summer, when in his innocence he had believed that anything was possible if one were in love, they had secretly pledged to be true to each other forever. Two years later, he had gone off to join the army, secure in his belief that Matilda was his to claim upon his return.

What a fool he had been, Harry thought, bitterness flooding back. The one and only letter he had received from Matilda had broken his heart. Less than a year after he had left Castleton Abbey, she had married his brother, Nigel. The betrayal still rankled. Nigel's behavior did not surprise him. His brother, heir to the title but not to Black Harry's dashing good looks, had always wanted whatever was Harry's. It was only natural that he should want Matilda, and according to that one tear-stained letter she had written, her father had made sure that the heir to the Davenport estates got what he wanted.

Well, now she was a widow, he thought with a certain grim satisfaction. Childless too, as old Hamilton had informed him, and without any claim whatsoever on the estate. Nigel had left her without a feather to fly with, so she had gone back to nurse old Sir Gerald Woodall and take up her former duties as hostess of Woodall Manor.

Impatiently, Harry thrust all thoughts of Matilda from his mind. His romantic ideal of the fair princess had died the day he received that letter, he reminded himself. And even if it hadn't—which of course it had, he reminded himself again— he no longer believed in love matches. His marriage to Miss Walters would put an end to any last vestige of such nonsense that might still linger in his heart.

* * *

It was after five o'clock that afternoon before the major found himself free to mount old Duke, his campaign gelding, and take the exercise he so badly needed.

The Park was thin of company so late on a sunny July afternoon. Most of the nobility had long since removed to the country for the summer, and Harry wished he could have done the same. He was anxious to see his home again, and London life had never pleased him overmuch. Unlike his brother, his tastes were simple and he longed to set his hand to restoring Castleton Abbey to its former splendor.

But before that was possible, there was something he must bring himself to do, he thought, as he cantered along a shady bridle path, deliberately avoiding the few carriages which dotted the street. Although it was unlikely anyone would recognize him after seven years away, Harry had no wish to call attention to himself and provoke idle questions which he would undoubtedly find embarrassing to answer.

And that, of course, was the rub. He would have to marry the Walters chit if he were to save the Abbey from his father's creditors, and himself from ruin. Of course, footloose as he would undoubtedly be if the Cit's daughter turned him down, he could always go to the colonies. He had heard that with hard work and a little luck, fortunes could be made there. But the Kent countryside of his youth called to him, and Harry knew, deep in his heart, that he wanted to return home to stay.

Lost in his thoughts, Harry had paid little notice to his surroundings. Now he became aware of a rider ahead of him among the trees. It had to be a lady, since a liveried groom on a neatish cob rode at a decreet distance behind her, and the splash of scarlet riding habit and saucy plumed hat could only belong to a lady of the first stare.

Harry drew Duke down to a sedate walk. He had no desire whatsoever for female company, but a meeting seemed to be inevitable since Duke's long, mile-eating strides were quickly decreasing the distance between them.

He was about to draw rein and swing the Duke around to retrace his steps, when something about the female form ahead of him made him pause. He examined her more closely. The waist, impossibly slim, flared out enticingly into softly rounded hips. She rode with a certain flair and self-confidence which reminded him of someone. Her hair, tucked primly under the smart black beaver hat with its daring scarlet feather, was as dark as midnight.

At that moment, the lady stopped her horse and turned to say something to the groom, and Harry recognized her. Even had he wished, he could not have avoided the encounter when her smoky eyes stared in startled recognition directly into his, and a spontaneous smile of welcome flashed on her lips.

"Major Davenport, well met, sir." Angela smiled at him as he brought his rangy gray gelding abreast of her own mount.

"Miss Walters, an unexpected pleasure, ma'am." Major Davenport bowed slightly at her greeting and then seemed to take a sudden interest in her horse. "Is that not a rather skittish mount for a lady, Miss Walters? I confess I am not particularly fond of Arabians myself. Too temperamental by half, or so I've heard." He favored her with a fleeting glance from those dark blue eyes which threatened her composure.

Had she imagined it, she wondered in confusion, or had there been a gleam of approval in the major's eyes before he veiled them with that cool, impersonal stare he favored? The gleam was gone so quickly that Angela convinced herself she had been mistaken.

"Oh, I have been riding Black Star for over ten years," she replied calmly. "And never once has he shown any sign of temperament. My father found him as a rather scrawny, mistreated colt at Tattersalls just before my twelfth birthday. I had wanted a horse of my own and Papa said that as soon as he saw Black Star, he thought of me. We were both so scrawny in our early years, you see." She laughed companionably at the recollection. "An uncomplimentary comparison, and so I told him, but true nevertheless. We grew up together, Black Star and I. And Papa was right, we were both gangly and awkward in those days."

"But true no longer, as I hardly need point out, Miss Walters," the major remarked in a voice that was soft without being flirtatious.

"Yes, we are both a good deal older and wiser," Angela remarked, deliberately ignoring the implied compliment in the major's words. "And how is Jeremy?" she said, changing the subject. "Does he not ride?"

"Oh yes," the major laughed shortly. "The lad is a bruising rider. Neck or nothing, unfortunately. I fear he will come to grief before he is very much older."

He had deliberately not answered her first question, Angela noticed, and suddenly it was vitally important for her to know if the major had proven her wrong in supposing he would not spend the bank draft she had given him. She lacked the courage to ask him directly, however, and before she could think of a way to extract the information from her reticent companion, he seemed to take pity on her and volunteered the information she was so anxious to hear.

"As a rule he would be with me now, since riding is such a passion with him, but I left him trying on his new finery, Miss Walters. He has developed an unsuspected weakness for sartorial splendor, I'm afraid," the major said with a rueful smile. "He is anxious for your approval, ma'am," he added in a noncommittal voice. "I have promised he may call on you tomorrow morning, if that is agreeable to you."

An unexpected glow of pleasure made Angela's blood sing in her veins. He had passed the test. He had spent her money. And he was coming to call on her again tomorrow morning. Just a minute, she chided herself sternly. Of course he had done so; what other choice did he have? Her Papa had made no bones about the state of the major's finances; his pockets were decidedly to let. He was an ex-soldier with no income at all, no prospects to speak of, a ruined estate, and a mountain of debts. How could he refuse the astoundingly generous proposal Mr. Walters must have made him through his man of business?

Angela's heart sank, and her surge of happiness quickly dissipated. What a fool she was to imagine that he might, just might be doing this for her sake. What a simpleton she was, indeed. How lacking in worldliness to imagine for a single second that it could be otherwise. Whichever way she looked at it, the picture was crystal clear. Her dearest Papa, wishing to fulfil her mother's last dream and concerned with his only daughter's single state, had dangled a carrot too large to be ignored before this man's cynical gaze. She did not know the exact figure that had been discussed, but she did know her father and the enormous resources at his disposal. In all likelihood, the major's debts and obligations would not even make him blink. He would pay them all without counting the cost to a man's pride.

Or to a woman's either, she thought, momentarily threatened by a fit of the dismals. For the first time in her life, Angela regretted her father's vast fortune. It had been insufficient to save her from that insulting proposal from Roger. Oh, Roger, she thought with a twist of longing she had imagined was a thing of the past. What a gorgeous, deceitful, charming, hypocritical Adonis you were. I loved you much more than you deserved.

In an effort to dispel the image of irresistible blond manhood that threatened to destroy her composure completely, Angela turned to the dark man who rode at her side and was surprised to find his quizzical blue gaze fixed on her face.

"I trust it will be convenient for us to call on you tomorrow, Miss Walters?" he repeated rather stiffly.

Angela sensed that there was more to this simple request than the words suggested. This sounded perilously like capitulation. Was the major implying that he was ready to accept her Papa's terms? In a flash of insight, she realized that she had guessed correctly. A less punctilious man might well have seized this chance encounter to bring things to a head between them. She was glad the major had enough delicacy to give her one last chance to turn aside the impending agreement. She could so easily plead another engagement. And if she did so, she knew instinctively that she would never see the major or Jeremy again.

She gazed into the unreadable depths of his eyes and smiled. "I look forward to seeing both of you, Major."

After a restless night, during which Angela examined her impending relationship with Major Harry Davenport from every conceivable angle without finding the comfort she was hoping for, she rose betimes and sat at her open bedroom window, watching the summer dawn break over the rooftops of London.

Although these ruminations in no way caused her to waver from her decision to accept the major's offer when it came, the soul searching did provide a clearer view of her own motivations. Tomorrow she would be twenty-three, and she was well aware that, for all her father's fortune, she was unlikely to contract a more comfortable alliance with such a minimum of fuss. The major would hardly expect her to play the blushing bride, and she was more than certain that he would be a civil rather than an amorous bridegroom. On the other hand, the man exuded—even at his most cynically aloof—a virility which Angela found to be highly tantalizing, and which made her breathless even now, just thinking about it.

This was all to the good, she told herself calmly, watching the nearby chimneys begin to belch wisps of thin smoke into the morning air. Such a man would undoubtedly consummate their marriage without delay, and she would welcome this fact if she wished to have children of her own. And she most definitely did want them. This truth had hit her forcibly when she met Jeremy and began to imagine what he had been like as a baby. What would it be like to have the major's child? she wondered. Her stomach gave a peculiar little lurch at the thought. She was determined not to be missish about what she had heard referred to as conjugal intimacies. Conjugal intimacies, she whispered aloud, savoring the taste of the words in all their mysterious implications.

Her experience with intimacies of any kind was decidedly limited, she had to admit. Aside from a few inexpertly stolen kisses from inexperienced suitors, she had encountered nothing vaguely resembling the earth-shattering emotion she had been led to expect from the opposite sex from her occasional indulgence in romantic novels purchased from Hatchard's Bookshop. Until Roger, that is. Roger had fulfilled her every romantic illusion with his golden curls falling in careless disarray over his laughing eyes. And his mouth had seduced her utterly with kisses both sweet and incredibly provocative. But his hard, lean body had been the worst temptation of all, making her dizzy with a desire that had almost ruined her. Small wonder he had lost all respect for her, she thought. Her behavior had been positively wanton.

At that moment the clock in the hall downstairs struck six, and the echo was immediately taken up by several church towers in the neighborhood. Angela sighed and rose to tug the bellrope to summon Rosie, the little maid who brought up her chocolate every morning. She would have to learn to put the memory of Roger away in mothballs for good. After today, that part of her life would be gone forever, and best forgotten if she were to make the major a satisfactory wife, she thought.

On impulse, Angela decided to spend an hour or two in the music room that morning, going over her favorite pieces. Music always managed to restore her peace of mind, and she would need all the tranquility she could get if she were to face the major with equanimity when he came to call.

So it was there, in the sunny music room, that Higgins found her at a quarter to ten that morning to announce that he had shown the major and that young person into the morning room once more.

Angela found the major at his usual place before the window, but Jeremy stood facing the door, obviously in anticipation of her arrival. A broad grin broke across his face as soon as she entered.

"Good morning, Miss Walters," he exclaimed, rushing up to grasp her hand in both of his with obvious pleasure. "Uncle Harry says I have you to thank for my new clothes, and I do indeed thank you very much. Tell me if they meet with your approval." He turned slowly for her inspection, his eyes fixed anxiously on her face.

Angela regarded him, her own eyes brimming with merriment. "I declare I have not seen anything finer in a long while, Jeremy. You have excellent taste."

"Oh, Uncle Harry chose them," he explained naively. "I'm sorry I missed meeting you in the Park yesterday. Uncle Harry says you have a bang-up piece of blood and bones. What's his name?"

"I call him Black Star."

"Are you going riding again today?" he asked eagerly. "May I go with you, please? I would like above anything to see Black Star. May I, Uncle Harry? Please say I may." Jeremy turned toward the man still standing at the window, regarding the scene with amusement.

Angela raised her eyes to meet his and was struck once again by the change in their hue. Today they were almost a sapphire blue, no longer the brooding, midnight shade of yesterday, but filled with glints of suppressed laughter. She found them very attractive indeed.

"Yes, Major. Please say that he may." She added her plea to Jeremy's as she advanced to offer her hand, a welcoming smile on her lips.

Major Davenport bent over her hand with his usual stiff bow, but this time Angela distinctly felt his lips rest briefly on her fingers. A small victory, she thought, but it pleased her nevertheless, and she rewarded him with a brilliant smile.

"Well?" She looked up at him. "Perhaps you would like to ride with us, Major? The Park is usually deserted at this hour." Now why did she say that? she wondered as soon as the words slipped out. The major would think she did not want to be seen with him when, in fact, all she meant was that it was unlikely that any of his friends would see him in the company of a Cit's daughter.

"If there's no one around, I can show Jeremy some of Black Star's paces," she added, trying to correct her blunder and wishing that she did not have to watch her tongue so carefully.

Jeremy greeted this announcement with a series of joyous cries which caused his uncle's face to soften.

"Very well, brat," he said. "On the condition that you take yourself off this instant to the stables so that Miss Walters and I can have some peace and quiet."

Angela swallowed. Here it comes, she thought with a sudden flash of panic. I am about to receive an offer of marriage from a man I met two days ago. Automatically, she pulled the bellrope to summon Higgins and, in a voice that sounded perfectly calm in spite of her inner agitation, instructed the butler to keep Jeremy amused below stairs until Major Davenport was ready to leave.

In the sudden silence that fell after the door closed behind them, Angela racked her brain for something to say. By this time the whole house must know why the major was closeted in the morning room with her. She had seen the knowledge in Higgins's usually inscrutable face. Heaven help her if this interview turned out to be a false start. The notion that perhaps the major intended to hedge off and not make her an offer at all startled Angela out of her reverie.

"May I pour you a cup of tea, Major?" she inquired, indicating the refreshment tray Higgins had placed on the low table before the hearth. "Or would you prefer a glass of sherry?"

"Tea will do nicely, thank you, Miss Walters," he replied, leaning an arm on the marble mantel and looking down at her.

"Tell me," he said, as she passed him the delicate Wedgwood cup, "why do you always address me by my military title?"

Angela had expected anything but this, and she felt herself relax as she looked up at him and laughed. "To tell you the truth, I prefer to think of you as a soldier," she confessed.

"You have something against hereditary titles?" His voice was curious and, she thought, faintly amused.

She hesitated for a second, then decided to tell him the truth. "Yes, as a matter of fact, I do."

"May I ask why?"

"You will probably think me nonsensical, but I had a rather unpleasant experience with a titled gentleman when I was only nineteen. I was very young and foolish. And very much in love," she added, determined not to misrepresent her part in the ugly affair.

"And what happened?" he said softly.

Angela paused, regarding him closely for any indication of censure in his eyes. She found none, so she continued with a small sigh. "It was brought home to me, in no uncertain terms, that gentlemen of the nobility do not make respectable offers to females like me." She had tried to keep the bitterness out of her voice, but it was there. After all these years, she was still unable to be neutral about Roger's betrayal.

A deep silence followed Angela's confession, during which she kept her eyes firmly on her teacup. The ticking of the ormolu clock on the mantel was the only sound to disturb the paralysis which seemed to have afflicted both occupants of the room.

The major finally moved to set down his cup. "So, based on that one unhappy experience, the idea of becoming a countess holds no appeal for you, I gather."

"No." She could not trust herself to look up to him.

"Am I right in assuming, however, that you might not be averse to becoming a plain soldier's wife?"

Was this meant to be an offer? she wondered, her eyes still lowered. If so, it was a strange way for an earl to go about it. But she must answer his question truthfully, whatever the cost.

"No." she repeated. "That would certainly be preferable."

"A plain Mrs. Davenport, then?" he said gently. "Mrs. Harry Davenport, for example?"

This time there could be no mistaking the nature of his question. It was undoubtedly an offer of marriage. Angela's eyes flew to his face, and she was surprised to see compassion there—and something else which made her heart leap into her throat.

"Yes." she whispered, and quickly dropped her eyes again as a faint blush stole up into her cheeks.

Before she could gather her wits about her, she felt the major take the cup of cold tea from her equally cold fingers and place it on the tray. Then he took her by the hand and raised her to her feet. A whiff of the Holland water he used assailed her nostrils and brought home to her how very close together they stood. Her eyes were riveted on his white cravat, a bare three inches from her nose.

"Then it is all settled between us, Angela?"

Surprised and pleased at his use of her given name, Angela raised her head and stared up at him. There was neither cynicism nor bitterness in his eyes, but only kindness, and perhaps hope, she speculated. His voice, gruffer than she had yet heard it, betrayed unsuspected emotion.

When his gaze slid down to rest on her mouth, Angela instinctively raised her face to receive her major's first kiss.

4

The Family Dinner

It had been much easier than he had imagined, Harry thought, looking down into Angela's smoky eyes as he bent to brush his lips firmly but briefly upon hers. She had made it easy for him and had made no demands on him at all, beyond raising her face for his kiss. But even that had only been in response to his own unspoken decision. She had read his intention and responded without missishness or false modesty. He liked that about her. She seemed like a sensible female, and for the first time since this marriage had been proposed to him, Harry felt that it might not be as bad as he had imagined.

"I take that to mean that things are indeed settled between us, my dear?" he murmured, wondering what was really going on behind those magnificent, mysterious eyes of hers.

"Yes, of course," came the brief answer, with a flicker of a smile.

"What made you change your mind, Angela?" he wanted to know. "I could have sworn that yesterday you meant to send me packing. Am I not right?"

She regarded him with surprise. "Yes, that is true. I had thought that . . . well, that we would not suit."

"And what changed your mind?"

She turned away from him to resume her seat on the yellow brocade settee, to give herself time to compose her answer. Harry wondered if she would tell him the truth and not throw a sop to his pride. She had already shown that she could share painful memories with him without flinching. He found himself hoping she would trust him enough to be honest with him.

"I realize that your initial impression of me could not have been very favorable," he prompted.

To his relief, she laughed. "That is very much an under-statement, Major. You were totally repellent, if you must know the terrible truth. You could barely bring yourself to ad-dress me at all and made me feel how totally unacceptable I was to someone of your social standing. I was crushed until I remembered that I could—as you put it—send you packing." She smiled at him to take the sting out of her words. "Then it occurred to me that your position was even less comfortable than my own."

Well, he had wanted the truth, he thought ruefully, and she had given it to him. He cursed his stubborn pride which had blinded him to anything but his own humiliating need for funds. He had not stopped to regard her feelings at all.

"I apologize for any pain I have caused you, Angela," he said, wondering if she realized how much this confession was costing him. "But unless I am mistaken, that kindness on your part could not have been the only factor in changing your mind."

Angela's face registered surprise. "You are very percep-tive, Major." she replied with another of her startling smiles that lit up her whole face and caused glints of humor to dance in the smoky depths of her eyes. "And insistent, too. I see I shall have to reveal all."

She paused for a moment, as if to collect her thoughts, or perhaps to find the courage to answer honestly. "I shall be twenty-three tomorrow, Major," she began.

"A ripe old age, indeed," Harry remarked lightly.

"By some standards, perhaps. For the past three years, ever since that incident I spoke of, I have been indifferent to the passing of time. I was firmly resolved to remain single. I have been very happy here with my music, my horses, my books. My father adores me and I him, and I have been mistress of this house since my mother died when I was fifteen. I lack nothing. I thought I had my life laid out for me. And I did, of course, until you brought Jeremy here yesterday. Seeing him made me realize that perhaps my life was not as complete as I had imagined."

Angela paused and looked away, a faint blush betraying her reluctance to be more specific.

Harry took pity on her. "You found out that you wanted children of your own?" he asked quietly.

She nodded. "Yes. It took me quite by surprise."

"And since you could hardly set up a nursery without a husband, you realized I might be the answer to your prayer?" For some reason, the prospect of being accepted for his reproductive services failed to amuse him.

Angela choked back a nervous laugh. "I do not recall actually praying for such a thing, but it did occur to me that you might wish for an heir."

"I already have an heir," he said, more brusquely that he had intended. "Jeremy is a Davenport, as were his father and grandfather before him. He is Black Harry's only great-grandson, and stands next to me in line for the title."

As he spoke, he strode over to the window, conscious that his leg had begun to throb. It always did when he became angry, and for some reason he did not dare examine too closely, he was angry now. With an effort, he controlled his sudden, irrational flare of temper and turned back to Angela. If he were not careful, the wench could still reject him.

"I am sorry, Angela," he said, limping back to stand in front of the hearth. "I did not mean to fly off the handle at you. My deuced temper sometimes gets the better of me." He suddenly noticed that she had gone pale and that her eyes, so recently full of amusement, were now two pools of undecipherable emotion.

"I see," she said at last, her voice cool and distant, as if addressed to a stranger. For the space of several moments Angela stared at him as if he had committed the most deplorable faux pas imaginable.

When she did speak, it was with a polite formality which made him curse himself for a bumbling clodpole. "Now, if you will please sit down, Major, you might be more comfortable. And there are two other matters which we need to discuss."

"I should think there are many more than two, my dear," he replied curtly, settling himself in the leather wing-chair beside her. "Which two are you thinking of in particular?"

"Your own wardrobe, for one," Angela said bluntly. "My father has accounts with Weston, Stultz, and Scott, and has bought his boots from Hoby for years. He suggested to me this morning that you might like to charge any new items you need to his account until your own affairs are settled."

Harry leapt to his feet with such alacrity that his wounded leg nearly buckled under him. He turned a white, furious face to Angela, who regarded him with so bland an expression in her gray eyes that he wondered if she had set out deliberately to provoke him.

"I will do nothing of the sort," he growled, wishing his leg would not throb so. "And I would like to remind you, Miss Walters, that I have been clothing myself for years without any help from a . . ." He stopped abruptly, horrified at what he had almost said. "From anybody," he corrected himself hastily. "And I have no intention of accepting any now."

"Very well," came the cool reply. "As you wish, Major. But I fail to see why you must fly up into the boughs over such a trifle."

"I will accept nothing from your father until I have fulfilled my end of the agreement," Harry said, his voice still edged with angry overtones. "What is the second matter you wished to discuss?"

"My father will expect you to seek an interview with him to make the final arrangements," Angela pointed out. "So I would like to know if you are free to have dinner with us this evening."

Harry felt himself cringe. Here it comes, he thought. This is what he most feared from this whole arrangement. Not only must he take a Cit's daughter to wife, but he would also be expected to socialize with a whole family of merchants. His lip curled faintly at the thought. He noticed that Angela was watching him, her wide, intelligent eyes missing nothing. Intuitively he knew that she had read everything in his mind, every sordid, unkind thought, and he felt a stab of shame.

"Cannot the arrangements be made through your father's man of business?" he argued.

No sooner had this thoughtless remark left his lips than Harry became aware that he had committed an unpardonable sin. Angela sprang to her feet, her eyes dark with fury. She faced him, fairly bristling with suppressed rage. He was at least six inches taller than the top of her glistening black curls, but the look of disdain on her face made him feel very small indeed.

"So," she lashed out at him, every word a rapier point. "The grand Major Davenport is too good to sit at my father's table, but not too top-lofty to accept his money, is he? Well, you can think again, Major. I will not tolerate even a suggestion of a slight against my father. He is everything that is good, and kind, and generous in my life, and he deserves better than the contempt of a penniless soldier like you." The contempt in her voice was patent, and she tossed her head angrily. "I do not ask that you love him as I do, but I do demand, yes, I *demand* that you respect him. Not for what he is not, but for what he *is*. You owe him that, at least, as my father. But you owe him a great deal more, and if you so much as dare to look down that supercilious nose of yours at him, I shall never, ever speak to you again. Is that quite clear?"

Her breast was heaving with emotion, and her cheeks were flushed to a delicate pink. Harry thought she looked quite magnificent, and for a moment he was at a loss for words. Her outburst—admittedly justified—brought back bittersweet memories of his beloved governess, Miss Hayworth, the only person he knew who could make his stomach twist with guilt as it did now.

"All I asked, Miss Walters," he said finally, "was whether the arrangements could not be made by our men of business. I never meant to imply—"

"I would much prefer that you not treat me as if I were a fool, Major," Angela said coldly. "Your thoughts were on your face for all to see. So don't try to gammon me, because it won't fadge. You were appalled at the thought of actually having to dine at my father's table. Admit it."

"I admit no such a thing." He was beginning to recover from the shock of her attack, and his temper flared, not so much at her accusations as at the fact that she had read him so accurately.

"So, can we expect you to dine with us tonight?" Her voice was mocking and slightly bitter, as if she already knew the answer he would give to her question.

"We shall see," he replied tersely, wondering how he could keep from throttling this impossible female.

"Yes, of course, Major, we shall all see what kind of a man you really are, won't we? I can't imagine what maggot got into my head to imagine that you could be any different from Roger. You are cut from the same mold, after all. Selfish, cynical, unscrupulous, puffed up with your own petty importance." She paused, as if at a loss for words.

"Have you quite finished, Miss Walters?" Harry silently congratulated himself on his restraint; his burning impulse was to curl his fingers around her slim white neck and shake his newly betrothed until her teeth rattled.

"Finished? Of course I'm not finished," she fairly spat on him. "But I will be tonight if you cannot bring yourself to dine with your future father-in-law." Angela swept regally to the door and threw it open. "We dine at eight," she remarked over her shoulder, as an afterthought. "I will send Higgins to see you out."

And she was gone.

Harry took out a handkerchief and mopped his brow. A regular termagant, an archwife, a virago of the worst kind. That's what Miss Angela Walters had shown herself to be. He would be well rid of her, he thought irritably. Order him to present himself when and where it pleased her, would she? Well, Harry Davenport was not some cursed Johnny Raw who would dance attendance on any female with a pretty face. Miss Walters would soon find out that she had missed her mark if she thought he could be brought to heel so easily. It would serve her right if he washed his hands of her entirely.

Angela had never been so outraged in her entire life. After leaving the morning room, she went up to her sitting room and slammed the door, something she could not recall ever having done before. It did not help to decrease her fury in the slightest, nor relieve her frustration at the man she had just left.

An hour of pacing the length and breadth of her elegant sitting room did nothing to calm her jangled nerves, and when the luncheon hour came and went without either Higgins or any of the other domestics approaching her, she knew she had set the household on its ear.

At two o'clock, she went down to the music room, but neither Haydn nor Bach, her two most cherished composers, were able to console her troubled spirit. After she had changed into her scarlet habit for a ride in the Park, in the hope that fresh air and exercise would restore her tranquility of mind, she remembered that she had promised to ride that afternoon with Davenport and his ward. Immediately she ordered Clothilde to help her out of the habit again. She would not go, she decided. Instead, she chose an afternoon gown of bright blue silk until she realized—after Clothilde had painstakingly fastened the long row of buttons from neck to waist—that the color reminded her of a certain pair of eyes she would rather not think of.

Disgusted at herself, Angela changed the gown for a daring green one of soft muslin with several flounces and wide Brussels lace at the neck. She regarded herself critically in the cheval mirror, as Clothilde stood behind her, eyes watchful and wary. Angela laughed at her dresser's sour expression.

"I don't like this one either," she remarked. "But it will have to do. I will wear the new apricot silk for dinner, Clothilde, if you have fixed the hem."

Remembering that she had not finished the latest novel by Mrs. Radcliffe, purchased from Hatchard's before the major had come into her life, Angela went in search of it and took it out into the enclosed garden at the back of the house. Here she ensconced herself in a comfortable garden chair and finally with the help of the warm sun, the smell of summer flowers, and the occasional song of their resident thrush, she began to regain her composure.

At four o'clock, when Higgins brought her a tea tray and some welcome pastries, Angela felt more herself. She was no less angry with the major—he had, after all, demonstrated a crass insensitivity quite consistent with her expectations of a titled gentleman—but she had become more philosophical about the outcome of their first battle.

She chuckled to herself as she recalled his startled reaction to her attack. For a brief moment, she had seen a gleam of frank admiration in his eyes. Though why this fact should please her, she did not know. He was almost as bad as Roger in his stiff pride in his name and inability to see any worth in her at all.

Her amusement died as she remembered the humiliating snub she had been forced to endure. So a Cit's daughter was not good enough to be the mother of his children, she thought, her fury rekindling. He already had his heir in Jeremy; he had made that quite clear. And, of course, Jeremy was a Davenport, directly descended from this Black Harry the major seemed to hold in such high regard.

Angela sighed. In all likelihood, the major would not put in an appearance at all that evening. And that would be that, she told herself firmly. Her pride would have to endure one more bruise, and then she could announce to the whole household that she had decided against matrimony after all. Her dear Papa would start making plans to take her to Brighton, and Julian would undoubtedly be pleased at her decision. Like all men, she thought, Julian liked to be proved right.

Angela preferred to be right herself, of course, but this time her instincts seemed to have misled her. The sooner she put the whole affair behind her, the better it would be for her peace of mind, she thought.

She kept this resolution firmly in mind that evening as she dressed for dinner in the elegant apricot silk gown. The fact that its rustling folds had been cut with an eye to revealing every seductive curve of her feminine form without transcending the bounds of good taste gave her perverse pleasure. The only thing that marred her feeling of triumph was the unfortunate circumstance that the major would not be present to witness it.

"You look *absolument ravissante*," Clothilde exclaimed as she gave a last twitch to the silken folds around Angela's long legs. "*Monsieur le comte* will be, how you say, *étonné*."

"Bowled over, I imagine," Angela laughed, satisfied with the reflection of the long-legged seductress in her mirror. No need to tell Clothilde that her precious *comte* would not be there to be bowled over. On impulse, she took out the diamond necklace and earbobs her father had given her on her twenty-first birthday.

"You are a grown woman now," he had told her seriously as he presented her with the exquisitely cut diamonds, which had probably set him back several thousand pounds. "And it is only fitting that you wear jewels to reflect that status."

Clothilde arranged her dark curls in a sophisticated pile on the top of her head, allowing several ringlets to fall gracefully on her white shoulders. The glittering diamonds were exactly right tonight, she thought. They matched the militant glitter of her eyes.

She would accept her Papa's invitation to spend a month in Brighton, she decided. The more she thought about it, the more the idea appealed to her. She would order a dozen new gowns—or perhaps twenty would be better. She would promenade along the glazed red brick pavement of the Marine Parade, attend the local assemblies at the Old Ship and Castle Inns, drink the waters in the Pump Room, browse in Donaldson's Circulating Library, and drive her new curricle among the holiday traffic. And if any titled gentlemen was foolhardy enough to approach her, she would give him the cut direct. Even if that gentleman happened to be the Prince Regent himself.

The thought of a Cit's daughter rejecting a summons from the Regent to attend a select dinner party at his Marine Pavilion, with its excess of domes and minarets, caused Angela's lips to curve into an enchanting smile. This smile still lingered on her lips as she descended to the main drawing room that evening, a good twenty minutes later than her usual hour.

Higgins opened the door for her, and Angela swept into the room, a laughing apology on her lips for keeping her dearest Papa waiting so long. The apology never was completed. Two gentlemen rose at her entrance. One of them was, of course, her father, his tall, slender frame dressed as always in elegantly simple black evening clothes. The other was dressed in the unmistakable uniform of the 7th Hussars, a crack cavalry regiment much touted for its bravery and the sartorial splendor of its officers.

For a moment that seemed to Angela to last forever, she stood rooted to the plush Axminster carpet beneath her feet. Then, she recovered from the shock and took another step into the room, her face unfreezing into a dazzling smile.

Major Harry Davenport covered the space between them in four strides and bowed—with no hint of his previous stiffness in his tall frame—over the hand she extended. The kiss he bestowed was warmer than strictly conventional, but less than ef-

fusive, and he did not release her hand when he rose to his full
height and looked down at her.

"Surprised to see me, Angela?" he said softly, a glint of
amusement in his eyes. "I would not have missed this for anything, my dear." His eyes, startling sapphire tonight, Angela
noticed, lazily examined her face and then dropped to her low
décolletage. "You are stunningly beautiful tonight, Angela,"
he murmured in low tones. "But then, of course, you already
know that, don't you m'dear?"

Angela frowned at this blatant flattery. "You are looking
very fine yourself, Major," she said crisply. "And to answer
your first question, no, I did not expect to see you tonight. Or
ever again, for that matter."

"So sorry to disappoint you, Miss Walters," he replied, the
humor fading from his eyes.

"Don't be ridiculous," she said without thinking. "I am
very glad you did come. I behaved abominably this morning,"
she rushed on before she could regret her impulse. "And I am
heartily sorry I ripped up at you as I did. I am not apologizing
for what I said, mind you. I meant *everything* I said. But I
wish I had chosen a more civil way of expressing myself."

The major laughed. "I doubt there is a civil way of telling a
fellow he is a selfish, cynical, unscrupulous cad."

"I shall have to discover one, nevertheless, Major, for I
may well need to repeat it."

"Your father is right, then, in telling me that your only flaw
is your temper?"

Suddenly noticing that her father was regarding their whispered exchange with quiet amusement, Angela withdrew her
hand from the major's clasp and swept over to give Mr. Walters a very affectionate embrace.

"I see you have already made the acquaintance of Major
Davenport, Papa," she said, wondering just what her father
was thinking behind his polite expression. "Where is Julian?"
she asked, suddenly aware that her foster brother was not
there.

Before Mr. Walters could answer, the door opened again
and Julian Scarborough strode in, an apologetic grin on his
pleasant face. When his eyes fell on the major, however, he
paused, his square jaw rigid with disapproval.

Angela moved forward quickly to make the introductions, but it was clear to her from the outset that her dear Julian was determined to dislike Major Davenport. The major reacted predictably to Julian's stiff brow of acknowledgment by assuming a superior attitude toward him which Angela knew would only infuriate her brother still further. A glance at her Papa told her that Mr. Walters found the antagonism between the younger men vastly amusing. Why, oh why, she thought, did gentlemen feel obliged to indulge in such ridiculous posturing with each other? She knew that it would take every ounce of her skill as a hostess to make this dinner the civilized event it was intended to be.

5

The New Countess

Harry Davenport had not quite known what reception he would get at the Walters dinner party that evening, once he had made up his mind to attend. Of one thing he was certain, however. It was not what he had steeled himself to endure.

His first surprise had been Mr. George Walters himself. When Harry had been shown into the downstairs drawing room punctually at half past seven, he had found himself quite at home in surroundings similar to any of the *ton* drawing rooms he had frequented as a young man. The solitary man who had risen to greet him might have been any of the elderly gentlemen Harry had encountered dozens of times in the inner sanctum of White's.

Mr. Walters was neither jovially rotund nor vulgarly attired, two characteristics which Harry had been prepared for. His elegant black evening coat had obviously been cut by Stultz himself, and his spotless cravat tied by a master. And there was not the least hint of obsequiousness in his demeanor. He greeted his guest cordially and with an innate dignity which put Harry instantly at ease.

Harry's second surprise had been his betrothed. When Angela swept into the room, he had frankly been stunned. He had known her to possess a regal figure and passable good looks, but the apricot silk and diamond vision which met his eyes had caused him to stand there gaping like some uncouth gapeseed.

She had obviously not expected to see him, a discovery which had gratified him intensely. In fact, he had started to feel that he might actually enjoy the evening until Julian Scarborough had entered the room.

The antagonism between them had been instantaneous and

virulent. Scarborough, almost a head shorter than Harry, though equally as broad, and dressed with the same elegance as their host, had made it plain that he disapproved of Harry's presence. He especially seemed to resent the cordiality which Angela displayed towards the major. He had scowled when Harry claimed the privilege of leading Angela into the dining room and had sat throughout the meal saying little beyond polite commonplaces.

When Angela finally left the gentlemen to their port, Harry requested the private interview with his host he had been dreading.

"I must ask your lordship's indulgence with my son, Julian," Mr. Walters said as he took his place behind the wide oak desk in the library and motioned the major to a wing chair opposite. "He has been Angela's elder brother for so long he is reluctant to relinquish that responsibility." He smiled, and some of Harry's resentment against the disgruntled young man evaporated. "Has my daughter explained how Julian came to be a part of our family, my lord?"

"I understand that Mr. Scarborough's father was a partner of yours, sir," Harry replied.

"That is true. But our alliance goes back still further. Julian's grandfather started the partnership with my father, who built this house back in 1762, before I was born. Julian is my partner but not my heir. His own holdings are considerable, inherited from his father. I had hoped for a son to take over from me, but I was blessed with a daughter, who is the light of my life." Mr. Walters paused, regarding his guest searchingly, and Harry felt a twinge of envy at the closeness which must exist between this man and his daughter. His own family relationships had been uneven at best, and after his father's death, they had deteriorated still further. He had despised his brother, Nigel, and never been a favorite with his mother. Since the death of his cousin Charles, Jeremy's father, the only relative he felt the slightest affection for was his sister, Sophy, who probably regarded him as the black sheep of the family.

"I have tried to keep Angela away from the business side of our affairs, my lord," his host continued. "But she has a high degree of intelligence for a female, and an excellent head for figures. She is also willful and has a mind of her own." He smiled ruefully at his guest, who had to agree with his assessment.

"She takes after her grandfather in that respect, I'm afraid," Mr. Walters continued. "So I must confess that, in spite of all my efforts to confine her to ladylike activities, Angela probably knows as much about sea trading as Julian himself."

There was a slight pause while Mr. Walters refilled their port glasses.

"Angela has informed me, my lord, that—"

"I would prefer to keep my military title, if it is all the same to you, sir," Harry interrupted. "Miss Walters also prefers it that way," he added with a grin.

Mr. Walters did not look surprised. "I see my daughter has revealed something of her unfortunate experience with a titled gentleman." He paused, and Harry noted that his host's face had become somber. "A deplorable incident. If I had been younger, and of his own set, I would have called him out. As it was, I took other measures which will probably be more painful in the long run to the gentleman he professes himself to be."

Harry was startled at the quiet anger in his host's voice and the cold intensity of his gaze. As suddenly as it had appeared, however, it was gone, and Mr. Walters's countenance regained its urbane expression.

"Another of my daughter's besetting sins, I am sure you have already guessed, Major," he smiled. "A lamentable tendency to speak her mind—rather forcefully at times, I am afraid."

Harry laughed. "I have already been privileged to hear Miss Walters express her opinions, sir. It is a failing we have in common."

"I am particularly wishful that you be aware of these flaws in my daughter's character before we come to any formal agreement, Major. There is still ample time to reconsider, you know. With no hard feelings, naturally. And I pray you will be perfectly frank with me, sir. I do not want my daughter to be hurt again, you understand."

As Harry considered his host's words carefully, he realized that Mr. Walters was actually not at all eager to relinquish his daughter to an earl. He was not—as Harry had imagined him—an ambitious father grasping at a title to puff up his family tree, but a man concerned primarily for the happiness and well-being of a beloved daughter. The discovery surprised and humbled him.

He cleared his throat and spoke words which never in a hundred years had he dreamed of speaking. "I would take it as an honor, Mr. Walters, if you would consider my offer for your daughter's hand in marriage."

Mr. Walters regarded him from under bushy brows. "Is there already an understanding between you?"

"Miss Walters has expressed a preference for the title of Mrs. Harry Davenport over that of Countess of Castleton, sir," Harry replied with a slight smile. "I have presumed to take that as encouragement for my suit."

"Saucy minx," her father remarked fondly. He sighed. "You understand that the outcome rests entirely with my daughter, Major. I will not force her into an alliance that is distasteful to her. It would seem that she favors you, however, so let us go over some of the conditions."

And go over them they did for the better part of an hour. When they emerged from the library and went to join Angela in the drawing room, Harry was astounded at his new father-in-law's generosity. Not only would Mr. Walters discharge all the Davenport debts accumulated since his father's time, but he would also buy up all mortgages on Davenport properties, including the London residence. When Harry had argued that the London house could well be sold, Mr. Walters insisted that a house that had been in the Davenport family for six generations deserved to be maintained.

The terms of the settlement were so generous, in fact, that Harry felt a great wave of relief at what he would now be able to do to restore Castleton Abbey. Unfortunately, he also detected, in the recesses of his mind, a flicker of resentment which he immediately repressed, ashamed at the serpent which he had glimpsed coiled at the heart of his new prosperity.

The morning of her twenty-third birthday dawned blue and cloudless. In spite of the restless night Angela had passed, she rose before six to sit at the open window, as was her habit when her mind was troubled. And this morning her mind was certainly troubled. The evening before, events had picked up an alarming speed and seemed to be racing forward beyond her control. She shuddered slightly at the realization that her future was taking shape around her as if it had a life of its own.

Dinner had gone better than she had dared to hope, considering that Julian did nothing but scowl and answer all comments addressed to him in curt monosyllables. She could hardly blame Major Davenport for ignoring him. She loved Julian dearly, but his attitude toward her proposed marriage to a titled gentleman had sorely tried her patience. While the major had been closeted with her father after dinner, Julian had done his very best to talk Angela out of giving her consent to the arrangement.

"But I have already given it, Julian," she had said, for perhaps the third time.

"Nothing is yet final, Angela," he insisted. "Father will certainly give you the final say in this matter. All you need say is that you have changed your mind, my dear, and this military coxcomb will have to take himself off to find his fortune elsewhere."

"I have already had my final say, Julian. So please do not tease me; you will give me a headache."

Her brother looked at her for several seconds, his face clouded and his brown eyes filled with anger. "I hope you will not be disappointed in your precious earl," he said, making the title sound like a particularly unpleasant disease. "And if he makes you unhappy, I swear I will give him such a proper melting he will not walk for a month afterward."

"I hope you will do nothing so rag-mannered, dear," Angela laughed, slipping her arm companionably through his. "Come over to the pianoforte, and I will sing you a song to banish those ungenerous thoughts from your head."

And so the major and her father had found them an hour later, although Angela doubted that Julian's thoughts were any more charitable toward their guest. He had been right in one thing, however. Her Papa had made it quite clear that, although he and the major had agreed on the terms of the marriage settlement, she would have the last word in the matter. If she disliked anything about the connection, including the date proposed for the marriage, she had only to say so. Her wishes would be respected.

And then Mr. Walters had pointedly challenged Julian to their evening game of billiards and declared that they would be back to take tea with Angela and the major in an hour.

She rang for her morning chocolate, and when Rosie had placed the steaming cup beside her on the window ledge, Angela allowed herself to relive the hour she had spent in the major's company last night. . . .

"Your father is a most extraordinary man, my dear," he had said as soon as they were alone. "But I get the distinct impression that he is not particularly anxious for you to wed."

"That is not so surprising, is it, Major?" Angela remarked, running her fingers softly over the keys. She wondered what the major really meant by extraordinary. He had seemed rather bemused after his interview with her father, but she sensed a tension in him, too, as if he were not quite comfortable with the way things were going.

"I am his only daughter, after all," she continued, then added diffidently. "I trust the settlements will be sufficient to restore your home."

He looked at her sharply, and Angela saw his jaw tighten before he turned away and began to look through the music scores scattered on top of the pianoforte.

"Your father has been very generous indeed," he replied, and Angela thought she detected a slight reticence in his voice. "Much more than I had a right to expect. But it will be your home, too, Angela. Unless, of course, you plan to cry off when you hear just how quickly I would like to conclude this business and get down to Castleton Abbey. There is so much to do there."

There was a teasing note in his voice now which Angela responded to with a smile, although she quailed inwardly at his reference to their marriage as a business to be concluded in haste.

"Tell me something of the Abbey," she encouraged him. "You have said that your mother has been living there with your sister. What are they like?" What she really wanted to know but dared not ask was whether his family would receive her kindly or consider her as an encroaching mushroom and treat her with disdain and contempt.

"Sophy was only fifteen when I saw her at my father's funeral two years ago," he replied. "She was a shy little thing but very good-hearted and always ready to help anyone in distress. I imagine she will be glad of your company, my dear." His face softened as he spoke of his sister, and Angela was comforted to think that she might find at least one ally at the Abbey.

"And your mother?"

The major's soft expression disappeared, and Angela saw his lip curl as a mocking note entered his voice. "I would not count on getting a warm welcome from my mother," he said with brutal frankness. "I was never one of her favorites, even as a child. It was always my brother, Nigel, who could do no wrong in her eyes. She invariably took his side against Sophy and me. It was enough for Nigel to want something that was mine, even . . ." His voice trailed off suddenly, as if he had revealed more than he had intended.

"Even what?" she prompted gently.

He looked at her then, his eyes an angry midnight blue. "Even my betrothed," he snapped.

Angela gasped, and her hand flew out in a comforting gesture which was never completed because he turned away and strode over to the hearth.

"You are better off without a woman with so little regard for you that she could betray you with your own brother," Angela remarked after a considerable pause. "I hope she lived to regret her decision."

The major turned to face her, a grimace of a smile curling his lips. "Of that you may be certain," he said curtly. "Nigel was not known for his kindness or generosity. But he was the heir to the title, and from what Matilda told me, both her father and my mother were quite set on the match."

"She told you so herself?" Angela was appalled.

"Not in person. I was on the Peninsula at the time. My father had purchased a pair of colors for me when I was twenty-one. Convinced me that I should make a career for myself in the army. I often wondered if that was not my mother's doing, to get me out of the way." He paused, eyes bleak and hooded.

He is still hurting, Angela thought, distressed at the story of love and betrayal that had so suddenly emerged from the major's past. She wondered if he still loved this Matilda, the unknown woman who had broken his young heart so many years ago.

"I had been gone scarcely six months when I received her letter. The only one she ever wrote. I wondered why I didn't hear from her, and then I found out. She was already married to Nigel when she wrote it."

His voice had turned harsh, and from the sound of it Angela knew the memory of this past betrayal still affected the major deeply. A horrible thought suddenly occurred to her.

"Does she live at the Abbey?"

He laughed mirthlessly. "Luckily we will be spared that. Nigel left her without a feather to fly with, of course. Technically, my mother has the use of the Dower House during her lifetime, and since there were no children, Matilda chose to return to her father's house. He is an invalid and was glad to have her."

Angela's conflicting emotions must have been revealed on her face, for the major regarded her searchingly and said in a kinder voice, "I hope this sordid tale has not given you a distaste for all Davenports, my dear. But it is better you hear the facts from me rather than get them from the local gossips at Castleton."

When she made no reply, her thoughts still in confusion, the major came over to the pianoforte and took one of her cold hands in his. "I did not mean to shock you, Angela, and I beg you will not refine too much on what is now past history."

"I confess that your tale took me rather by surprise, Major," Angela replied with a smile. "I have always believed that my own unpleasant experience was the worst that could happen to anyone, but I see that I was wrong." She noticed that his eyes had returned to their sapphire brilliance and were fixed upon her with a glint of amusement.

"Let us put both experiences behind us, Angela," he said, still holding her hand in his. "I want to talk about our own marriage. Would you be opposed to getting married by special license? I know that such haste is unseemly, and your father is not pleased with the idea. But I do need to get down to Castleton Abbey as soon as possible. There are so many details that require my attention. And yours, too, my dear. From what my solicitor tells me, the house is in serious disrepair and will need considerable refurbishing."

Angela regarded him apprehensively. "Just how soon did you wish to leave London?"

"The day after your birthday."

Angela stared at the major in utter amazement. "The day after tomorrow?" she repeated weakly. "You cannot be serious, Major."

He regarded her with a hint of annoyance. "Oh, but I am very serious, my dear. I cannot get the license until late tomorrow afternoon. But we can be married the next morning, before we leave London for Kent."

"But . . . that is so. . . sudden," she gulped. "I had not thought it would happen so soon."

He frowned, and Angela felt that he was on the verge of losing his temper at her missishness. She herself had heard the echoes of panic in her voice as she protested the haste with which he intended to tie the knot.

"If we are agreed on the terms, I see no reason for waiting," he said. "What else is there to say, my dear?"

What else, indeed? Angela wondered, hoping that her disappointment did not show. What did she expect after all? For him this marriage was just a business agreement between two men that wanted but her consent to be concluded satisfactorily. Her father had insisted that she could withdraw at any time, but did she really want to do so?

Schooling her features into a mask of polite acquiescence, Angela withdrew her hand from the major's clasp and played the opening bars of a Bach fugue.

"Nothing that I can think of," she said. "Nothing at all."

"It's all settled, then," he said, and Angela distinctly heard the relief in his voice.

The day passed in a blur of activity. In the morning, she supervised the packing of several trunks with a selection of clothes she deemed appropriate for an extended stay at a country house. Clothilde, who had not taken kindly to the news that her town-bred mistress was suddenly about to become a countess and mistress of a country establishment, muttered ominously as she worked. She was furious when she learned that Miss Walters was to be married in an ordinary morning gown. When Angela pointed out to the truculent dresser that the morning gown in question was anything but ordinary, and was quite the *dernier cri* of current London fashion, Clothilde sniffed disparagingly.

"This is not at all *comme il faut*, Mam'selle," she grumbled. "I know Madame Marceau will be most distressed when she finds out that you have allowed this *comte* person to talk you into doing something so . . . how you say? . . . *capricieux*."

Angela had to agree with her dresser on this. Privately however, she thought that her expensive French modiste was much more likely to regret not being called upon to outfit one of her most valued customers with an entire trousseau.

"I am not being at all capricious, Clothilde," she laughed. "And do not bother to pack any of my winter gowns. I will need more light muslins and perhaps a few more silk or brocade evening gowns. It will be warm in Kent at this time of year. I can send for my winter things later."

By mid-afternoon she was exhausted and had just retired to her favorite place in the garden for a few minutes' rest when Higgins bustled out with a bouquet of white roses from the major. The accompanying note, written in a bold, slanting hand, informed her that he looked forward to conveying his birthday greetings to her in person that evening at dinner.

Angela had no recollection of what their cook served for dinner that evening. She did notice, however, that Julian was polite to the major and seemed resigned to her marriage.

After dinner she opened her presents in the drawing room as she had done all her life, and the three gentlemen toasted her with champagne. Among other things, her father gave her a length of heavy Chinese silk in an unusual bronze color with huge chrysanthemums outlined on it in gold thread. Julian chose a jade statuette of a dainty Chinese lady in a flowing kimono, and an intricately patterned shawl of green silk. But it was the major's gift which surprised her the most.

"Your father invited me to visit one of his warehouses this afternoon," he explained as Angela exclaimed in wonder at the exquisite jade rose set in a heavily engraved gold setting. "I thought a ring would be appropriate under the circumstances."

So the hoity-toity major had actually deigned to tour a lowly warehouse with a Cit to find her a present, Angela thought. Although, as she well knew, her father's warehouses were anything but lowly, stuffed as they generally were with exotic treasures from all parts of the world, brought back to London on his fleet of merchant vessels. It had always been her father's custom to take his daughter down to the warehouses whenever a new shipment arrived from the Orient or from India. Angela recalled many a happy afternoon spent wandering through these treasures and daydreaming of romantic princesses in faraway lands.

For some reason she did not examine too closely, Angela wore the ring to bed that night, and the next morning the unfamiliar feel of it on her finger brought back the sharp realization that today was her wedding day. She lay still for a paralyzed moment, while the knowledge that a significant part of her life was about to end forever washed over her.

Impatiently, she pushed the disturbing thought aside and jumped out of bed. There was still much to do before the major arrived at ten o'clock with that special license that would make her his countess. Angela wondered, not for the first time, whether she was doing the right thing. She had desperately wanted to be Roger's countess, and when he had found her unworthy of that honor, she had suffered a crushing blow to her self-esteem from which she had not thought to recover. Yet here she was, about to become leg-shackled to a man she hardly knew and who probably regarded her as equally unworthy to carry his name. If not for the circumstances of his father's ruinous debts, the Earl of Castleton would never have glanced her way. Worse still, Angela thought as she rang for her dresser, they would never have met.

Ten o'clock arrived all too quickly, and before she had adequately reconciled herself to her changing status, she found herself standing in the middle of her father's drawing room, her future husband by her side. As she listened to the voice of the minister and responded automatically to the question he put to her, she suddenly knew, beyond a shadow of a doubt, that the path she had chosen would not be strewn with roses. The major would not be an easy man to live with. He had shown himself to be proud, moody, quick-tempered, and autocratic. Besides these less than ideal qualities, she knew his heart to be scarred—possibly beyond repair—just as her own had been by Roger's cruel disdain.

Actually, Angela realized as her new husband briefly set his lips to hers in a sealing kiss, they were well matched, since both had suffered grievously at the hands of the opposite sex.

Why was it then, she wondered, that when her dear Papa clasped her to him and gruffly wished her happiness in her new life, Angela had an almost irresistible urge to burst into tears?

6

Castleton Abbey

Although Harry had hoped to start their journey south to Castleton Abbey somewhat earlier, the elegant, well-sprung Walters' traveling chaise, drawn by four blooded horses, did not set forth from St. James Square until a little after twelve o'clock that day. Driving his light sporting curricle—when he had had a curricle to drive—Harry had been known to make the journey down to the Abbey, five miles outside Bromley Green in south Kent, in just under five hours. This kind of speed was impossible with the heavily loaded chaise carrying the new countess, her dresser and maid, his ward, Jeremy, and a moderate amount of luggage.

Riding ahead of the coach on his campaign gelding, Duke, Harry could easily imagine that he was returning home alone, as he had done so often in his youth. Only when he reached a rise in the road and glanced back did reality impinge upon his daydreams. There would be no father at the Abbey to greet him with recriminations on his mediocre performance at Oxford, or a brother to flaunt a new gun or horse or woman for his benefit. Above all, there would be no Matilda, her pale gold hair in a halo around her small face, waiting to raise her eager lips for his welcoming kiss.

Damnation, he thought savagely, what was the matter with him? He would have to stop mooning over a woman who had spurned him seven long years ago for the sake of a mere title. It had been easier when he was on the Peninsula, where his duties occupied all of his days and many of his nights. But here, so close to home, Harry felt the old hurt pulse once again deep in his stomach.

Well, he thought with a certain amount of grim satisfaction, he had the title now, and if Matilda had but waited for him, as she had promised, she would have had it too. Instead, she had allowed herself to be dazzled by Nigel's expectations as his father's heir, or, worse still, permitted her father to force her into a loveless marriage with Nigel. Harry had preferred to believe the latter possibility although he could not ignore the brash charm his brother had exercised over many young ladies of Matilda's class.

None of this mattered anymore, he told himself bitterly. Not that he would have wanted to take his brother's widow to wife. He wondered briefly if Matilda was expecting him to do so. Well, it was a moot question now. He already had a wife, a very rich wife, and he would spend all his energies in restoring his estate and not in senseless regrets over a woman who had betrayed him so damnably. Matilda would have to lie in the bed she had chosen, Harry decided, letting Duke lengthen his stride into a canter.

After a brief stop at the posting inn at Rochester to change horses and partake of some light refreshment, Harry decided to push on to Maldstone, where they would spend the night. Twilight was falling when the coach finally pulled into the courtyard of the Blue Stag Inn on Maldstone's Highstreet. Harry, who had ridden ahead to make sure that suitable rooms would be ready for his bride upon her arrival, stepped forward to hand Angela down from the coach.

"The Blue Stag was always a favorite of mine when I used to frequent these roads as a young lad," he remarked as he led her into the private parlor he had procured for their use. "Old John Oakhill, the innkeeper, tells me that they still serve the roast duck and deep venison pie I enjoyed last time I stopped here."

While Angela went upstairs with her dresser to wash her travel-stained face and tidy her hair, Harry drank a tankard of locally brewed ale in the taproom with his old friend Mr. Oakhill.

"Yer looking more like yer grandfather every day, Master Harry," the innkeeper remarked jovially. "Give me a fair start, ye do, walking in like that. Been expecting ye, of course, ever since we heard about your brother. Sorry business, that. But can't say I'm sorry to see the Abbey come to ye, my lad. Reckon ye'll do more for the place than yer brother ever did. Begging your pardon and all, but Master Nigel never was much liked in these parts."

His host's wrinkled face closed into a scowl, and Harry remembered that ten years ago Nigel had taken a fancy to old Oakhill's saucy youngest daughter and would have ruined her if Harry had not ridden over in the middle of the night to spike Nigel's planned elopement.

"And how is Peggy these days?" he inquired, his mind still lingering on the intended victim of Nigel's licentious nature.

"Ach, me little Peg's as saucy as ever and doin' very well for herself over in Rochester. Married a butcher, she did, and has three young 'uns to keep her out of trouble." His honest face became wreathed in smiles. "Spunky little tykes they are, too. Take after their mother, no doubt about it." He glanced speculatively at the major. "Jimmy Dunn was in here yesterday on his way to the Abbey. Told us ye was comin' down with yer lady wife, Major. Yer grandfather, old Black Harry as we all called him around here, will be resting lightly in his grave tonight, knowin' that his namesake is fixin' to fill the Abbey with little Harrys. If you'll pardon me for saying so, Major, things just ain't been the same since Old Harry went to his reward. No sir, they ain't at that."

Harry smiled at his old friend's garrulity and wondered if perhaps he had been premature in assuring Angela that he already had an heir in Jeremy. The idea of fathering a son and heir with the daughter of a tradesmen had been repugnant to him from the start. The marriage had been inevitable, and Harry had reconciled himself to it as the only means of saving his heritage. But a Davenport with tainted blood? What would Black Harry have done in his place? he wondered.

Later that evening, as Harry sat across the supper table watching the candlelight play on the shining dark ringlets of his new bride, it came to him in a sudden insight that Black Harry would have lived up to old Oakhill's expectations. He would undoubtedly have filled the Abbey nursery with little Harrys. The major was not quite sure he was ready to take that step.

Their reception at Castleton Abbey the next morning was everything Angela had dreaded it would be. Even the butler, a lanky, stooped individual with hostile eyes half-hidden in a thicket of grizzly eyebrows, barely acknowledged their presence as the major escorted her into the marble-tiled hall. No one else was in sight, and Angela was glad that she had four of her own servants with her. If the taciturn butler's attitude was any indication of the welcome she could expect from the Abbey staff, she would need them.

"Where is everyone, Hodges?" the Major snapped, evidently put out by the cool reception.

"Her ladyship is feeling poorly this morning, my lord. She is taking her nuncheon on a tray in her chamber, I believe."

"And my sister?"

"Lady Sophia is with her ladyship, my lord."

"Get Mrs. Hodges up here at once," the major said curtly. "And have her ladyship's trunks taken up to the master suite immediately."

The butler gave a discreet cough behind a gloved hand, and Angela could have sworn he was concealing a smirk. "Excuse me, my lord," he began but was interrupted by an exclamation from the stairs.

"Harry!" A slight form flew down the remaining stairs and threw itself into the major's arms. "Oh, I'm so glad you're back safely, Harry. Why ever didn't you let us know you were coming, dearest? The house has been in a uproar ever since Jimmy Dunn arrived yesterday with the news. Mama is in such a miff, Harry, you have no idea."

"Unfortunately, I have a pretty good idea, Sophy," Harry replied, giving his sister a bear hug and a sound kiss. "Angela, come and meet my little sister, Sophia." He drew Angela forward, and she found herself being scrutinized by a tiny, golden-haired girl of no more than seventeen, whose blue eyes were serious beyond her years.

"Please call me Sophy," she said in a soft voice, rising on tiptoe to kiss Angela's proffered cheek. "I am so glad that Harry is married and come home to us at last. Only . . . oh, Harry. The bailiffs were here," Sophy cried, casting a frightened glance at her brother. "They will be back next week, they said. To sell off everything, even Mama's pug, Hercules. Whatever will we do, dear?"

"They are welcome to Hercules, Sophy. They can take the

nasty fat beast with my blessing. But the Abbey is safe now."
He looked over Sophy's head at Angela, and she saw, for the
first time, a glimmer of gratitude in his gaze. He said no
more, however, and Angela was disappointed that he could
not bring himself to acknowledge her role in saving his home
from the bailiffs.

"Ah, there you are, Mrs. Hodges," the major exclaimed,
turning to the tall, spare figure of the housekeeper, who had
materialized beside the butler. "Escort her ladyship up to the
master suite and get her settled in, will you? And send up a
tray of refreshments for us. Care to join us Sophy?"

The complete silence which greeted the major's request
should have warned Angela that all was not well, but she was
unprepared for Sophy's stammered explanation.

"Oh, Harry," she whispered, a furious blush suffusing her
pale cheeks. "Mama has not yet removed from the master-
suite. Your message only came yesterday, you see, and she
has been so unwell."

Angela was appalled at the explosion of pure fury she saw
in Harry's eyes. When he spoke, however, his voice was so
controlled she wondered if she had imagined his violent reaction.

"Mrs. Hodges, I want to see my mother out of that suite
within the next two hours. Put her somewhere in the West
wing. Is that perfectly clear? If she is not, I will carry her out
myself. You may tell her so."

"Hodges," he turned to the quivering butler, "we will have
our refreshments in the drawing room."

The two domestics slipped silently away, and Sophy
looked appealingly at her brother.

"I could not persuade her to move, Harry. And I tried, truly
I did."

"Where did she expect my wife to sleep?" Harry asked
harshly. An odd expression suddenly crossed his face.
"Where did my brother's wife sleep if my mother continued
in the master-suite?"

"Matilda preferred the room on the other side of Nigel's,"
Sophy replied in a small voice.

The major gave a snort of derision. "Preferred?" he barked.

"Do you take me for a flat, Sophy? Did she ever have a choice?"

Angela felt impelled to intervene. "I would be quite happy in another room, Harry. There is no need to inconvenience her ladyship if she is feeling poorly."

"Well, I would not be happy at all," the major snapped at her. "The mistress of the Abbey occupies the master-suite, and my mother is no longer the mistress here. She will have to get used to that fact, Sophy, and the sooner she does so, the better for all of us."

Sophy glanced nervously at Angela. "I am truly sorry that you have to witness this uproar, Angela," she said. "Mama can be very difficult upon occasion, but it is not always so unpleasant."

"No," put in the major cynically. "Sometimes it is much worse."

"If only you would not fly off the handle with her, Harry," his sister suggested mildly.

"I will be master in my own house, Sophy, and that's final."

Sophy took Angela by the hand. "Do come up to my room and refresh yourself a little, Angela," she urged. "That will give Harry time to simmer down."

Feeling very much out of her element and intensely uncomfortable at being caught in the middle of a family quarrel, Angela followed her new sister-in-law up to her airy bedchamber on the second floor. Although she knew Sophy was only seventeen, Angela felt that the younger woman possessed a calm, sensible disposition that made her seem much older.

"Oh, what a beautiful gown that is," Sophy exclaimed as she helped Angela out of her pelisse and bonnet.

Angela glanced down at the elegant green braided traveling dress she had chosen that morning as appropriate for this first encounter with the major's family, and smiled ruefully. Compared to the simple white muslin worn by her hostess, modestly trimmed with a single flounce of lace at the hem, the modishly cut green dress was indeed rather grand, she thought.

"I fear you will put me to the blush," Sophy continued

naively. "I have nothing that would hold a candle to that. Mama always says that girls my age should not call attention to themselves."

"She is probably right," Angela replied, conscious of the hint of wistfulness in Sophy's voice. "But you will soon be making your come-out, won't you? Then you will have all manner of elegant clothes."

"I doubt it. Mama says we cannot afford a come-out for me, so I have quite given up on the idea. I don't really regret it, you see, because it has always been difficult for me to talk to gentlemen. All except Harry, that is," she added. "He is my very favorite person. If only he would not fly up into the boughs as he did just now, we could all still be comfortable here."

"I imagine that his leg is bothering him after spending so long in the saddle," Angela remarked.

"His leg?" Sophy exclaimed in surprise. "What's wrong with Harry's leg?"

Angela stared at her in amazement. Could it be that the major had not told his family about his battle wound? She wondered if perhaps she had said more than she ought. Well, it was too late to worry about that now.

"He received a saber wound in his thigh six months ago," she replied. "He has not discussed the details with me, of course, but I understand that it is still painful."

Sophy's initial shock turned to exasperation. "It is so like Harry to keep something like that from us,"she complained. "He always used to make light of physical pain, which I think is rather silly of him, don't you? I shall tell him so."

Angela had to agree with Sophy's opinion of the major's stiff-necked refusal to make any allowances for his impaired condition. She rather doubted, however, that he would take kindly to being told that such reticence was silly. Her attempt to persuade her new husband to ride down to Kent in the carriage had earned her a withering look of contempt which she had found hard to ignore. She had held her peace, however, and she now suggested to Sophy that perhaps it might be best not to mention anything to the major which might put his back up.

"I see you have learned to deal admirably with my dear

brother," Sophy laughed. "And you are quite right, of course. Harry has the devil's own temper if he is crossed." She put her arm companionably around her tall guest's waist as the two ladies descended the stairs. "But you must not let him intimidate you with that scowl of his," she confided. "Harry's bark is a good deal worse than his bite, you know."

Angela did not know it, but she was relieved to hear that this little slip of a girl was not daunted by her brother's blue-deviled starts. She hoped that, in time, she could learn to be as comfortable with the major as Sophy obviously was.

That first afternoon and evening served to reinforce the tone of rejection which Angela had sensed earlier in the attitude of Hodges, the Davenport butler. She could understand, having been a mistress of her father's establishment for many years, that the domestic staff at Castleton Abbey would have strong feelings of loyalty to the dowager. This did not bother Angela, for she knew that, under normal circumstances, it would not take her long to establish herself as the new mistress of the household. Unfortunately, she soon began to suspect that the circumstances at the Abbey were anything but normal.

By mid-afternoon, she had been installed in the master-suite bedchamber traditionally reserved for the mistress of the Abbey. The eviction of the dowager from this exalted position had not been accomplished without a Cheltenham tragedy of major proportions. Although Angela had not yet had the privilege of meeting her mother-in-law, the dowager's tearful progress through the upstairs halls had been heard throughout the house.

"Mama is very high-strung," Sophy explained apologetically as a particularly piercing screech echoed down the main staircase and into the drawing room where Hodges had finally set out their refreshments.

"She also enjoys making scenes," the major remarked with his usual cynicism in referring to his mother. He got to his feet impatiently. "I am going down to the stables, Sophy. I depend on you to see that Angela is made comfortable."

After he had gone, Angela wondered how anyone could ever feel comfortable in a house where bedlam seemed to reign. How could she live in this constant state of confusion? she thought as another burst of high-pitched voices, accompanied by the shrill yapping of the pug, Hercules, penetrated the drawing room.

Her hostess must have guessed her thoughts, for she grinned sheepishly. "Harry always could cast Mama into strong hysterics," she said. "Nigel was her favorite, you see, and poor Harry never could do anything right."

"In that case, I imagine she will not approve of me."

"Perhaps not at first," Sophy admitted reluctantly. "But she will soon come about when she realizes she cannot bullock you or put you in a quake with her overbearing starts."

Angela had to laugh at this frank appraisal of the dowager's character. "And how do you know she cannot put me out of countenance, Sophy? I'm sure your mother can be rather formidable when she chooses."

"Oh, yes. She can reduce me to a jelly at times, I confess it. But then, I am such a goose, and you are made of sterner stuff, Angela. Anyone can see that."

"I trust you are right, Sophy," Angela said. "But let us hope that it will not come to open hostilities between us. I, for one, would vastly prefer it. ''

Angela realized that this wish would not be granted when, later that afternoon, a sullen Hodges approached the two ladies in the garden to inform them that her ladyship had removed to the West wing.

No sooner had Angela opened the disputed bedchamber door than the full extent of her mother-in-law's dislike became abundantly apparent. Even Sophy was taken aback at the state in which her disgruntled parent had left the room. The bed had been stripped but not remade, and the pale pink eiderdown lay crumpled on the floor. Wardrobe doors and dresser drawers hung open drunkenly, and the carved cheval mirror sported a jagged crack from top to bottom where a jar of face cream had been thrown at it. Discarded silk stockings, a broken fan, and various mismatched satin slippers littered the floor. And over it all hung the heavy odor of unwashed dog.

"Phew!" Angela crinkled her nose in distaste. "It would seem that your mother's pug is sadly in need of a bath."

She trod gingerly over to the high window, partially covered by heavy purple drapes. "We need some air in here immediately. Pull the rope for me, will you, Sophy? It will take an army of maids to clean this mess."

Angela tugged at the curtains, which sent a shower of dust billowing into the room. Then she struggled with the window, which refused to open at all. Even with Sophy's help, she could not release the bronze catch, which seemed to have rusted in place.

"Mama had a fear of draughts," Sophy explained. "She refused to have the windows open at all, even during summer."

"This is a job for a carpenter," Angela decided. "Ah, Hodges," she said to the butler, who had put in a belated appearance in the doorway. "Send up every able-bodied maid you have below stairs. This room needs a thorough cleaning. I want the carpet taken up and cleaned, and the drapes removed. And get a carpenter to fix this window immediately. We cannot breathe in here."

Hodges seemed to be somewhat taken aback by this torrent of activity his new mistress was about to release, for he mumbled an unintelligible reply and shuffled off.

Two hours later, Angela surveyed the results with a gleam of satisfaction in her eyes. The broken mirror had been removed, the bed remade with fresh linen, the pug-stained carpet taken up, and the floor scrubbed until it gleamed. The hideous purple curtains had been disposed of, and the big windows stood wide open to the gentle summer breeze. Best of all, the room no longer exuded the odor of her ladyship's fat pug.

Clothilde, her nose in the air and her back rigid with disapproval, stood by the wardrobe, carefully hanging up her mistress's gowns. Angela's maid, Rosie, who had accompanied the new countess to Kent, was arranging her ladyship's underthings in the dresser, while Angela herself stood at the open window with Sophy, admiring the view of the West Park.

"Which gown will you wear this evening, my lady?" Clothilde inquired in her clipped manner. "This yellow silk perhaps?"

"Yes, that one will do nicely, Clothilde. But I will need a bath first, if you can get some hot water for me, Rosie."

Shortly before the dinner gong sounded that evening, Angela heard a tap on the door to the adjoining sitting room, and the major strolled in. Angela started at the unexpected appearance of her husband and wondered if he would make a habit of walking in on her without warning. During the first night of their marriage, spent as it had been at the Blue Stag Inn in Maldstone, where Angela had slept in a room with Clothilde and Rosie, the question of wedded intimacies had not arisen. This casual presence of the major in her bedchamber, however, brought home to Angela that she would be expected to admit this stranger to her bed. The thought made her nervous, and Clothilde must have sensed it, for the dresser calmly continued her task of arranging her mistress's dark curls, then clasped a jade necklace round Angela's neck and threw a light shawl over her bare shoulders before making her curtsy and leaving the room.

The major cast an approving glance around the room. "This is a great improvement already, my dear," he said. "What happened to the carpet?"

"It smelled of dog, so I had it removed to be cleaned," Angela replied. "And I had the carpenters open the windows. The odor of pug was too rank for my taste."

He regarded her for a moment without speaking. Then a crooked grin flickered on his lips. "I trust you will not allow my mother's animosity to set your back up, Angela. Sophy has told me the wretched state this room was left in. She is most favorably impressed with your fortitude, I should tell you."

Angela smiled and was about to express her own favorable impression of her sister-in-law when there was a slight tap at her door and Sophy herself appeared to escort Angela downstairs.

"Mama wants to know what is keeping you, Angela," she said. "She is awaiting us in the drawing room and is eager to make your acquaintance."

"That's a whisker if ever I heard one, Sophy," the major remarked in his cool way. "Come, let us escort Angela into the presence of the dragon."

"Oh, Harry, don't talk like that," Sophy cried. "You will throw Angela into high fidgets with your nonsense. Mama is hardly a dragon."

"You surprise me, little sister. I distinctly recall hearing you refer to her as such on various occasions," the major drawled, regarding Sophy with obvious affection. "And you need have no fear that Angela will be cowed by our irascible parent. She comes from stronger stock than that, my dear."

Although he had spoken in a teasing tone, Angela felt a stab of anxiety at the mention of her background. Could this be a disparaging reference to the solid yet undeniably common roots from which she sprang? She had known from the start that the major was fiercely proud of his own noble lineage and had resisted an alliance with a Cit's daughter with every fiber of his being. Was she to be condemned for the rest of her life to endure subtle yet cutting reminders that she carried the unforgivable smell of trade about her? she wondered. But perhaps she was refining too much on this sensitive subject, she told herself firmly. You are what you are, she thought. He will have to accept that sooner or later, or they would both be miserable.

A more immediate hurdle to be cleared was this first meeting with the dowager, and as she accompanied the major and Sophy down the wide staircase, Angela felt her nervousness increasing. Nothing she had yet heard about her new mother-in-law had suggested that Augusta, Lady Castleton, would be anything but hostile. So it was with considerable trepidation that she entered the drawing room and allowed Sophy to lead her over to the turbaned figure seated majestically on a green brocade settee before the small fire.

7

Clash of Wills

Angela's heart sank as she stood looking down into the frosti-
est pair of eyes she had ever beheld. There was not the slightest hint of welcome in them, and when the dowager finally
spoke, after what seemed like an eternity to Angela, her voice
was as querulous as the whine of the sausage-like pug curled
on her lap.

"So there you are, girl. I must tell you that we pride our-
selves on our punctuality here at the Abbey, you know. None
of your ramshackle town manners for us, thank you." She
glared up at Angela as if her daughter-in-law were personally
responsible for every depraved custom in the country.

"The gong has only just sounded, Mama," Sophy said in
her quiet voice.

"When I want your opinion, young lady, I shall ask for it,"
her mother snapped. "There is nothing wrong with my hearing. Now, pour me a glass of sherry, Sophia. I have been kept
waiting quite long enough."

Sophy obediently went to the sideboard and poured three
glasses of sherry, two of which the major carried across the
room to his mother and Angela.

The dowager sipped her drink for several moments, observing Angela over the rim of her glass with small, hard eyes
not unlike her pug's. "You should not wear yellow, my girl,"
she announced suddenly. "Not your color at all. Makes you
look bilious."

Taken aback by this unexpected rudeness, Angela responded with restrained politeness. "I shall endeavor to remember that in future, ma'am. And I thank you for pointing it
out to me."

"I think Angela looks charming in that particular shade of

yellow," Sophy put in, evidently trying to soften the impact of her mother's criticism.

"Well, that only shows how little you know about the matter," her ladyship retorted with conviction. "I trust you found the master bedroom to your liking?" This latter remark was clearly addressed to Angela, and for a moment she could not believe her ears. Harsh words of recrimination rose to her lips, but then she caught the major's sardonic gaze on her. Did he imagine that she would disgrace herself by losing her temper? It might well come to that eventually, but for now, Angela bared her teeth in a polite smile and responded sweetly.

"Oh, yes, indeed. A most delightful room. I appreciate your ladyship's kindness in vacating it so swiftly." She had been unable to resist the sly reference to the major's unceremonious eviction of his mother from the master-suite. It was all she could do to keep a straight face as the major choked on his sherry, and Sophy stared at her with round-eyed alarm.

Even the formidable dowager seemed to be at a loss for words. Her heavy jowls quivered alarmingly, and her considerable bosom—festooned with a youthful array of lace and bows—swelled with repressed indignation. Finally she chose to ignore the remark entirely and pass on to firmer ground.

"Tell me about your family," she commanded. "I understand your father is in trade?" She pronounced the last word as if it tasted bitter on her tongue, and her thin lips curled slightly. Hercules, the pug, must have sensed her disdain, for he raised his lip in a silent snarl.

Angela sighed. She would do well to gird herself for a long and vicious battle, she thought unhappily. The dowager was evidently determined to expose every flaw—both real and imagined—in her new daughter-in-law. But two can play that game, Angela told herself. And perhaps the dowager would not be so eager to persecute her if she showed no reluctance to disclose—and perhaps even exaggerate a little—the infamous details of her common background.

"Oh, yes," she replied in a bright, innocent tone. "And my grandfather and great-grandfather before him. I come from a long line of successful tradesmen. Unfortunately, my mother was the daughter of an earl, but even the best families have their black sheep, wouldn't you agree, ma'am?"

This bizarre announcement was met by profound silence, broken eventually by a snort of amusement from the major and a horrified gasp from Sophy. The dowager looked as though she had received a mortal blow; her face paled noticeably, her mouth hung open, and her eyes registered severe shock. Hercules whined piteously and hid his nose in the voluminous folds of the dowager's purple gown.

Finally she shut her mouth with a snap, and turned weakly to her daughter. "Run up and fetch my vinaigrette, Sophia. I fear I am quite overcome with palpitations. I see that in future, I shall have to keep it by me constantly if I am to survive these assaults on my delicate constitution." She glared at her son. "I fail to see what you find so amusing, Harold," she said stiffly. "If I fall into a fatal decline and go to an early grave, it will be entirely your fault, I want you to know. Hush, my pet," she crooned to the agitated pug. "Mama will not let anyone hurt my little precious."

Revolted by the spectacle of the pug's bloated stomach, which he had exposed to be tickled by the dowager's beringed fingers, Angela spoke soothingly. "I hope I have said nothing to offend you, ma'am. May I pour you another glass of sherry?"

"No, you may not," the dowager snapped. "Thank you," she added stiffly. "I must say I find your attitude toward your mother very unnatural, child. I can understand how her own family might consider her a black sheep for running off with a commoner. They were married at Gretna Green, no doubt. A highly disreputable practice, if I may say so."

"Oh, no such thing," Angela said with a trill of artificial laughter. "There is no higher stickler for the proprieties than my dear Papa, ma'am. He would never have done anything so havey-cavey as run away to Gretna Green. My parents were married in St. James's Church, close by the house my grandfather built on St. James's Square."

The dowager was undaunted by this information, however. "A sorry affair it must have been, nevertheless. Your mother's family must surely have disowned her, regardless of where she was married," she insisted.

"Why, of course they did," Angela replied promptly. "They would have nothing to do with us at all. Which was a very good thing, since both the earl and his two sons had such deplorable reputations as rakes and gamesters, my grandmother would never have received them anyway."

Angela was saved from having to listen to the dowager's response to this outrageous piece of nonsense by the appearance of Hodges, who announced in his tired voice that dinner was served. She stood up and shook out the folds of the yellow gown which had inspired her mother-in-law's censure.

The dowager had also risen and, handing Hercules to a waiting footman, motioned imperiously to her son. "You may take me in to dinner, Harold," she commanded, grasping his arm firmly and propelling him toward the door. As Angela followed the major and his mother out of the room, accompanied by a subdued Sophy, she wished desperately for an excuse to escape upstairs, away from this obnoxious woman with her impertinent questions. She had lost her appetite and dreaded having to endure the dowager's snide remarks throughout an entire meal. She wondered what further indignities were in store for her, and began to feel her anger rise at the major's apparent indifference to his mother's cavalier treatment of his new bride.

No sooner had she entered the dining room than she realized she was about to be subjected to another of the dowager's manipulations. The major had taken his place at the head of the table, but by the time Angela made her entrance, the dowager was in the process of allowing the butler to seat her at the foot of the table, a place Angela knew was hers by right.

Determined not to be cheated out of her rightful place by a scheming old harridan, Angela stepped up to the dowager and said mildly, "I believe you are in my place, ma'am. Hodges, be so good as to seat her ladyship over beside Lord Castleton."

Hodges gave no sign of having heard her but looked expectantly at the dowager, who turned a limpid gaze up at her daughter-in-law.

"What fustian you do talk, my dear. As if it made any difference where we sit. This is my usual place, you should know. Even my poor Matilda deferred to me in that. I see no reason to change things, do you?"

Angela felt a surge of anger flood through her. So this impertinent, platter-faced old fidget thought she would get the better of Angela Walters, did she? Well, she was about to find out differently.

"Actually, I do," she replied coldly. "Change is inevitable, and one must learn to adapt to it. But I refuse to haggle with you, ma'am. Sit wherever you wish. I can just as easily have my dinner in my room. Under the circumstances, it might even be preferable."

"And as for you"—she turned, eyes blazing, to the major, who had stood throughout this speech regarding her intently—"I would like to see you as soon as you have finished your dinner."

Then, without a backward glance, Angela turned and swept out of the room.

Angela did not sleep at all well that first night under her own roof. Her dreams were filled with dragons with the dowager's piercing eyes and enormous pug dogs drooling all over her bed. Finally she arose and, wrapping herself in her silk robe, went to sit at the open window to watch the dawn break over the wide park land to the west of the house.

As she stared out over the still landscape, Angela wondered how soon the major would keep his promise to show her the estate and introduce her to the tenants. He had come up to the sitting room last night after dinner as she had requested, but she had seen from his scowl that he was not in an amiable mood. He had surveyed the half-eaten remains of her dinner tray and made a caustic remark about her fastidious tastes, which had seemed unfair to Angela.

"I have never been a finicky eater, my lord," she protested patiently. "But I do object to cold, greasy food served on chipped plates."

"It tasted all right to me," he said curtly. "But I assume you did not bring me up here to discuss the deficiencies of our kitchen staff." He moved over to lean against the mantel, and when Angela noticed that he was limping again, her anger evaporated.

"Please sit down, my lord," she said, ignoring his remark. "You will be so much more comfortable."

"I am very well as I am, thank you."

Angela sighed. This interview was going to be much harder than she had imagined. "Very well, my lord," she said, forcing herself to keep her impatience from showing. "If you insist on behaving in this boorish fashion, you must be exhausted, so perhaps we should postpone this discussion until tomorrow morning."

He swung round to face her, and his eyes were an angry midnight blue as they glared down at her. "Are you dismissing me, my lady?" he demanded harshly.

Angela met his gaze unflinchingly. "Of course not, my lord," she replied calmly. "I am merely suggesting that since your wound is obviously paining you—"

"It is doing nothing of the sort," he cut in sharply. "And I can do without your pity, thank you."

This is getting ludicrous, Angela thought. The time has come to speak frankly to this irascible man.

"I do not pity you at all, my lord," she replied. "Quite the contrary, I find you exasperating and pig-headed beyond bearing." She rose to her feet and began pacing to and fro before the shabby gilt settee. "You have the audacity to stand there and tell me that you are not in pain. What kind of flat do you take me for? I can see perfectly well that you are in pain. And why do you feel you have to dissemble with me is beyond my comprehension. Do you not trust me enough to tell me the truth?"

Warming to her subject, Angela stopped in front of the major, and regarded him searchingly. His eyes had lost their angry glow and held something that might have been amusement.

"I had hoped we could at least have been friends, Harry," she continued in a softer voice. The sound of his name felt good on her tongue. "This marriage is going to be difficult enough as it is without this constant bickering between us. Sophy will be a good friend to me—I can feel it already—but your mother is set against me. I will need your support if I am not to be overwhelmed by her hostility."

"You have my support, my dear. I am sorry if I have given

you reason to doubt it. And Sophy will stand by you; she has said as much to me."

Angela was reassured by his words, but she knew that the kind of support he offered would not be enough. "This is not a happy house," she said hesitantly.

The major's crack of laughter held no amusement. "It never was," he said. "There has always been conflict here, for as long as I remember. My mother was usually at the heart of it. Nothing much has changed in that regard."

"Well, we must make it change," Angela said stoutly. "There can be no happiness where there is such deeply rooted discord."

"Happiness?" The major's laugh was bitter. "What little happiness I have ever known proved to be a false rainbow, a fool's paradise. I shall not aspire so high again."

Angela regarded the major's grim features with a sense of shock and felt compassion well up in her breast. Yes, she thought, she had been mistaken. She did pity this man, after all, for his lack of faith in his own capacity for love and friendship. He was deliberately cutting himself off from human companionship and trust. He was cutting himself off, whether he realized it or not, from her. The thought depressed her.

"I trust you will not object too much if I pursue my own personal rainbow," she said lightly. "I am unaccustomed to conflict and bickering and much prefer friendship and contentment."

"You will find little enough of that here, my dear. What do you propose to do about it?"

Angela looked up into his eyes, which had lost some of their bleakness. "I propose to ask your support in removing the dowager to the Dower House," she said firmly, unsure of his reaction. She was surprised at his amused laugh.

"That would be an admirable solution, if only the Dower House were habitable, which it isn't."

"It could be made habitable, couldn't it?" she replied eagerly.

"No," he replied shortly. "It would take more than I could afford at the moment. There are a hundred more important things to spend money on, my dear. Tenant cottages, farm equipment, livestock, seed for crops, even the Abbey itself needs repair. No, the Dower House will have to wait."

"It wouldn't have to if you let me—"

"No!" the major exclaimed so sharply that Angela jumped. "I will not have you asking your father for any more money. He has been more than generous already. I could not bear to go begging for more." His face had taken on an obstinate expression which made Angela's heart sink.

"I had not intended to ask Papa for anything, Harry," she said. "Have you forgotten that I have an income of my own which is doing nobody any good?"

"I will not have you spending your own fortune on things that are my responsibility."

"Harry, please listen to me. It would take so very little to bring us all a great deal of peace and quiet. Besides," she added quickly, when she saw his frown deepen, "I want very much to do this. After all, this is my home, too, isn't it? Surely I have the right to contribute something to make . . ." She hesitated, then finished in a rush of enthusiasm: "To make that rainbow more accessible. Do say you will, Harry."

Something in the quality of his gaze changed abruptly, and Angela suddenly realized that, in her enthusiasm, she had grasped his arm with both her hands, and was leaning against him in an alarmingly intimate way. His eyes had lost that somber hue and in their depths Angela caught a flicker of latent emotion which made the blood leap into her cheeks. She drew back self-consciously and lowered her eyes in confusion.

When he finally spoke, his voice had a caressing note in it that Angela had never heard before. "If that is a sample of your powers of persuasion, my dear Angela, I can assure you that there is little I would not grant you."

"You are teasing me, sir," she murmured, glancing up at him through her lashes.

"And you are flirting with me, you minx."

"I am not," she replied hotly, her blush receding. "I never flirt. At least, I don't remember ever doing so," she corrected herself. "At least, nothing to signify."

This time the major's laugh was genuine. "I think I will

stay and have a cup of tea with you, after all," he said. "And I will even sit down to do it, if you will have me."

"Does that mean that I can start the repairs on the Dower House?"

The major had finally agreed that she could undertake the refurbishment of the Dower House and that, as soon as it was habitable again, he would see that his mother was removed from the Abbey. Angela felt a renewed glow of pleasure at the memory of that hour they had spent together last night. The major's bad humor evaporated after she had clung to him so immodestly. He had even teased her about flirting with him, she remembered. This was absurd, of course. She wouldn't dream of flirting with a man who had shown no attraction to her at all. No self-respecting female would have such poor taste as to attempt to attract a man who was so obviously still under the spell of another.

On the whole, Angela was well pleased with the progress she had made in establishing a cordial relationship with her husband. *Harry, my husband.* She murmured the words aloud to test the flavor of them on her tongue. Perhaps husband was not the right word to use to describe their relationship. Harry was that, of course, but he would be a friend rather than a lover. He had made that clear last night when he had made no attempt to claim his conjugal rights.

Had she been disappointed? she asked herself, staring out at the expanse of green park. No, of course not; she had not really expected him to, had she? Perhaps the tiniest bit in the most secret corner of her heart. But being friends would have to be enough, she thought. It would have to be, and that was that.

The next morning, as Harry prepared for his morning ride, he looked back on the forty-eight hours of his marriage to Miss Walters and found that he was not entirely displeased with the way things were going. He had known that his mother would disapprove of his choice of a bride, even had he chosen a duke's daughter. He suspected that she had cherished the notion of him marrying someone like his brother's widow. Matilda had been a particular favorite of hers, and she would have welcomed a docile daughter-in-law. So it came as no surprise to him to witness the dowager's attempts to embarrass Angela and put her out of countenance. What did disturb him was the degree of virulence his mother exhibited in her dealings with his wife.

Angela, as he had found out in their very first encounter, was no docile, insecure miss willing to be guided by her mother-in-law. Harry smiled as he allowed Jimmy Dunn to help him into his old green hunting coat and ease the wrinkles across his broad shoulders.

"We should be thinkin' of gettin' ye some new clothes, Major," Dunn observed as he handed his master a fresh cravat. "This old coat has seen better days, and no mistake."

"All in good time, Jimmy," Harry replied. "There are more important things that need attention before I waste money on clothes."

It was good to be back, he thought, slipping the cravat round his neck and tying it in a simple fall. Even if his mother had not improved with age. Of course, it was too early to be sure, but in Angela, Harry sensed he had an ally in keeping the dowager at bay. The chit had spirit, he thought, which under normal circumstances he would have frowned on as unbecoming in a lady of quality. But her performance last night in the drawing room had been splendid, he had to admit. Shocking, unexpected, and perhaps even immodest, but splendid nevertheless. His mother had been foiled on every front by the outrageous innocence of Angela's responses to the dowager's impertinent questions.

Yes, he thought, his new wife had the force of character required to keep his mother in her place. The skirmishes might be bloody, but he would put his money on Angela to win this war. With his support, of course. And last night in their sitting room, she had asked for his help, he remembered with a feeling of pleasure. And he had promised her that support and also given in to her plea to repair the Dower House.

The memory of that moment caused an unfamiliar tingle of excitement to run through his tall frame. She had been most persuasive. He had accused her of flirting with him, he remembered. But he was sure she had been completely unaware of the effect her closeness had had on him. Those mysterious smokey eyes alone might have swayed him, he thought. But she had clasped his arm and pressed against him. The memory was still disturbingly fresh in his mind. He had clearly felt the pressure of her firm breasts, and the unexpected sensations that this simple act had triggered in him had shaken him out of his black humor.

"Will there be anythin' else, Major?" His batman's voice brought Harry out of his reverie.

"Have Duke saddled for me in about half an hour, if you will. I am riding out with Crofts to see what needs to be done most urgently. I fear it will take months before Black Harry would recognize the estate for what it once was."

"That's as may be," Dunn replied shortly. "But at least you have the blunt to do it now, Major. Which is more than we could have said a week ago. So count yer blessings, Major. Count yer blessings."

And Harry reminded himself of this fact once again as he descended to the breakfast room, expecting to have it all to himself at this early hour.

He was wrong. His wife stood at the sideboard, examining the contents of a dish of coddled eggs.

"These eggs are overdone beyond recognition," he heard her say to the rigid form of the butler, who stood at her side.

"Her ladyship prefers them this way," Hodges managed to say through his thin lips.

"I understand that her ladyship always takes her breakfast on a tray in her room," Angela replied coolly. "So, please take these back to the kitchen and ask Cook to make up another serving. I like mine moist, tell him."

At that point she saw him standing in the doorway and waved the butler away.

"Good morning, my dear," Harry said, taking his seat at the table and accepting a cup of coffee from the affronted Hodges. "I gather you are not happy with the breakfast fare we serve here either," he remarked.

He had not intended to sound critical, but when Angela glanced at him apprehensively, he smiled. "I don't care much for it myself," he admitted. "Never have. I've had better fare in the army." He looked into each chafing dish in turn and then settled for toast.

"I see you are dressed for riding," he said, wondering if

Angela was expecting him to dance attendance on her. "I would accompany you, my dear, but I am off with Crofts to see what needs mending most urgently. I fear you would be bored with such things." On the other hand, he thought, perhaps it might be as well if she saw the enormity of the task ahead of them. He rephrased the invitation and was gratified when Angela accepted.

They spent the whole morning together, Angela saying little but listening intently to old Crofts enumerate the items that needed the new earl's immediate attention. Harry grew increasingly morose as he began to realize just how run-down the estate had become. Their progress was slow, for each of the remaining tenants was eager to receive the lord of the manor and his lady with every mark of respect. This entailed innumerable glasses of homemade elderberry wine, freshly baked rolls or currant cake, and the inevitable parade of new babies and small children born since Harry's last visit.

Harry had known most of his father's tenants since childhood, and could recognize any number of them by name. He had expected them to receive him kindly, and more so when they discovered that he intended to make extensive repairs on their cottages. He was not prepared for their evident delight in his new countess, however. There was something about Angela's unpretentious acceptance of their hospitality, her unfeigned interest in their welfare, and the delight she showed in dandling their various offspring that overcame their natural reserve.

" 'Er ladyship is a rare jewel, my lord," one weather-beaten farmer went so far as to say. "And so fond of the young 'uns, too." He indicated the spectacle of Angela exclaiming over a gurgling baby held on her lap by its beaming mother. "A good sign that is, my lord. A blessing from heaven it is to have a good wife. You'll see the truth of that when yer own young 'uns start comin', Master 'Arry. That'll be the day, and no mistake."

Yes, Harry thought to himself as he rode beside his wife back to the Abbey. That will indeed be the day.

8

Angela Takes Charge

After that first morning, during which Angela had seen with her own eyes the extent of the deterioration suffered by the Davenport estate during the tenure of the last two earls, she discovered in herself a strong streak of the crusader. Her life in London had been both pleasant and protected, but she began to realize that it had been sadly lacking in purpose. True, she had run her father's house and been the perfect hostess to his friends; true, she had learned enough of his affairs—much against his wishes, of course—to be able to converse intelligently on all aspects of the Oriental trading business. This was all to the good, she decided. One day she would inherit all of this vast empire; at least she would not be a total flat when that day came.

During her first week at the Abbey, however, Angela realized that her London existence had been placid to the point of boredom. Her competent domestic staff could have run the house without her, and often did. In her new home, on the other hand, the staff was insolent and slovenly, the house needed cleaning and refurbishing, the estate books were in disarray, and the tenants in dire need of her help.

And on top of everything else, she thought one evening as she sat listlessly at the dinner table, she had to listen to the dowager's disparaging comments on her gown—this time green silk made her look consumptive.

Angela looked down at the overcooked vegetables and undercooked lamb on her plate and realized that if she were not to fritter away her life listening to this fusty, bran-faced old tabby and eating unappetizing food, she would have to take strong, immediate action. By hedge or by stile, she thought, with a surge of sudden enthusiasm, she would triumph over this chaos.

She glanced down the table and caught the major's eye. He looked faintly amused, as always, at his mother's imprecations. But he would help her, Angela reminded herself. He had promised. He would help her to remove this bumptious female from the Abbey, and he had begun to listen to her recommendations for the tenants' welfare. The thought raised her spirits, and she turned to the dowager with a bright smile.

"Perhaps I am consumptive, my lady," she said sweetly. "And bilious, too, of course, as you so kindly pointed out the other evening. I only hope it is not catching."

The dowager glared at her suspiciously. "You cannot mean it, girl. So inconsiderate of you to suggest such a thing, although I should have expected it, of course. I declare, I have quite lost my appetite." But since she proceeded to do more than justice to the sweet custard and fruit pastries served for dessert, nobody took this pronouncement seriously.

The very next week, after the carpenters and painters had completed the restoration of the Dower House, and new rugs and curtains, ordered specially from London warehouses, had been installed, Angela took action on her new resolution.

"Hodges," she said one morning as she entered the breakfast room, "immediately after breakfast, I will see you and Mrs. Hodges in my study."

When the two truculent domestics stood before her, Angela wasted no time in pleasantries. "It has come to my notice," she said briskly, "that you are not happy in my employ. It seems that neither of you has been able to adapt to the new circumstances here at the Abbey." She paused to let her words sink in and saw the first signs of apprehension on their faces. "Your loyalty to the dowager is, naturally, commendable, so I shall beg her to keep you on in her employ when you leave mine."

The butler's face took on a mutinous look, but Mrs. Hodges showed signs of bursting into tears. Angela felt almost sorry for them until she reminded herself of the countless snubs and subtle insolence she had endured at their hands.

"We shall see what her ladyship has to say about this," Hodges said rudely.

"Yes, indeed," Angela replied, deliberately misunderstanding his meaning. "You had best speak to her ladyship immediately about your new positions. My own butler and housekeeper will be arriving from London sometime this afternoon."

As soon as they were gone, no doubt bent on filling the dowager's ear with this latest outrage, Angela relaxed. She had brushed through that rather well, she thought. Of course, the old tabby was bound to kick up the deuce of a dust, but she could weather that storm if only Harry would support her in this. She had not actually told him that she intended to dismiss half his domestic staff, but he had said she could make any changes she thought necessary. And this was one change she would insist on.

But she could not afford to rest on her laurels, she told herself, glancing at the clock on the carved mantel. There was one other important step she must take before she could escape on Black Star for her morning ride. That incompetent cook also had to go. In spite of her polite requests, he had continued to ignore every one of her suggestions and produced meals to suit the dowager's indiscriminate palate rather than making any effort to please his new mistress. Well, she thought resolutely, this evening the Abbey would have a new cook, and perhaps her coddled eggs would not be inedible in the mornings.

Before she could leave the room, however, the door burst open, and Jeremy ran in, obviously in high gig.

"Angela," he cried excitedly. He had dropped the more formal *Aunt* very early in their relationship. "What is going on? Hodges is in a rare taking. He told me I could jolly well pour my own chocolate this morning, because he had more important things to attend to."

Angela laughed. "I imagine he is a little upset because I have just dismissed him," she explained. "But that was very rude of him, I must say. Did you have your chocolate after all, Jeremy?"

"No, I thought it best to play least-in-sight until this rumpus blows over. That old platter-face has gone rushing up to complain to the dowager, no doubt. I say, Angela," he ex-claimed as a thought struck him. "Hadn't we better make our-selves scarce? Old parrot-face is bound to kick up a dust when she gets an earful of that fuddlecap's bibble-babble."

"Jeremy!" Angela cried, torn between dismay and amuse-ment. "Haven't I told you to keep that kind of talk for the sta-bles? That is no way to speak of her ladyship—or Hodges, for that matter. I know he can be tiresome, but that is no excuse for calling him an 'old platter-face.' "

"Oh, but he is," Jeremy insisted.

"Who are you calling platter-faced, Jeremy?"

Both Angela and Jeremy jumped guiltily at the sight of the major standing in the doorway, a quizzical gleam in his eyes.

"I thought you had gone out already, sir," Jeremy said in-nocently. "Angela and I were just leaving, weren't we?" He looked at Angela expectantly.

"Yes, as a matter of fact, we were, Jeremy," she laughed. "You could make yourself useful and saddle Black Star for me. I'll meet you in the stables in ten minutes. There is some-thing I must do in the kitchen before we go."

"Ah! I think I can guess what that is," Jeremy giggled. He ran to the door, then turned and addressed the major in an ex-aggerated whisper: "Best lope off while you can, sir. Old par-rot-face—I mean, Great-aunt Augusta will raise the devil of a breeze when she gets wind of what Angela is up to."

Angela, who had followed the lad out into the hall, admon-ished him gently. "You do run on like a fiddlestick, Jeremy. Off with you, now."

The major gazed after his retreating nephew with a be-mused look on his face. "Between the two of you, I am all aquake," he remarked. "Just what *are* you up to, if I may ask, my lady?"

Angela threw him a dazzling smile as she turned away. "Nothing to get into a pucker over," she laughed. "I am merely going to dismiss that dreadful cook, my lord."

"The major stared after her briefly before taking his nephew's advice and striding out to where his own horse awaited him.

* * *

By the time Angela had made the two calls on outlying farms she had planned for that morning, it was well past noon. In spite of Jeremy's reluctance to brave the wrath of the dowager, she could find no excuse for staying out any longer. Besides, she wanted to be at home when the new domestics arrived that afternoon.

Jeremy, however, had no such compelling reason for returning to the Abbey. "Do you mind if I go off to find Uncle Harry, Angela?" he asked as she turned Black Star's head toward home. "If we have no cook, there'll be nothing to eat at the Abbey anyway, and Uncle Harry might take me into Bromley Green."

"So, you're leaving me to face the music alone, Jeremy? Shame on you," Angela laughed. At his crestfallen expression, she relented. "Go along with you, then. But I want to see both of you back for dinner."

As she watched him canter away, Angela felt an unfamiliar ache in her heart. She had developed a great affection for Jeremy, who had accepted her without reservations. He had, in fact, attached himself to her with almost the same devotion he showed for his Uncle Harry. She knew that she fulfilled a strong need in the boy for motherly love and comfort, and felt flattered that, in the absence of his own mother, he had chosen her as a substitute. Between them, she and the major were the only parents Jeremy would know.

And what about herself? she thought. Jeremy had been a strong influence in her decision to accept this arranged marriage with the major in the first place. She had been prepared to turn him down, she recalled. And then he had brought the child to her house, and it had suddenly dawned on her what she would be missing if she never married. The thought of spending the rest of her life as a childless spinster had forced her to regard the major in a different light. And although she was all alone in the middle of an open field, Angela blushed at the immodest aspirations she had suddenly acquired in regard to Major Davenport.

Of course, he had scotched those dreams ruthlessly with his announcement that he already had his heir in Jeremy. Apparently he had meant that she was not to be allowed to share that side of his life. And so far, he had shown no sign of wishing to change his mind. Except for that first evening together at the Abbey, she remembered. The memory of that raw emotion that had flashed in his blue eyes had often returned to haunt her. Even now, in the bright sunlight of the deserted meadow, the thought of it made her shiver with secret delight.

But in the evenings that had followed, cozy evenings spent together in their private sitting room going over plans for improving various aspects of the estate, she had never seen that look again. And she had wanted to, she finally admitted to herself, half ashamed at the direction of her unruly thoughts. She had fed her fantasies in other, less satisfying ways. Unobtrusively, she watched the ripple of muscles across his broad back as he bent over the table, the way the cloth of his breeches outlined the strong line of his thighs as he walked, the dark curls that fell carelessly over his brow and which her fingers itched to brush back. She sighed as the frustration of it all washed over her.

As the days had turned into weeks, the major had grown more comfortable with her, Angela realized. He discussed estate affairs with her and listened to her suggestions. He had even accepted her offer to set the books in order until he could find a reliable secretary. They were well on the way to becoming friends and allies in restoring the Abbey to its former grandeur. Unhappily, Angela had begun to feel that this was all he wanted from her. He wanted a reasonably intelligent, competent wife to run his house, and with whom he could discuss local affairs. He did not want a mother for his children, since he had made it clear that he did not want children.

Angela was beginning to doubt that this would be enough for her, but what she could do about it, she did not know. Perhaps Jeremy would be all the children she would ever have, and she had better accept the idea. She wondered, not for the first time, who would share her husband's bed in the future. Would it be the elusive Matilda? she thought. And where was this former love of her husband's? All Angela knew was that the major's widowed sister-in-law was not at Woodall House, her father's estate adjoining the Abbey. The possibility that, at any moment, the beautiful Matilda might arrive to upset the tenuous relationship Angela was building with her husband made her uneasy.

Jeremy had long disappeared from view, and Black Star's patience was wearing thin. The horse gave a snort and shook his head vigorously. The movement brought Angela out of her reverie, and she turned the horse toward home.

When she arrived at the front steps, there was no footman waiting to take her horse, so she rode round to the stables. Her own groom appeared immediately, accompanied by her father's coachman.

"Good day to you, Miss Angela," the coachman greeted her. "Or, my lady, I should say, begging your pardon."

"Nonsense, John," Angela laughed. "I don't want to hear that kind of formality from you." John had been her father's coachman for as long as Angela could remember, and although she drew comfort from his presence, she wondered if he might not prefer to resume his post in London. "Tell me, John," she asked, "do you miss London? I can send you back if you prefer."

"Why, no, Miss Angela," the old man replied without hesitation. "Unless, of course, you no longer want me here." He smiled. "I think it best if I stay around to keep an eye out for you, miss."

Angela laughed at this frank speech. "Oh, I agree with you, John. You must know I need all the support I can get."

"Well, you can count on me anytime, miss," the coachman declared in his bluff way. "Me and Joseph here both." He indicated the groom. "And Jimmy Dunn, the major's man, is of a like mind, let me tell you. An army man and a real right 'un is Jimmy Dunn."

Angela felt cheered to know that she had three stalwart champions on her side, and she entered the house through the kitchen, ready to face anything the dowager might have to say.

The kitchen, however, was deserted. When Angela got up to her room, she found Clothilde and Rosie there, both considerably agitated.

"Oh, *Dieu merci,* you are back, my lady," Clothilde exclaimed with less than her usual sang-froid. "This house had gone mad. The . . . how you say, *bouleversement* is everywhere. Even in here we hear *la vieille comtesse* screaming out her . . . how you say? *elle lâche des gros jurons partout.*"

"That's true, my lady," broke in Rosie. "The old lady threw a rare fit, she did. Swore like a sailor, too, just as Mam'selle Clothilde says. I would never have believed it if I hadn't heard it with me own ears, ma'am. Something dreadful it was. She threw a vase full of flowers at Mam'selle Clothilde, too. Quite beside herself was her ladyship. I hope I never have to see that again, my lady. Gave me the spasms, it did. I swear it." Rosie was overcome at the memory of this outrage and burst into tears.

Angela's response was forestalled by a light tap at the door and the entrance of Sophy, looking harried and exhausted.

"Angela, wherever have you been, dear? I've been looking for you everywhere. Hodges says you have dismissed him. And Cook, too. Is that true? Both he and Mrs. Hodges woke Mama up this morning with the news, and you know how she hates to be disturbed before noon. She went into high fidgets at the idea that you could do such a thing without consulting her. You were nowhere to be found, so she ripped up at me, dear. I have spent the most dreadful morning imaginable."

"I did not realize I needed to consult her on managing my own household," Angela said, a note of coolness in her voice.

"But the Hodges have been here forever," Sophy wailed. "They are devastated."

"There is nothing to prevent your Mama from giving them positions in the Dower House," Angela said with a hint of impatience. "And that goes for Cook, too, as I pointed out to him. Your mama actually *enjoys* his coddled eggs. And I don't; it's as simple as that. By this evening, when their replacements arrive, we should have some order restored below stairs. Any of the other domestics who are unhappy with that should apply to the dowager for new positions."

This was Angela's last word on the matter, and since the major, ignoring his mother's strident complaints, upheld her decision, the matter was soon considered closed.

The changeover did not occur as smoothly as Angela had hoped, but by the following afternoon both Hodges and the cook had moved down to the newly remodeled Dower House, accompanied by the dowager's favorite footman, two upstairs maids, her personal abigail, and a scullery maid who was walking out with the footman.

Jaspers, the new butler, and his wife assumed their duties quickly and efficiently, and in no time had the Abbey household functioning as well as Angela could have wished. The new cook, a volatile Frenchman named Monsieur Gaston, had more difficulty finding competent kitchen help, but with some diplomatic encouragement and the promise of a new stove from Angela, he was soon entrenched in his private domain and regaling the Davenports with dishes the like of which the Abbey had not seen since the days of old Black Harry, a notable gourmet.

When it came to the physical removal of the dowager herself, however, Angela ran into what began to seem like unsurmountable obstacles. No sooner had she been persuaded to drive down to inspect the new furnishings than the dowager launched into a litany of complaints.

"I simply cannot live with puce curtains in the drawing room," she announced firmly one evening at the dinner table.

Angela looked at her in surprise. "You particularly wished for that color, ma'am. As you know, I consulted you on everything that was ordered for the house."

The dowager snorted and turned to the vicar, who was their guest that evening. "I could never have done anything so addle-brained, my dear Mr. Reynolds, for I cannot abide puce. If you had paid the least heed to my wishes, Angela, you would have ordered green velvet, as I specifically requested."

Since her irate mother-in-law was, at that very moment, swathed in a voluminous puce gown of dubious fashion, Angela wondered that she had the nerve to say she disliked the color.

"That can be easily changed, my lady," she replied soothingly, determined to be civil in front of the vicar. "I will send away to Ashford for samples tomorrow afternoon, and you can choose the one you prefer."

"You can save yourself the trouble, my girl. They will not

have the exact shade I want in Ashford," the dowager said, sending Angela a withering glance from under lowered brows. "There is nothing of any consequence in Ashford, as everyone knows."

"Oh, Mama, you know that you found that length of green satin you liked so much at Hardcastle's in Ashford only last spring," Sophy put in unwisely.

"I cannot think why you insist on contradicting me, child. Such rag-mannered starts are all very well for commoners, but vastly unbecoming in a Davenport, as you must know."

"We can send to London for the samples if you wish, ma'am," Angela said quickly, ignoring this indirect insult. She was anxious to divert the dowager's wrath from Sophy, who was easily cast into a pucker by her mother's unkind comments.

The dowager glared at her, unappeased. "London," she snorted. "I suppose that is all it's good for these days. The place has become so full of tradesmen that a lady of any breeding at all would do well to avoid it. Of course, I fear we are hardly safe from such encroachment even here in the country. Wouldn't you agree, Mr. Reynolds?"

During this insulting speech Angela noticed that Sophy had blushed deeply with embarrassment and cast her an appealing look. She also felt sorry for the poor vicar, who was having difficulty swallowing the baked haddock he had just put in his mouth.

"Let me remind you, ma'am, that were it not for those same tradesmen," she said, her patience wearing thin, "there would be no lengths of silk and satin for us to buy. And no velvet curtains of any color at all. Without them our saloons and wardrobes would be very dull indeed."

"That's all very well for you to say, my girl. But if that garish carpet you had installed in my bedroom is your idea of high fashion, then all I can say is that I prefer to be dull, thank you. I can tell you now that I will never sleep in a room with that unsightly thing on the floor. It would give me nightmares."

Angela gritted her teeth. The carpet in question was an extremely expensive Axminster from her father's warehouse, which Angela had felt certain would please her difficult mother-in-law.

"I am sorry to hear you do not like it, ma'am," she remarked quietly. "I confess, I was tempted to keep it for myself when I saw it, so now I can indulge my whim. Tomorrow I will have it moved up to my room, and we will order you another, less colorful, one."

"Yes, please do," the dowager exclaimed, evidently cross that by rejecting the offensive carpet, she had gratified her daughter-in-law. "But be sure to allow me to choose my own colors next time."

It had obviously slipped her ladyship's memory that Angela had, in fact, consulted her on the color and style of every item purchased for the Dower House. Or she was deliberately forgetting the painful hours they had spent together poring over fashion plates and samples.

As the days and weeks slipped by, and the complaints continued, and the changes were made, it gradually dawned on Angela that her ladyship had no intention of moving to the Dower House at all. The discovery infuriated her. She would be damned before she allowed that old tabby to outwit her, she vowed. Sophy was no help at all, for she kept begging Angela to have a little more patience with her dear Mama. Sooner or later, Sophy assured her, the dowager was bound to find everything to her satisfaction.

Angela's patience was running out, however, and as August turned to September, and the trees in the park began to lose some of their summer color, it came to an end. The incident that triggered the explosion occurred during one of the light nuncheons the ladies usually took together in the small dining room. Since Harry was rarely present at this hour to protect his wife, these were the occasions the dowager often chose to vent the most crushing of her criticisms. That day was no exception.

"That coachman of yours is an insolent ruffian," she declared as soon as they had taken their seats. When Angela made no response, her ladyship continued angrily. "Of course, I cannot expect you to care that the servants disregard my orders. But that fellow actually refused to bring round the carriage this morning when I specifically requested it. He sent round the groom with the tilbury instead, and you must know how unseemly it is for the Countess of Castleton to go jauntering around the countryside in such a vehicle."

"Were you going into Bromley Green, Mama?" Sophy inquired quickly, before Angela had a chance to remind her ladyship that she was now the *Dowager* Countess. "I would have been glad to accompany you."

"No, my love, I was going to the Dower House to check on the new curtains in the master bedchamber. Which reminds me, Angela. The new carpet you ordered for that room won't do at all. It is still far too gaudy for my taste. My nerves simply cannot tolerate such bright colors."

Angela, who had been wondering why anyone would need a carriage and four horses to drive the short distance down the driveway to the Dower House, bristled instantly.

"The carpet *I* ordered?" she said, a dangerous gleam in her eyes. "I beg to differ, ma'am. *You* were the one who ordered that carpet. I had no say in the matter at all. Sophy was there, and she can confirm that it was *your* choice exclusively."

Caught in the cross fire, Sophy could only nod and stammer in agreement. "Why, yes, Mama. You said you particularly liked the muted shades of green and brown. I remember distinctly."

The dowager let out a shriek of frustration, and her face became an alarming red. "There you go again, you unnatural child," she cried. "Always taking that hussy's side against me. Hounding your poor mother to death, you are. Oh, how I wish my dear Matilda were still the mistress of this house. *She* would have more charity than to banish her husband's mother to the Dower House, that I do know."

Angela clearly heard, over the drumming of the angry blood in her veins, Sophy's gasp of horror at the dowager's ugly accusations. Quietly she rose to her feet and, ignoring Sophy's anguished glance, swept out of the room. This time, she told herself as she climbed the stairs to her room, that pestilential harridan had gone too far.

When Sophy found her an hour later, Angela was busy supervising the packing of a small trunk. Both Clothilde and Rosie were bustling around, eagerly selecting the clothes their mistress would need on this sudden trip.

"What are you doing, Angela?" Sophy exclaimed, her face a study of alarm and astonishment. "You cannot be leaving?"

"And why not?" Angela demanded coldly. "Do you think I enjoy being insulted and criticized every moment of the day by that dragon you call mother? I have had quite enough, thank you. I am returning to London, where, according to your mother, those of us in trade have a place."

"You will never go off and leave me alone?"

"Of course not, silly," Angela said. "You have your dear Mama to tell you how to go on. Her taste is impeccable, after all."

"That's what I mean, exactly," Sophy wailed, her eyes filling with tears. "She will make my life impossible. I cannot bear it. Oh, Angela, what am I to do?" She collapsed on Angela's bed in a fit of wild sobbing.

Angela regarded her little sister-in-law with compassion. "Well," she began tentatively, "there is a way out of your dilemma if you are brave enough to take it."

Sophy raised her tear-stained face to stare at Angela. "Do you mean it? Tell me, quickly, dear. I can bear anything but Mama's constant criticisms."

Angela regarded her, a smile of anticipation beginning to curl her lips. The idea was somewhat outrageous, but it appealed to her sense of humor.

"Go and pack a small bag, immediately," she said briskly. "And say nothing to your abigail. Take Rosie to help you. We have no time to dawdle, though, I'm warning you. The coach will be ready in half an hour."

Sophy's eyes grew round with alarm. "The coach? What are you talking about, Angela," she murmured. "Why would I need to pack a bag?"

"Just trust me, Sophy. And do hurry. I have to write a note for Harry before we leave."

"Leave?" Sophy echoed. "You must have taken leave of your senses, Angela. Where are we going?"

"You and I are going up to London, my love. And don't argue with me. It will be for the best, believe me."

9

False Alarm

After several days back in London, Angela felt her rage at the dowager dissipate entirely, but as the days passed, so did her euphoria at being once again safely ensconced in her father's house.

Her unexpected arrival with Sophy had delighted Mr. Walters, who had not expected to see his beloved daughter again until the Christmas season. He accepted without question her excuse that she had brought her young sister-in-law up to town to replenish her wardrobe. But Angela knew that she could not pull the wool over her brother's eyes so easily.

"If you think I believe that Canterbury tale, you have more hair than wit, Angela," he declared roundly as soon as they had a moment together. "Something has put you out of curl, my dear, and I want to know what it is with no roundaboutation."

"Oh, Julian," she replied lightly, "you are all about in the head, dear. Only you could take a perfectly innocent shopping excursion and turn it into a Cheltenham tragedy. Fie on you, sir. I thought you would be glad to see me," she added, smiling up at him sweetly.

"Don't try to turn me up sweet, Angela, for it won't fadge. I know you too well, my dear. Something has sent you posting up here to London, and I want to know what it is." He observed her keenly for a moment before a frown appeared on his brow. "It's not that soldier fellow you married, is it? Because if he has given you so much as one unhappy moment, I shall draw his cork for him. Of that you may be quite sure." He ground his teeth ominously, and his eyes clouded with anger.

Angela knew the signs all too well. Julian had always been

subject to these fits of protective rage whenever he felt she had been slighted. The last time she had seen him in this state, he had administered a bloody nose to Roger Hyland, in this very room, over three years ago. Angela shuddered at the memory of Roger's startled face as he watched the blood dripping onto his impeccably white cravat.

"It has nothing to do with Harry," she said quickly. "He has been everything that is correct."

"What made you angry enough to run away, then?" he demanded. "Because you were angry when you arrived. I could tell."

"I didn't run away," she protested, annoyed that Julian had, as usual, put his finger on the weak spot in her argument. Would Harry also think she had run away? she wondered, suddenly anxious.

"What made you angry, then? I want to know."

Angela sighed. She knew from experience that her brother would badger her until she told him the truth. "It's the dowager," she said finally. "She has fought me every step of the way. I can please her in nothing, Julian. And I have tried, I really have." Angela heard her voice quavering with suppressed tears. "But the worst thing is that she refuses to move into the Dower House. I know this will sound like some silly squabble to you, but she keeps finding things wrong with the furnishings. The last straw was when she criticized that lovely carpet Papa sent down for me. I changed it for her, and now she doesn't like that one either. I simply cannot bear it any longer."

Quite unexpectedly, Angela burst into tears.

"There, there, my love," Julian said bracingly, one arm around her shaking shoulders while he fished out his handkerchief and held it at the ready. "I can see that I will have to go down to Kent and draw that old harridan's cork for her. I might even break her nose; that will give her something besides carpets to worry about."

Angela gurgled with laughter against her brother's damp cravat and accepted the handkerchief he offered her.

"Oh, Julian, do be serious," she choked. "Although I must admit, I have wanted to plant her a facer myself a time or two." She paused to blow her nose vigorously. "Then there is Hercules," she added. "I cannot start to refurbish the Abbey until I get him out. He leaves hair on all the settees."

"Who's Hercules?"

"The dowager's pug," she replied. "The ugliest little beast you ever saw, Julian. And he smells terrible! I can't wait to get rid of him."

"Don't allow a little thing like that to put you into the hips, Angela. I shall ride down tomorrow and strangle the animal, damned if I won't. And while I'm there, I'll send that old tabby to the right-about. I'll warrant you she'll give you no more trouble, love."

"Oh, do be serious, Julian," Angela laughed. "Let Harry take care of it. I've told him that I won't come back until his mother is out of the Abbey. I need you here to escort Sophy and me about town. I want her first stay in London to be a success, and I am depending on you to make her feel at home with us."

"She seems a nice enough chit," he replied. "A trifle young to be out on the town, though, don't you think?"

"She is nearly eighteen," Angela said. "And once I get rid of those dowdy gowns her mother insists she wear, I think she will surprise you, Julian. She has been a great comfort to me, you know, so I want you to help me keep her amused. Please say you will, dear," she wheedled, hoping she had managed to take his mind off bloodthirsty thoughts.

Julian grinned at her affectionately. "You have only to command, my dear, and you will be obeyed." His frown suddenly reappeared. "But I warn you, Angela, if that soldier of yours cannot put his house in order, I won't answer for my actions."

With this, Angela had to be content, and indeed, she found very little to complain about in the days that followed.

A willing and amiable host, Julian escorted the ladies to many of London's most fashionable entertainments, and to others that were not quite so elegant but just as much fun. They attended Drury Lane to see Mr. Kean in his famous rendition of *Macbeth*, a performance which caused Sophy to declare that she finally understood why her governess had

insisted on her reading the Bard's plays. They visited the
Royal Academy at Somerset House to admire the hundreds of
paintings displayed there, and the Royal Italian Opera House
on the corner of Pall Mall and Haymarket.

On a less formal level, Julian took the ladies to spend an
evening at Vauxhall Gardens, which adjoined the Royal Hos-
pital in Chelsea. This popular pleasure garden, opened in
1742 with much fanfare, had in later years lost most of its re-
spectability and glitter. This did not prevent Sophy for deriv-
ing a great deal of enjoyment from watching the strolling
groups of boisterous revelers and savoring the supper of
Yorkshire ham, savoy cake, pastries, and blancmange Julian
ordered in one of the booths.

Shy at first, especially in the presence of the gentlemen,
Sophy soon became comfortable with Julian. Angela noticed
that her brother, usually reserved with the fairer sex, treated
her guest quite as one of the family, even teasing her on her
transformation from country mouse to a young lady of fashion.

These and other sightseeing excursions, supplemented by
numerous visits to a modiste for fittings and morning rides in
Hyde Park, made the days fly by for the carefree Sophy, who
was having the time of her life. For Angela, however, the return to her father's house was less pleasurable than she had
anticipated.

After the first week, she began to look forward to the arrival of the morning post with growing anxiety. Why, she
wondered every morning when there was no letter for her on
the hall tray, did Harry not write to tell her that the dowager
had retired to the Dower House? Could it be that she was still
at the Abbey? Had Harry got her note? Now, that is a foolish
notion, she told herself sharply. How could he not have seen
it, propped so prominently on the mantel of their sitting
room?

She continued to plague herself with such thoughts, and by
the end of the second week she was imagining the worst. Had
Harry washed his hands of her entirely? Now that she thought
of it, he had ever been unwilling to engage his mother in ver-
bal battle, preferring instead to ignore her irritating starts. Per-

haps he was glad that his wife had taken herself off. Angela shuddered at this unpleasant possibility.

At night she lay awake racking her brain for plausible excuses to return home. It came to her as somewhat of a shock that she now considered the Abbey her home, and that she dearly wished to return there. She missed her morning rides about the estate almost as much as she missed her quiet evenings with Harry in the private sanctuary of their sitting room. She missed the bustle of activity in planning the refurbishing of the Abbey, and the almost daily visits to one tenant or another. She missed Jeremy's company and his enthusiastic prattle. But most of all, she had to admit, she missed seeing Harry every day—at the breakfast table, riding around the estate, even at the dinner table, where she had to share him with the dowager.

Why did she bother to think of him at all? she asked herself at least once a day, when he obviously was not thinking of her.

So much did the thought of Harry's perfidy pray on Angela's mind that she had finally convinced herself that he had, indeed, cast her off. Consequently, she was paying little attention to Sophy's happy chatter as they rode through the park with Julian one afternoon toward the end of their third week in town. She was jolted out of her morbid reverie by Sophy's startled cry.

"Oh, Angela! That is Harry's man, is it not? Over there, on the roan gelding."

Angela jerked her head up and recognized the figure riding some distance in front of them as Jimmy Dunn, her husband's batman. Mindless of the impropriety of her action, she kicked her horse into a canter and pulled up beside the roan gelding.

"Jimmy!" she exclaimed. "Whatever are you doing in London?"

The man touched his forelock respectfully. "Came up last night with the major, my lady," he replied.

"Why didn't the major let me know he was coming?" Angela asked, her anxiety of the past weeks beginning to turn to anger.

"Ain't much for writing letters is the major," Dunn pointed

out. "More a man of action, if you know what I mean, my lady."

"But where is Harry?" Sophy wanted to know, having overheard the last part of this conversation.

"Racking up with Captain Woodall on Jermyn Street, ma'am. The captain served with Major Harry on the Peninsula," he added by way of explanation.

"I don't care whom he served with on the Peninsula," Angela said icily. "Why did he not come to St. James's Square?"

"Couldn't rightly say, my lady," Jimmy replied mildly. "But knowing the major, I'll wager he had a good reason."

"That I can believe," Sophy laughed. "But Harry was never one to explain his reasons."

"If you'll excuse me, my lady," Jimmy said, addressing his mistress, "when I left him, the major was on his way to St. James's Square to see you."

Angela's heart leaped up into her throat. Harry had come to see her. Perhaps she had worried needlessly after all. "Was he indeed?" she said, trying to sound unconcerned. "I trust that there is nothing amiss at the Abbey?"

"No, my lady. Leastways, not to my knowledge."

"Thank you, Jimmy."

After he had ridden away, Angela turned anxiously to her brother, who had been regarding her keenly during this exchange. She had been about to suggest that they cut short their outing and ride home, but a disagreeable thought occurred to her. What if Harry were angry with her for rushing off in such a madcap fashion? What if he had done nothing about the dowager?

These doubts still tormented her when, twenty minutes later, they arrived back at St. James's to be met with the news that Major Davenport was closeted with Mr. Walters in the library. Angela had also had time to brood on what she considered her husband's cavalier treatment of her. Consequently, she became increasingly incensed at that gentleman for causing her so much anxiety, and by the time she burst into the library, she had convinced herself that Harry was to blame for the whole affair.

Both gentlemen rose at her precipitate entrance, and it did

not improve Angela's mood to see that her father seemed to be extraordinarily pleased with the major's company.

"So," she snapped waspishly, quite unable to control her temper, "you have finally put in an appearance, have you?"

A startled expression crossed the major's face. And then he smiled lazily. "So it would seem, my love." He came across the room and casually kissed her cheek, quite as though he had not ignored her entirely for three whole weeks, Angela thought crossly. "I trust I find you well, Angela."

No, she wanted to scream at him. I am not at all well, thanks to you. Angela had a sudden, overpowering desire to stamp her foot, throw a book at him, smash a Ming vase—in short, indulge herself in a tantrum. It would give her immense pleasure, she thought, to wipe the smug look from both their faces. Even her doting Papa seemed to be regarding her with the same amused tolerance she saw in Harry's eyes. Had he taken the major's side against her? She knew the thought was ridiculous, but in her present agitated state it was enough to cause a lump to form in her throat.

"As well as can be expected," she answered, a catch in her voice.

"There, there, my dear child," Mr. Walters said, advancing on his daughter and taking her gently by the arm. "Come and sit down, my love, and do not agitate yourself. We know just how you must feel."

"You do?" Angela glanced up at him, puzzled at his strange behavior.

"Yes, my dear. Harry has told me all." Angela was startled at the silly grin on her father's face.

"He has?" she muttered. "All what?"

"I only wish you had told me yourself, Angela." he smiled benignly at her.

"Told you what, Papa? What Banbury tale is this, pray?"

Mr. Walters laughed at this, as though it were a huge joke. Then he pinched her cheek, regarding her all the while with a besotted look on his face, the like of which Angela had never seen him wear before.

"You are a naughty minx, Angela. Fancy letting me go for three entire weeks without informing me that I am about to become a grandparent. Shame on you, love."

"About to become a *what*?" Angela gasped faintly, feeling the blood drain from her cheeks.

"Don't be a silly peagoose," her father said. "Harry has told me all about your fits and starts. Your mother was just like that when she was carrying you, my dear. These moods will pass, as I told Harry here, and then everything will be plain sailing. Trust me, Angela. I've been through this before."

But Angela was hardly listening to him. She stared accusingly into the sapphire depths of her husband's eyes, noting with a mixture of anger and panic that he appeared to be enjoying her discomfort hugely. How dare he play such a scurvy trick on her? she wondered. And worse yet, she thought with sudden fury, how dare he deceive her poor father with such a patently false alarm? How could she be increasing? For a wrenching moment she had a joyful vision of what it might be like to carry Harry's child. But Harry, of all people, must know that this was impossible. How could he be so cruel to her?

Angela felt the tears start into her eyes. Before she could make a complete cake of herself, she rose unsteadily from her chair and rushed blindly out of the room.

The unexpected pain and confusion Harry had glimpsed in his wife's eyes before she ran from the room had startled him. Not for a moment had he intended to hurt her feelings with the whisker he had told his father-in-law. True, he had wanted to wring her neck when he read that curt note she had left on the mantelpiece three weeks ago. He had, he remembered, been so incensed by her autocratic tone that he had flung the offensive missive into the fire. She should have known better than to lay down the law to him. His murderous rage had been short-lived, however, and by the end of the first week after her departure, he had ceased to invent various pithy comments he would use to teach the headstrong chit better manners.

Midway through the second week, he began to suspect that Angela meant what she said. She would not come back until the dowager was removed from the Abbey. And, to tell the truth, his mother had only contributed to his ill humor with her constant bickering. As if it were his fault that his rag-mannered wife had persuaded Sophy to go jauntering off to London with her. If the dowager's dire predictions held even a grain of truth, the two wayward hoydens were even now indulging themselves with every conceivable immodest entertainment that decadent city had to offer.

The dowager's lamentations only increased with the arrival of a letter from Sophy, in which she described, with a wealth of detail, the numerous entertainments she was enjoying and the number of new gowns Angela had insisted on ordering for her. Harry suspected that his little sister's obvious enjoyment of her stay in London was especially painful for the dowager to bear.

"It offends every sense of propriety that you would sit here and allow that tradesman's daughter to drag your own sister through the mire," she told him one evening as he sat morosely at the dinner table. "One would think, to see you, that you had lost all sense of what is due a Davenport."

"Cut line, ma'am," Harry interrupted. "If you had moved down to the Dower House, where you belong, none of this would have happened."

"Ah!" the dowager snorted angrily. "So the sly little baggage has set my own son against me. Never did I imagine, when your poor father died, that I would live to be insulted in my own house." She drew out a scrap of lace and sniffled into it ostensibly.

"This is not your house," Harry snapped, finally losing his patience with her. "And tomorrow you will move to the Dower House, if you please. It has been ready and waiting for you this past month."

The dowager fell into a fit of the vapors at this ultimatum and retired directly to her room, in high dudgeon, to find solace—as she put it—in memories of happier days when she was not treated like a leper by one of her own children.

Remorseful as he was for his angry outburst, Harry stood by his word, and by the following evening the dowager was gone. When he came home after a full day spent purchasing livestock at the county fair in Ashford with his bailiff, the house was depressingly empty. It suddenly hit him forcibly that he missed his wife's light step in the hall, her calm voice as she spoke to the servants, her smile at some amusing incident he had recounted for her benefit. In short, the Abbey no longer seemed to be the haven he had thought it to be.

At first Harry thought he was coming down with something, but the feeling persisted until he could no longer deceive himself. He wanted his wife back. She must be better company than he had thought, he told himself. Why else would her absence affect him so adversely? Once he had identified the cause of his malaise, Harry rose one morning before dawn and ordered Jimmy Dunn to saddle their horses. They were going to London.

He knew he had done the right thing as soon as Angela entered the library, where he sat with his father-in-law. She looked magnificent, her fashionable green braided riding habit molding her slim, shapely figure and her smoky eyes flashing. Her curt greeting had surprised him momentarily, but when it occurred to him that his wife had expected him to come after her much sooner, he had relaxed. The little minx had missed him, he thought with a glow of satisfaction.

If only he had not had the misplaced notion of inventing that Banbury tale about a possible grandchild, Harry thought ruefully, he might have brushed through this affair tolerably well. The truth was, he reflected, Mr. Walters had caught him off guard with that remark about his daughter's odd moodiness. Rather than confess that his mother was responsible for Angela's sudden presence in London, Harry had blurted out the first reckless excuse that came to mind. He had been unprepared for his father-in-law's delight and his wife's tears.

Harry sighed. Never had the old adage of acting in haste and repenting at leisure seemed more appropriate to him.

When the ladies came down to dinner, Harry had eyes only for his wife, who wore a low-cut gown of watered emerald brocade, with a flounce of Brussels lace around the hem.

He moved forward to greet her as she entered the drawing room, taking her small hand in his and raising it to his lips.

"You are looking in high gig, my dear," he said softly. "I trust I am forgiven," he added after a short pause, looking directly into her eyes.

"No, you are certainly not, my lord," she replied stiffly,

withdrawing her hand quickly and brushing past him to sit in a brocade wing chair near the hearth.

"Harry!" Sophy's delighted squeal distracted him from his wife's cool reception. She threw her arms round his neck and kissed his cheek affectionately, then stood back shyly for his approval.

"Do you like it, Harry? This is but one of the beautiful gowns Angela has insisted I will need if I am not to look dowdy when we come up to London in the future."

Harry regarded his sister with surprise. Although he loved Sophy dearly and considered her a taking little thing, he had never thought of her as beautiful. But seeing her in these new surroundings, wearing a fashionably cut gown of palest pink silk, festooned with darker pink rosebuds at the hem and low neckline, he had to admit that she looked very well indeed. Her pale golden hair, usually worn in careless ringlets about her face, had been gathered in a simple yet elegant twist of curls on top of her head, giving her a more mature and confident appearance. Her blue eyes sparkled with a vivacity he had not seen in them since they had been children together, and Harry felt a sudden sadness in his heart that his own sweet Sophy had needed a Cit's daughter to bring her the kind of carefree happiness she should have found in her own home.

"By Jove," he exclaimed with sincere admiration. "And who is this enchanting young lady who bestows her kisses on complete strangers? Surely this cannot be my little Sophy, turned into a princess as soon as I let her out of my sight?"

"Oh, Harry, you are a sad tease," she gurgled happily. "Who else would it be, silly?" A sudden frown marred her cheerful expression. "It was very naughty of you to blurt out Angela's secret without consulting her, Harry. I can think of nothing more provoking than having such a special announcement made by someone else at the wrong moment. She is exceedingly put out with you, I should warn you," she added in a low voice. "I fear she will make you pay for it, my dear, so prepare yourself."

And Sophy was right, Harry discovered to his chagrin. All through dinner Angela said not one word to him and answered his direct questions with monosyllables. Had it not been for Sophy and Mr. Walters, who kept up a flow of lively conversation during the entire meal, Angela's silence would have been more noticeable. As it was, Harry found himself drawn by his host into discussing the various improvements he had started to make to his estates. Mr. Walters seemed to possess more than a cursory understanding of estate affairs, and Harry was surprised and gratified to discover in his father-in-law such an attentive and informed audience.

When the gentlemen joined the ladies in the drawing room afterward, Angela was seated at the pianoforte and Sophy was singing an old country song in her clear, childlike voice. Julian was immediately persuaded to join Sophy in a duet, and Harry noticed for the first time the easy friendship which had sprung up between them.

How different from their family evenings in the drawing room at the Abbey, he thought with a pang of envy. The Walters seemed to be a loving family, one which now obviously included Sophy. He thought with disgust of the endless evenings spent listening to his mother's often malicious bickering about everyone she knew, both living and dead. He caught his wife's eye, and when she looked quickly away, Harry felt left out, excluded from the warmth the others shared.

He felt this even more keenly when Sophy remarked that they would have to forgo their usual hand of whist, since they were now five, and instead challenged Mr. Walters to a game of piquet. Angela spoke up at this point to insist that Harry take her usual place at the card table, since she felt a headache coming on and wished to retire early.

Unable to decline without sounding rude, Harry found himself paired with Mr. Walters at the card table. It was, therefore, after ten o'clock when he climbed the stairs to the comfortable room the housekeeper had prepared for him. There he found Jimmy Dunn, who had transferred their belongings from Captain Woodall's lodgings to St. James's Square earlier that evening.

"Her ladyship's in a rare takin', she is," Jimmy greeted him, his face studiously devoid of expression. "Gave me a message for ye, Major, she did. Fair made me quake, she was that chilly. And I'm thinkin' ye should know the rumor that's runnin' rife below stairs, sir. Somethin' about her ladyship bein' in an interestin' condition, as they say." He coughed self-consciously. "Can't say I noticed anythin' meself, but ye never know with these things, now, do ye?"

Harry cursed under his breath. He should have known that the story he had started would not be safe from the domestics, who always seemed to know everything their employers were doing.

"Am I to congratulate ye, Major?" Jimmy asked skeptically, obviously unwilling to give the rumor any credence.

And with good reason, Harry thought ruefully. For if anyone could have guessed that he had not been near his wife in the short months of their marriage, it was bound to be Jimmy Dunn.

"What was the message?" he demanded shortly, ignoring his batman's question.

"Ye're to come into her sittin' room as soon as ye come up, sir," he replied, gesturing toward the connecting door. "Seems her ladyship is wishful of boxin' yer ears for ye, Major. Likewise, that's the impression I got, if ye'll forgive me for sayin' so, my lord."

Harry debated several moments, wondering whether he should simply disregard the summons. Perhaps by morning Angela's anger would subside, and he would avoid a scene. On the other hand, she looked splendid when she was enraged, as she had been this evening in the library. He had a sudden yearning to see her smoky eyes flashing at him. In fact, if he were honest, he would have to admit that he yearned to do much more than look into her eyes again.

Harry felt a faint pulse of desire. A slow smile lit his face as he opened the adjoining door and walked into his wife's sitting room.

10

Lady Steele to the Rescue

After dinner that evening, Angela had managed to slip away upstairs early on the pretext of having a headache. She felt quite unable to face an entire evening of being cosseted by everyone, including her mendacious husband, when she knew her condition did not warrant it. She was particularly distraught at her Papa's jubilant reception of the news that he would become a grandfather. How unfair, she thought as she allowed Clothilde to remove her gown and help her into her nightrail, that she was the unwilling accomplice in this dastardly deception.

She suddenly became aware that her abigail had been unusually silent during the ritual of preparing her mistress for bed. Silence was not Clothilde's *forte* and never had been. If something needed to be said, and often even if it didn't, Clothilde would not hesitate to do so. Something must be very wrong, Angela realized, for the voluble Frenchwoman to hold her runaway tongue for so long.

"What is it, Clothilde?" she asked finally.

"*Rien du tout,* madame" came the stiff reply. And then, unable to repress her natural inclination any longer, she added, "I am puzzled, madame, by the odd rumors I hear in the kitchen. *C'est tout.*"

"What rumors?" Angela asked obligingly.

Clothilde needed no further encouragement, but launched into a tirade against irresponsible domestics, unfounded gossip, and the lack of proper respect displayed by English servants for their betters. "For I know such a rumor is not true, my lady. I, of all people, would be the *first* to know if you became . . . how you say, *enceinte*. Yes, I would know at once. And this is not the case at all. And if I did know, I would not discuss such an event in the servants' hall, madame. Not Clothilde Artois, *certainement*."

Angela had to smile. "You are correct, Clothilde, it is not true, of course. But we will be going back to Kent tomorrow, and I will write my father from there to tell him so."

She had lacked the courage to contradict Harry outright in the library this afternoon, when it would have been appropriate to do so. Now she would have to pretend that she, not Harry, had made a mistake. Her father would be downcast, of course, thanks to Harry's thoughtlessness. Why the major had told such a Banbury tale at all was beyond her comprehension. He had told her quite plainly that he wanted no children with her. At least, she corrected herself, he had implied it.

A sudden thought made her uneasy. Could Harry have changed his mind? Now that she looked back on that scene in the library, she recalled that Harry's eyes had revealed a mixture of emotions. There had been a welcoming gleam in them, and a glint of admiration, and something else she had been too angry to identify at the time.

And then she remembered the warmth of his smile as he asked if she had forgiven him. Angela was glad she had not listened to the little voice in her heart which had told her to smile back into those sapphire eyes and give him the answer he wanted. No, she thought, he needed to be told, in no uncertain terms, that his cruel lie would cause pain and disillusionment to her dear Papa. She had not known that her father had such a strong desire for a grandchild. The discovery had saddened her, since she would not be able to give him this one thing he seemed to want from her.

The realization that her father would be disappointed in her increased Angela's anger. Impulsively she told her abigail she wanted to see Jimmy Dunn immediately in the sitting room. She would insist on an interview with the major that very evening, Angela determined. She would not sleep unless she told him, to his face, how inconsiderate he had been.

So she had curled up on the green silk settee with a new novel she had purchased at Hatchard's two days ago. At first the time went by slowly, but after an hour Angela had become so engrossed in the romance which was unfolding for the beleaguered heroine of Mrs. Radcliffe's novel that she fairly jumped when the adjoining door opened sharply and the major strode into the room.

"I hear you wish to see me, Angela." He stood with his back to the small fire Turner had had laid for her earlier and looked down at her with hooded eyes.

Angela closed her book slowly, her mind still filled with the fictional tribulations of her heroine. For a moment she gazed at her husband, marshaling her anger, which had dissipated under the spell of the romance she had been reading.

"Yes," she replied, taking the frontal attack she favored when angry. "I wish to know what possible reason you could have had for deceiving my father this afternoon." She rose to her feet and went to put the book on the mantel, then turned to face him. "I can think of no excuse whatsoever for misleading him as you did, my lord. It was most unkind of you."

The major regarded her for several moments, his hands clasped tightly behind his back. "If you had not run off in that hoydenish way," he said at last in a curt voice, "I would not have been placed in the intolerable position of having to explain to my father-in-law why his daughter came to London in a state of high fidgets."

Angela stared at him in amazement. "He never said anything to me on that head."

"Perhaps not. But he certainly asked me, my dear. Seemed to think I had mistreated you, or some such nonsense."

"But you *knew* why I came to London," she countered. "I left you a note to that effect. You had only to tell Papa that your precious mother drove me away." She paused, an unpleasant idea flitting through her head. "Or did you not wish to let it be generally known that your mother was at fault?"

A faint smile played over his angular face, and the hard look in his eyes softened. "She will not give you any more trouble, love. She has taken up residence in the Dower House."

"I am very glad to hear it," Angela said, momentarily diverted. "But that is not the point, sir. Why did you lie to my father?"

"He suggested it himself. Said something about your

mother going through a similar fit of the dismals. Had it all figured out in his own mind before I said anything. I merely confirmed what he wanted to hear."

Angela felt a wave of exasperation engulf her. How like a man to treat something like this so lightly. Didn't he see the awkward position he had placed her in?

"How could you even think of saying such a thing?" she cried. "When you *knew* it could not be true."

His smile had disappeared, replaced by an expression Angela had never seen in his eyes before. His gaze raked her leisurely before he replied, causing Angela to become uncomfortably aware that she was dressed for bed in her thin nightrail, covered only by an elegant scarlet brocade robe.

"Yes, I do know that, don't I, my dear?" His lips smiled, but there was no humor there. "How foolish of me not to have recalled that elementary fact. We shall have to do something to remedy that, won't we, love?"

Angela dropped her eyes and fiddled nervously with the belt of her robe. "You will tell Papa that it is not true, then?" she murmured, her throat suddenly dry. She wished she had not instigated this interview with her husband; he seemed to be in a strangely threatening mood which, rather than frightening her, had set her blood racing and awakened a new ache deep within her.

The major gave a crack of laughter, and Angela had the distinct impression that he was laughing at her. "That is not precisely what I was thinking of, my dear wife."

Her eyes flew open to search his face as she began to suspect his meaning. He had never called her *wife* before in that mocking tone which reminded her, as it must also remind him, that she was not his wife in the true sense of the word. In the physical sense of the word. Only on paper.

"Oh!" she murmured breathlessly, fighting a sudden desire to provoke the major into unleashing that latent passion she could feel emanating from his tall frame like a heady perfume. This is madness, she thought wildly, her mind struggling to impose order on her rioting emotions.

"I see you expect *me* to tell him. Is that it?" she managed to say.

"Wrong again, my dear." He had taken a step toward her

and now stood only a foot away, his eyes no longer cynical but intense.

Angela found she could not tear her gaze from those mesmerizing eyes, which seemed to be illuminated from within by a banked fire. She had seen something like it years ago in Roger's eyes and knew it to be a sign of male desire. But Roger's eyes had never had the power to paralyze her as Harry's were now doing. Part of her wanted to deny him, to break away and escape to the safety of her room. The other part . . . but she refused to heed what the other part was telling her to do.

So enthralled was she with the flood of new sensations which had invaded her body that when he put his hands gently on her waist and drew her to him, Angela made no resistance.

"That is not what I had in mind either, my love," he whispered against her neck, and Angela shuddered as his warm breath and questing lips explored her exposed skin.

The effect of his assault on her senses was immediate. She caught a familiar whiff of the Holland water he habitually used, but this time she was so close to him that the perfume was partially obscured by the smell of the man himself, an indescribably heady combination of maleness, soap, and tobacco, which made her head reel. Then there was the touch of his face against hers, the slight roughness of his shaved cheek, and the heat of it moving across her cheek and neck as his lips feathered against her skin.

But perhaps the most devastatingly sensuous response she experienced was triggered by the feeling of his body curved against hers. Angela had known the major was tall, but when her own slight frame was measured so intimately against his, she became acutely aware of the breadth of his shoulders bending over her, the strength of the arms that held her so lightly yet so inescapably, and, with a sudden shock, the tense hardness of his thighs pressed against hers.

When he moved his lips to claim her mouth, Angela felt the change in his mood instantly. One arm went round her slender waist and pulled her closer into the hardening curve of his body. The other slid up her back to cradle her head. His lips, so light and tender on her neck, covered her mouth with demands such had never been made of her before. His tongue became insistent, exploring, willing her to surrender her softness to him.

Angela felt herself melting against him, overcome in ways she had not dreamed possible. No other man, and certainly not Roger, had prepared her for the rush of passion that flooded through her at Harry's embrace. Her arms had somehow slipped around him, and she abandoned herself to the exquisite pleasure of the moment with a faint moan.

This expression of surrender on her part seemed to bring the major to his senses. Abruptly he pulled away from her and stood, breathing raggedly, staring down at her half-parted lips as though he had taken a sudden aversion to them.

After an endless moment of shocked silence, broken only by his harsh laugh and her own gasp of mortification, Angela felt herself stagger as the major pushed her roughly aside and disappeared into his room, slamming the door behind him.

Early the next morning, as Angela prepared for the journey back to Kent, she wondered how she could face the major with any degree of composure. The memory of his kiss and her wanton response to it had kept her awake long after the clock in the hall downstairs had struck midnight, and her dreams had been filled with disturbingly sensual visions. Consequently, she was rather subdued when she came down to breakfast to find Sophy sadly at odds with the major, who rose at his wife's entrance and settled her solicitously at the table.

Sophy had pleaded in vain with her brother to delay their return for a few days so that she could enjoy several of the entertainments Julian had planned for them. Even Mr. Walters's invitation to the major to prolong his stay in London for another week to allow the ladies to finish some last-minute shopping met with a firm denial. And although Angela sympathized with Sophy's desire to extend her sojourn in town, she was secretly glad that the major was adamant in his determination to return to the Abbey without further delay.

When the time for their departure arrived, Angela had to endure all manner of recommendations from both her father and Julian regarding her supposed delicate condition. Her nerves became quite frayed by the strain of having to keep up the pretense, and although she felt her husband's sardonic gaze upon her, she steadfastly refused to look at him.

The journey was accomplished quickly and comfortably in the well-sprung traveling chaise Mr. Walters had insisted they make use of until the major could procure a suitable carriage of his own. By the time they entered the gates of Castleton Abbey, however, the two ladies were heartily weary of traveling and looked forward to their dinner.

Coming home to the Abbey provoked an unexpected sense of satisfaction in Angela. When she expressed her feelings to Sophy, for whom the Abbey had always been home, her sister-in-law confided that she would find the Abbey dreadfully flat after the attention lavished on her in London by Angela's family.

Angela could not agree less. Her brief return to her father's house had confirmed what she had discovered upon her first arrival at Castleton Abbey. Much as she loved her father, he did not need her the way she was needed here in the major's house. Here, she had found a purpose to her life, a purpose that filled her days and gave her a deep sense of satisfaction. If only the major himself needed her as much as the estate did, Angela thought, her life would be complete.

But, of course, it was no use pining for things that could never be, she told herself firmly. For a heady moment, back there in her London sitting room, she had caught a breathtaking glimpse of what her life might be like if only Harry needed her as a man was supposed to need a woman. She would not ask for love. The Earl of Castleton could not be expected to fall in love with the daughter of a tradesman; that had been clear to her as soon as she had met him. His pride would never allow it. But she had been prepared to be the dutiful wife, to be content with friendship, with the comfortable companionship she had cultivated with him during their short time together. But now even that was in jeopardy.

For that brief moment in London, when Harry had finally taken her in his arms for the first time since their hasty wedding, she had been foolish enough to allow herself to believe that he had wanted her. Not just the money that marriage to her had brought, but Angela Walters as a woman, desirable

for herself. Perhaps her absence from the Abbey had made
him realize that he did need her, she had hoped. As she
needed him.

But she had been mistaken, of course. What a silly goose
she had been to imagine that the social chasm that existed between herself and her new husband could be bridged by a
mere civil contract, a business agreement entered into out of
necessity on the major's part. And now, through her own
fault, she had lost even the little regard he had developed for
her.

With a shudder Angela remembered the look of disgust in
his icy blue eyes as he had thrust her aside and slammed out
of her sitting room in London. What had she done wrong, she
wondered, to cause him to withdraw so abruptly from her embrace? Had she been too eager to surrender? And, in her own
mind, there was no doubt that she had been ready to acqui-
esce to anything the major might have asked of her. Should
she have shown more modesty perhaps? Had her eagerness to
please him been seen as wantonness, as lack of breeding?

This thought distressed Angela more than she cared to acknowledge, even in the recesses of her mind. She knew, of
course, that she was not the major's social equal, but she had
been educated as a lady by her mother, who had certainly
been as well-born as the earl. Had she betrayed her dear
Mama's teachings by behaving in a hoydenish, unladylike
manner? Had she thrown away any hope for a comfortable relationship with her husband?

As the days went by, Angela began to suspect that this was
indeed the case. The major rarely spoke to her at all and
seemed to avoid her, at the breakfast table, during her early
morning rides, her visits to the tenants, and even after dinner,
when he would retire immediately to his study and leave Angela and Sophy to entertain themselves.

Angela was glad that she had prevailed upon Sophy to
maintain her room at the Abbey when the dowager removed
to the Dower House. At Lady Castleton's insistence, her
daughter also had a room in the dowager's new residence, but
Sophy had enlisted her brother's aid in gaining permission to
spend a considerable amount of her time with Angela.

The dowager did not take this desertion placidly, and Angela felt the effect of her mother-in-law's resentment when the morning visits she received from the neighboring gentry dwindled down until the vicar, the Reverend Arthur Reynolds, was the sole visitor who frequented the Abbey. The few calls she had made herself had also been singularly unsuccessful.

At first Angela had been too busy with the refurbishing of the house to notice this desertion. But one morning, two weeks after their return from London, as she and Sophy were poring over samples of brocade sent from a London warehouse, a disturbing thought crossed her mind.

"I am beginning to believe that Lady Hastings was actually at home yesterday afternoon when we called, Sophy," she remarked, raising her eyes from the samples to gaze at the younger girl. "There was something about the butler's expression when he informed us that she had gone to the village that made me wonder if he was telling the truth. What do you think, dear?"

Unexpectedly, Sophy did not meet her eyes, but continued to flip through the samples on her lap.

"Now, why would she do a thing like that, Angela? What possible reason could she have for denying us?"

Angela regarded her in silence for a moment. "That's what I expect you to tell me, Sophy. If you are truly my friend, you will explain to me why we—or perhaps I should say, *I* am being ignored by the neighbors. I got little enough attention from them before, but now even that has dwindled to nothing. Only poor Mr. Reynolds still feels obligated to cross my threshold."

Sophy raised a guilty face and attempted a conciliatory smile. "You are imagining things, dear. The weather has not been favorable for outings this past week, remember."

"Fustian!" Angela replied. "Don't try to gammon me, Sophy. I am not so hen-witted as to believe such an obvious Banbury tale. Besides, it rained but once this past week."

When her friend lowered her eyes in confusion, Angela continued more kindly. "I sense your mother's hand in this, Sophy. Am I right?"

Sophy raised conscience-stricken eyes to Angela's face. "I had hoped you would not notice, dear. But that was silly of me, I know. And yes, you are right. I am ashamed to admit that Mama is indeed responsible for setting the neighbors against you. But I will not permit her to harm you any longer, Angela," she added more cheerfully. "In fact, this very afternoon we shall begin to fight back. And you are bound to win this battle, just wait and see."

No amount of cajoling could persuade Sophy to reveal the plan she had set in motion, except that it involved a visit to be paid that very afternoon to a neighboring estate.

In spite of her skepticism, when she entered the drawing room at Steele Hall later that day and was introduced to the vivacious, talkative, kindly Julia, Lady Steele, Angela felt she had found a friend. An attractive matron in her late thirties, Lady Steele had know the Davenports all her life and made no scruples about condemning the dowager's overbearing treatment of her new daughter-in-law.

"How did you know that she resents me, my lady?" Angela was prompted to inquire when it became apparent that Lady Steele was fully informed abut the new Countess Castleton's strained relationship with her mother-in-law.

"Sophy and my daughter Melissa are bosom companions, my dear. And Sophy wrote numerous letters to us in Brighton, whence we have just returned. We were to have taken her with us for a month, you know, but the dowager refused to let poor Sophy out of her sight. I am so glad that you were able to spirit her away recently, my dear. The child needs to get out from under her mother's oppressive eye. I can see a change for the good in her already," she added, casting an appraising look at Sophy, who blushed charmingly. "She is positively blooming. You have been a godsend to her, dear." Lady Steele regarded her guest with disconcerting candor.

"And for Harry, too, I have no doubt," she continued, and this time it was Angela's turn to blush. "The poor boy has had some most unfortunate experiences, thanks to his mother's meddling. And it's no use protesting, Sophy, for you know it to be true." Her warm glance scanned Angela's face searchingly. "I trust that he has found happiness at last, my dear. He must be a fool if he cannot see that you are worth a dozen of that milksop he nearly got himself leg-shackled to. That is one thing, at least, he can thank his mother for," she went on, seemingly oblivious of the effect of her candid remarks on her audience. "She wanted Matilda for her precious Nigel, but they all lived to regret it. Poetic justice, I call it, dear."

"Angela has not yet met Matilda," Sophy managed to say when her hostess paused for breath.

"Still up north visiting her aunt, is she?" Lady Steele sounded surprised. "I would have thought your Mama would have summoned her posthaste when Harry returned home. Such a biddable daughter-in-law she was, to be sure."

She must have caught the flash of pain in Angela's eyes, for she suddenly clasped her guest's hands impulsively. "Forgive me, dear. Sophy can tell you that I have a tongue that rattles on interminably. I did not mean to distress you. And besides, Matilda never had an original thought in her head, my dear, a hen-witted piece of fluff if ever I saw one. Isn't that so, Sophy?"

"Well, she always was rather missish," Sophy agreed cautiously. "But she is so very beautiful that the gentlemen don't seem to notice anything else."

Lady Steele made a sound that resembled a snort. "Pooh! All I can say is that I'm happy that Harry had enough sense to marry a gel with more spirit. And don't you worry, my dear," she squeezed Angela's hands before releasing them. "We will not allow Lady Castleton's rumors to make your life miserable, will we, Sophy? I will personally put a stop to that nasty little endeavor."

Angela was about to ask what endeavor Lady Steele referred to, but at that moment the butler appeared with the tea tray, closely followed by a lively young lady of about Sophy's age, and a young gentleman of no more than nineteen, whom Lady Steele introduced as her daughter Melissa and son Michael.

The young Steeles accorded Sophy a boisterous, affectionate welcome, and no sooner had they settled down to their tea and cakes than they insisted that she recount her London experiences for their benefit. This distraction allowed Lady Steele to converse privately with her new friend.

"For I do consider you a friend, my dear Angela," she said in her no-nonsense manner. "And I insist you call me Julia, if you please. I don't like to stand on ceremony with my friends."

By the time they took their leave an hour later, Angela felt that she did indeed have a friend in the outspoken Julia Steele. Not only had Lady Steele invited the Davenports to dinner the following evening, but she had also included Sophy and Angela in an alarming number of picnics, musicales, card parties, informal dances, and other amusements which the mistress of Steele Hall, the most popular hostess in the area, delighted in organizing.

Angela realized, with a glow of gratitude toward her new friend, that Lady Steele's sponsorship would assure her ultimate acceptance by all the gentry in the region, regardless of the dowager's opposition. As they drove home in the open carriage, Angela felt a surge of contentment at this small victory over the hostility of her mother-in-law. Now, she mused, if she could only win back the major's friendship as well, she would be in a fair way of achieving a definite place for herself at Castleton Abbey.

11

Man from the Past

The new Countess of Castleton soon found herself—as a direct result of her friendship with Lady Steele, she was convinced—in great demand from the principal families of the neighborhood. As if to make amends for their previous neglect, most of them now went out of their way to include Angela in every imaginable form of country entertainment.

She wondered just how she should broach the subject of the Steeles' dinner party to the major, but before she could decide on the best approach, Sophy blurted out the invitation and demanded to know if her brother intended to escort them.

Angela glanced at her husband and found his gaze fixed on her from the other end of the dinner table. Would he embarrass her before her new friends by refusing to accompany her? she wondered, suddenly losing interest in the braised pheasant pie her new cook prepared so exquisitely.

"Naturally I will escort you to an evening affair, Sophy. And the Steeles are old friends, after all," he replied in the cool manner he had adopted since their return from London. "I am glad to see that you are getting to know some of our neighbors, Angela," he added, staring down the table at her with an expression she found hard to decipher. "But don't ask me to waste my time attending afternoon teas or visits to ruins or amusements of that nature. I have far too much to attend to before the cold weather sets in."

And, much to Angela's surprise, he kept his word.

Although she felt a certain amount of apprehension at her first public appearance as the major's wife, Angela found nothing to criticize in his behavior toward her. He appeared to be on easy terms with Julia and her husband, Sir Joshua Steele, a jolly gentleman some ten years older than his wife.

Young Michael Steele stood in definite awe of the major and would have pestered him continually for stories of the Peninsular War had not Sir Joshua told his son and heir not to bother the major with his questions.

That first dinner at Steele Hall had been but the first of many evenings spent in the company of a growing circle of friends. Gradually, Angela began to entertain at the Abbey, first with a simple dinner with the Steeles as her only guests. Later, she undertook entertainments on a more ambitious scale, including all the important families in the immediate neighborhood. She began to enjoy a reputation as a popular hostess, thanks in part, she felt, to the expertise of her French cook, Monsieur Gaston.

She became more confident every day in the role of mistress of Castleton Abbey, and although the major still seemed aloof, Angela felt he approved of her ability to run his house and entertain his friends. Therefore, when disaster struck, it not only found her vulnerable and unprepared but also shattered all her hard-earned self-confidence.

One afternoon Angela went up to her room to change her dress and tidy her hair, since she was expecting Lady Steele to call. As Clothilde was fastening the last buttons down the back of a new gown of watered pink silk with Brussels lace at the neck, they both heard a carriage drive up to the front door. Impatient to see Julia again after several days of wet weather, Angela dismissed her dresser and left her room, hurrying along the hall to the staircase.

As she reached the head of the stairs, Angela clearly heard Lady Steele's voice, among a confused murmur of others, making an idle remark about the weather to Jaspers in the front hall directly below. She experienced a surge of well-being. Here she was, mistress of a grand house, entertaining her friends much as her mother must have done before she decided to marry Mr. Walters. What a pity Mama had not lived long enough to see her daughter established as a countess, Angela thought.

She had descended but two steps when a new voice from the hall below made her come to an abrupt halt, one foot poised above the third step. No, she thought wildly, a sudden frisson of panic causing her to sway against the banister. No, she must be imagining things. But the voice came again, a deep masculine voice, faintly bored but soft and caressing, a well-remembered voice that had filled her nightmares for months during that dreadful period three years ago when the world had fallen in on all her dreams.

No, she told herself again, this is impossible. Roger cannot be here at Castleton Abbey. But the voice wafted up to her rigid form yet again, and Angela could no longer doubt that it was indeed Roger Hyland, the man who had crushed her pride and destroyed her happiness so long ago.

In a panic she turned and mounted the stairs again, then stood, her mind in a whirl, grasping the banister for support. What should she do? She could not, *would* not go downstairs and confront Roger's handsome, smiling face again after all these years of trying to eradicate him from her heart. Wildly she looked around her. What should she do? Where could she hide? Then she thought of the major, and she knew she had to find him. He would help her, protect her.

The voices disappeared into the drawing room as Jaspers closed the door behind the visitors. Sophy was there; she could take care of them, Angela thought desperately. She would go to Harry. Silently she descended the stairs and turned away from the room that held the man from her past. Once out of earshot, she ran along the hall and flung open the door of the major's study. If he were not here, she would die, she thought. She would surely die before she would walk into that drawing room alone to meet her past again.

But he was there. Angela stood for a moment in the doorway, staring wildly at her husband. He stood up at her precipitous entry and came across the room, an expression of alarm in his eyes.

"What is it, Angela?" he said softly. "What has put you into this pucker?"

"Oh, Harry," she cried, relief making her voice quiver. "Oh, thank God you're here." Without hesitation Angela ran to her husband and grasped his lapels. "Help me, Harry," she moaned. "Please, please help me."

The major had spent a fruitful afternoon with his bailiff, going over plans for the changes the new earl wished to accomplish during the lull of the winter months, when outside activity was less pressing. They had discussed the purchase of new livestock to strengthen the estate's diminished herds and the need to reclaim the south farm, which had been allowed to go back to pasture. There were tenant cottages to rethatch, repairs to be made to the stables, and new varieties of seeds to be ordered for the spring plantings.

On the whole, Harry thought, after old Crofts had left him, he had managed to achieve a surprising amount of restoration with the ten thousand pounds Mr. Walters had transferred to his London bank on the day of his marriage last July. There would be another such sum transferred in January of the coming year, and two more payments at equal intervals over the following months. On top of this generous settlement, his father-in-law had bought up all the existing mortgages on the Abbey and Castleton House in London. This alone had amounted to over fifty thousand pounds.

And then there had been the debts, Harry remembered, cringing at the memory of the frivolous nature of his father's expenditures. Bills from fashionable modistes, milliners, jewelers, carriage makers, all long past due, had continued to accumulate on Mr. Hamilton's desk in London even though the late earl had known there were no funds to cover them. And when Nigel's equally extravagant purchases had been added to those his father had left unpaid, the sum had been staggering. Mr. Walters had paid them all without the slightest hesitation, and—what Harry had appreciated most of all—without any hint of condemnation. It was one thing for Harry to curse the spendthrift ways of his predecessors in the privacy of Mr. Hamilton's London office, but he could not have tolerated a word of blame from anyone else, much less from a mere tradesman.

That was unfair, Harry corrected himself. Mr. Walters was anything but a mere tradesman. In truth, if Harry were honest with himself, he would have to admit that his father-in-law was more gentlemanly than many noblemen of Harry's acquaintance. His generosity, his amiability, and above all his tact had rendered his son-in-law powerless to dislike him as Harry had been prepared to do. And his daughter was every inch a lady, Harry thought, every delectable inch of her.

Thoughts of his wife drove all others from his mind. Marriage to Angela had brought him over a hundred thousand pounds, which included the payment of debts, mortgages, and settlements. Thanks to her, he was completely debt-free, and his beloved home was well on the way to becoming a productive estate again. And what had he given her in return? he wondered.

A twinge of guilt made him uneasy. Yes indeed, he asked himself again. What had his wife received from him except the title of countess, which she set little store by? He cursed his own thoughtlessness in London for putting her in the uncomfortable position of having to deny his careless lie about her condition. It had seemed amusing at the time, but Angela had been right; he had caused unnecessary pain to others.

This train of thought brought him inevitably to their confrontation in London, when she had asked for an explanation of his behavior. And what had he given her instead of the apology she deserved? Harry grimaced at the scene which replayed itself in his mind, as it had done innumerable times in the past weeks. What a complete numbskull he was, to be sure. Instead of begging her forgiveness, as he clearly should have, he had, like some cow-handed clodpole, tried to seduce her.

The memory of his wife's compliant body in his arms flooded his mind again, setting his nerves tingling and his blood surging. Harry closed his eyes as the full force of the remembered intimacy hit him. The warmth of her response had surprised and delighted him. He felt again the softness of her skin under his lips, the heat of her mouth opening beneath his. She had been ready to surrender; he was quite sure of it. He had bedded enough women to recognize the precise moment when a woman was poised on the brink of surrender, ready to fall into his hand at a word from him. And Angela had reached that brink; he had felt it clearly in the way she had gone limp against him, in the little moan that had escaped her. But like a damned fool, he had thrown it all away.

And why? he asked himself for the umpteenth time. He knew very well why, but was loath to admit it even to himself. For at that last moment, when he had held his desirable wife in the palm of his hand, he had suddenly remembered his vow that he needed no other heir than his nephew, Jeremy. Although this notion now appeared both presumptuous and premature, it was enough to unsettle him and had abruptly cooled his ardor. And he had left her—left her with that startled, bereft look in her eyes. A look which still haunted him.

With an effort Harry tried to bring his mind back to the tasks ahead of him, but he was distracted by the sound of running steps in the hall. Then the door of his study was thrown open, and Angela stood on the threshold, staring at him with those same smoky eyes, now filled with panic.

"Oh, Harry," she cried, reaching out her arms to him. "Help me, Harry." He rose and strode toward her, alarmed at the panic he had never seen in her before. She came into his arms and grasped his lapels, gazing up at him pleadingly. "Please, please help me," she murmured, burrowing her face into his shoulder with a sob of relief.

"What is it, Angela? What has happened to distress you like this?" He stroked her trembling shoulders.

She murmured something which he did not catch. He took her chin in his hand and raised her face. "Tell me what has upset you, love," he said softly, now thoroughly alarmed at his wife's condition.

"It's *him*, Harry," she sobbed. "It's *him*."

"Who are you talking about, Angela. I don't understand. Who is this man who has overset you like this?"

"Oh, Harry. I can't face him; I simply can't do it. Please don't make me." She grew agitated again as he frowned at her.

"Who, my love, who?" he demanded. "Try to control yourself, Angela, and tell me the name of this villain who has frightened you so."

He took his handkerchief and gently wiped away her tears. She swallowed and regained some of her composure.

"It's Roger," she said in a small voice. "I don't know how he got here, but he's here, Harry. And I can't bear it." She looked up at him beseechingly. "I can't bear it; truly, I can't."

"And who is this Roger fellow, may I ask?" he inquired, a cold lump beginning to form in his heart.

Angela lowered her eyes. "I told you about it, Harry. Remember. He's the man who . . . well, he has a title and . . . I was silly enough to fall in love. I thought he wanted to marry me, but . . ."

She raised her eyes, and Harry saw they were filled with tears again. "He didn't," she finished in a strangled voice.

Harry pulled her against him and stroked her hair until her trembling stopped. "What is his name, love? Tell me his full name."

"Roger Hyland," she whispered. "The Earl of Medford. He told me his seat was in the north. Whatever can he be doing here, Harry? You won't let him hurt me again, will you?"

Harry felt a wave of tenderness for his frightened wife as he gazed down on her dark head cushioned against his shoulder. She had obviously suffered deeply from her entanglement with Medford, whom he vaguely remembered as one of the Norfolk Hylands. More than she had previously admitted, he guessed. A sudden uncomfortable thought made him pause. Gently he took her by the shoulders and held her at arm's length.

"Do you still love Medford, Angela? Tell me the truth."

She dropped her eyes, and Harry experienced a sick feeling in his stomach. He realized with a sudden flash of intuition that he did not want his wife to retain the least vestige of love for this man from her past. The very idea that she might still harbor tender feelings for Medford made him wince. He would kill him, he thought viciously. The devil take the man for intruding in their lives, for entering their very house, for threatening the tenuous relationship they shared.

Apprehension gripped him, and he shook her impatiently. "Do you, Angela?" he repeated, his voice harsh with fear.

She looked into his eyes and he saw indecision there. "I don't know, Harry. I really don't. It's been so long . . ."

"Well I hope not," he said roughly. "You are *my* wife now, Angela, do you understand? And I won't have you making sheep's eyes at another man. Do you hear me?"

He saw shock register in her eyes and wished he had not been so blunt. "Forgive me, my dear," he said, trying to overcome his own alarm at the thought of his wife with another man. "What I meant was that you must remember you are a married woman now. You are mine," he added more gently, folding her in his arms and resting his lips on the top of her head. "If you remember that, Medford will not be able to hurt you ever again."

Angela snuggled closer against his chest. "I shall try, Harry. But you will help me, won't you?"

"Of course, I will, dearest," he murmured against her hair. "Now, dry your eyes, and I will accompany you to the drawing room."

"No!" she cried, a shiver shaking her small frame. "I cannot face him, Harry. Please don't make me."

"But you must, love. Think how odd it will look if the lady of the house refuses to appear before her guests. You must be brave, Angela, and I will help you."

"How?" she asked unexpectedly, drawing back and gazing up at him anxiously. "How will you help me, Harry?"

He gazed down at her for a moment, wondering how he could convince her of his support. His eyes slid down to her lips, slightly parted and unconsciously inviting. He smiled a slow, caressing smile, suddenly knowing what he would do and anticipating the moment with pleasure.

"This is what I will do, my dear," he murmured, bending over her and brushing her lips with his mouth, at first with great gentleness and then with increasing pressure and warmth. She remained motionless in his arms, her body rigid against his chest. As his demands became more insistent, however, he felt her slowly relax, her mouth grow soft against his, and finally open to admit his probing tongue. He gloried in the feminine allure of her, which had already begun its insidious attack on his senses. Surely this must prove to her that she was his? he thought. Surely this, if nothing else, would be more than enough to drive intrusive thoughts of Medford out of her heart forever?

Reluctantly he raised his head and stared into her eyes, now faintly glazed with the first awakenings of desire. This time, however, he did not release her, but held her firmly against him.

He smiled possessively. "Did Medford ever kiss you like that, Angela?"

"No," she whispered, returning his smile hesitantly. "No, never."

"Well, remember that fact when we go into the drawing

room, my dear. Remember this kiss and think of this intimate moment we are sharing. Look at me across the room and think of this kiss when you must face Medford and welcome him to our house. Remember it if he tries to talk about the past; remember it, and you will be able to laugh at him and even pity him for being such a fool. This is the present, Angela. The past cannot hurt you unless you let it, my dear. This kiss will remind you that I am there to help you." He bowed his head and briefly kissed her again.

"Come, Angela," he said, slipping her hand through his arm and escorting her to the door. "We will face this man from the past together, and I will wager you will soon see that you have made much ado about nothing."

Angela was still in a daze of happiness when she approached the drawing room on Harry's arm. Jaspers was on hand to throw open the double doors, which he did with a flourish, since it was quite apparent that the Earl of Castleton was not about to relinquish his lady's arm. As a result, their entrance caused quite a stir, and as Angela felt all eyes turn toward them, it occurred to her that it must be obvious to everyone that Harry had been kissing her, since her lips felt slightly puffy.

Although she made an effort to control her expression, she felt sure that her happiness was written there for all to see. Quite irrationally, she did not care if they did. And why shouldn't she be kissing her husband if she felt so inclined? Even at three o'clock in the afternoon. *You are mine,* Harry had said. The words echoed through her mind in a captivating rhythm which Angela found quite intoxicating. *You are mine. You are mine.* Yes indeed, she thought. She was certainly his. Her heart was telling her so, too.

They paused several feet inside the room, and Angela caught Lady Steele's eye. She found herself being regarded with considerable interest by that lady, who raised a quizzical eyebrow and smiled at Angela approvingly.

"Julia," Angela said, advancing upon her friend and embracing her warmly. "Forgive me for keeping you waiting. Harry and I were reviewing some of the changes we are planning for the West wing," she added glibly. "Melissa,

Michael," she added, turning to Sophy's friends. "I'm glad to see you both. Sophy, have you asked Jaspers to bring in the tea?"

It was only when Lady Steele caught her hand and drew her toward a gentleman standing by the window that Angela suddenly remembered Roger. Harry had been right, she thought. That kiss had quite addled her brain.

"There is someone I want you to meet, dear," Julia was saying. "Someone who claims a prior acquaintance with you, Angela."

And then the moment she had so dreaded finally arrived. Angela found herself face to face with Roger Hyland, and the past came tumbling into the present. Her euphoria began to fade. He was still devastatingly handsome, she saw, and his pale blue eyes could still set off tremors in her stomach. He was observing her keenly from beneath hooded lids, and she forced herself to offer her hand, which he raised with mock gallantry to his lips.

"My dear Lady Castleton," he began in that odiously lazy, caressing tone he had used with her so often in the past. "What a pleasant surprise indeed. I couldn't believe my good fortune when Julia—who is my cousin, you know—let it drop that you were a close friend of hers. I shall enjoy my stay at Steele Hall even more than I had anticipated."

Angela murmured a polite response and withdrew her hand, which Roger had been holding overlong. She turned to watch for Harry, who materialized at her side and laid a steadying hand on her waist, a possessive gesture which was not lost on Roger, Angela noticed.

"Harry," she said. "I don't know if you are acquainted with the Earl of Medford."

"I believe we have met before," the major replied briefly. "Possibly at White's?" He extended his hand.

"Castleton, well met," Roger replied. "I gather I am to congratulate you on your recent good fortune in persuading Miss Walters to become your countess."

The major bowed briefly but said nothing and was soon claimed by Julia, who wanted to entice him to join a small expedition she was planning to show her cousin the local sights.

"Congratulations, Angela," Roger murmured as soon as

Harry was out of earshot. "I see that you have attained your heart's desire, my dear. A trifle under the hatches, the Castletons, of course, as everybody knows, but then, your dear Papa can easily replenish the empty coffers, can't he?"

Angela was surprised to detect, or so she thought, undertones of bitterness in Roger's voice. She was saved from having to devise a suitable reply to this disparaging comment on the financial embarrassment of the Castletons by the arrival of Jaspers with the tea tray.

Angela was soon to discover that the Earl of Medford meant exactly what he said about enjoying his stay at Steele Hall. As Lady Steele's houseguest, he was the object of numerous social activities devised by her ladyship to relieve the tedium of country living. So it was inevitable that the two ladies from the Abbey should find themselves more often in his company than one of them, at least, could wish. Angela envied her sister-in-law's apparent indifference to Roger's charm and classical good looks. While admitting that Lord Medford was indeed a fine figure of a man and undeniably handsome, Sophy preferred to talk about her short stay in London and the prospect of visiting the house on St. James's Square again in the near future.

As for Roger himself, Angela found that the cooler she was toward him, the more charmingly flirtatious he became. When he caught her alone, he let drop some pretty broad hints that he would be more than delighted to continue the relationship cut short three years ago by what he insisted on calling Angela's excessive prudishness.

"As a married lady, my dear," he would drawl in his caressing way that still had the insidious power to make Angela tremble, "you now enjoy a freedom from such petty restrictions. Among the *ton* who set the fashions, prudishness is considered the worst of sins, you know. Quite frankly, Angela, you disappoint me with these old-fashioned, provincial ways."

Whenever Angela could, she ignored these scandalous insinuations. When they occurred, as they often did, in a lowered voice in the middle of a country dance, or as Medford escorted her in to dinner or bowed mockingly over her hand or lifted her off her horse after an outing, Angela felt the tug of her old passion for him. Ironically, it was during Roger's most seductive assaults that Angela's thoughts flew to Harry. Her lips would glow again with the memory of his kiss, and she would glance around the room, searching for him. Invariably his dark gaze would be fastened on her, and as their eyes locked, she would see his lips twitch into a slow, secretive smile that made her forget, at least for the moment, the disturbing presence of the man from her past.

But Harry had the estate to attend to, and Angela could not expect him to accompany her on every excursion organized by Lady Steele for the benefit of her cousin. As a result, she frequently found herself in Medford's company when she was invited to accompany the Steeles on their afternoon calls around the neighborhood.

It was on one such afternoon, some three weeks after Roger Hyland's arrival at Steele Hall, just when Angela was beginning to feel that she had overcome her youthful infatuation for the man who had betrayed her, that a new threat appeared on the horizon.

There had been an early threat of rain on that autumn afternoon, so Lady Steele insisted that they take an early leave of Squire Rawson and his lady, with whom they had been taking tea, and return home. The skies had become dark with rain clouds roiling in from the south, and a chill wind had risen, so the party was in no mood to dawdle. Michael's suggestion that they take the shortcut across the Castleton estates was greeted with enthusiasm, and the horses, spooked by the impending storm, were barely manageable in their eagerness to reach home.

Angela gloried in the mad gallop across the open meadow and up a slight incline topped by a solitary old oak tree, which reached its gnarled arms up to the blackening sky. Her Black Star easily kept pace with the horses ridden by the two gentlemen, who had proposed a race to the top of the hill. Michael rode a wall-eyed bay gelding which Angela considered far too green a horse for pleasurable riding, and Medford bestrode a barrel-chested hunter of at least seventeen hands, whose labored breathing told Angela that his exercise had been sorely neglected of late.

In a fit of recklessness Angela touched Black Star's flank

with her booted heel, and the horse sprang forward in a surge of speed that left the others behind. When she drew rein beneath the spreading branches of the old oak, Angela caught her breath at the beauty of the pastoral scene that met her eyes. The slope was dotted with sheep, watched over by a barefooted lad with untidy hair and a pixie face who regarded her curiously.

"Ah, the joys of rural existence, my dear," came a bored sneer close to her ear. "It has a certain rustic enchantment, even I must admit. If only it weren't so deuced far from a decent tailor."

When Angela did not reply to this witticism, Medford continued in an insinuating whisper. "If it were not for the lure of your delectable charms, my sweet Angela, I don't think I could have endured spending more than a few weeks rusticating in such bland, boring surroundings. Although, what is that I see? Perhaps I have underestimated the delights of rural dalliance, after all. Ah, for a romp with a country wench," he murmured softly. "Doubtless one of the choicer advantages of being lord of the manor."

Angela sensed the change in Medford's tone, the sneer more pronounced, the mockery less subtle. Curious, she glanced at him and saw his gaze fixed on a distant grove of alders far to their right. Following his gaze, she realized that she had been so enthralled at the sight of the sheep that she had failed to notice a couple on horseback, deep in conversation among the distant alders.

The man sat with his back toward her, but Angela's eyes were drawn immediately to the lady, whom she could see clearly, although the distance between them might have been as great as a mile. Dressed completely in black, except for a green feather in her elegant hat, the lady rode a small-boned mare of pure white, which fidgeted nervously at the bit. The lady's hair was the palest blond Angela had ever seen, and it framed her small, heart-shaped face with graceful curls.

Angela had never seen this woman before, but a sudden premonition warned her that she was looking at her husband's first and only love. She felt herself go cold and rigid with apprehension. Unwillingly she wrenched her eyes away from the beautiful stranger and focused on the man. That broad back seemed uncomfortably familiar, but when Angela's gaze dropped to the horse he rode, she could no longer pretend to ignore what her heart was telling her. That was Duke, all right. No sense in trying to deny it. Harry's horse stood with one hip shot as if he had been standing in the same position for some time. How long had Harry been out here alone with this woman? Angela wondered. The thought of Harry, *her Harry*, with another woman sliced through her like a knife, and a wave of anguish deeper than any she had ever experienced washed over her.

"What have I been trying to tell you, my love? A little discreet dalliance is entirely acceptable. Obviously Castleton sees nothing wrong with it." The amused voice at her elbow had an undertone of triumph in it. "Don't look so devastated, my dear girl. Pull yourself together. Sooner or later, this was bound to happen. He was besotted with the chit before she chose his brother's title over true love, or whatever it was he offered our delectable Matilda in those days. Rather sensible of her, I should say."

The cruel words cascaded around her ears, but Angela barely heard them. She closed her eyes and breathed deeply, trying to recover her composure. When she looked again at the grove of alders, it was empty.

"*Voilà!* It was all a mirage, my dear," Medford murmured. "You saw nothing of great moment, after all. Castleton will be in your debt, you know, and will undoubtedly look the other way when you put aside your coyness, my love, and reward your most devoted admirer with a taste of your charms."

Resisting the impulse to slap Roger's smug face for him, Angela turned away, embarrassed that he had seen her distress so clearly. By the time Lady Steele, Sophy, and Melissa had ridden up, Angela had her emotions under control again. Michael, who must have seen the couple among the alders, glanced awkwardly at Angela several times and held his peace. She was acutely aware that Roger was enjoying himself hugely at her expense. Just the sort of despicable thing she might have expected of him, she thought after she and Sophy had parted from the Steeles and their guest and turned toward the Abbey, visible through the misty rain which had begun to fall.

"Is anything wrong, Angela?" Sophy queried as they made their way through the thickening fog which rolled in from the south.

What could possibly be wrong? Angela thought disconsolately. After all, I've just caught my husband in a secret rendezvous with another woman. What could be wrong about that? Perhaps Roger is right: Harry is still besotted with his precious Matilda. That must be it. Why else would he meet her in so isolated a spot? Barely four months wed, and he is already setting up a mistress. The thought of having to share Harry with another woman caused a painful lump to restrict her throat. She had thought about the possibility often, but now that the shadow of a mistress loomed in the immediate future, Angela discovered that she wanted Harry all for herself. Idle wish, she thought. He does not want me; why, oh why, had she allowed herself to believe that he might one day accept her for what she was?

"Angela?" Sophy's voice came eerily out of the fog. "What has set you in such a pucker, dear? Is it Lord Medford? I couldn't help noticing that he pays you particular attention. Harry has noticed it, too. I don't think he likes it very much, Angela."

"You are making much ado about a mere trifle, Sophy," Angela replied, consciously echoing Harry's comment about her fear of facing Roger. And what right has Harry to be upset about Roger's attentions to me? she wondered miserably. He has his precious Matilda to console him, but whom do I have? *You are mine,* he had told her the day Roger arrived, and she had read into those words what she had wanted to believe. That Harry had come to care for her. Now she would have to learn to live with the painful truth. Harry did *not* care for her. How could he, now that Matilda had returned?

A pox on Matilda, she thought savagely, giving Black Star his head and urging him recklessly toward the Abbey, as if she could outrun the demons that threatened to turn her dreams into ashes.

12

Lady from the Past

Harry ate a solitary dinner before the library fire that evening. Her ladyship had retired early to her room with a headache, Jaspers informed his master when he came in at dusk, his coat damp with the misty rain that had settled in for the night.

"Nothing serious, I hope?" Harry replied. It was unlike Angela to be afflicted with any of the usual ailments that laid the dowager low at regular intervals. He could not remember, offhand, ever hearing his wife complain of feeling out of sorts.

"No, my lord," Jaspers said in his toneless voice. "Her ladyship was out in the rain this afternoon with Lady Sophia. She seems to have caught a slight chill."

When Harry came downstairs later than evening, he discovered that Sophy had decided to have her dinner tray sent up to Angela's room. This did not surprise him greatly; he knew his sister had developed a strong fondness for Angela and was glad of it. Like himself, Sophy had not had a happy childhood. Aside from her friendship with Melissa Steele, his sister had no close friends, and her attachment to Angela was fortunate, he thought. It relieved him of the necessity of entertaining his wife.

At the thought of Angela, Harry felt a flicker of guilt. Had she seen him that afternoon out in the woods with Matilda? he wondered. Had anyone in that party Matilda had described to him as appearing suddenly on the distant hill recognized him? It had been a foolish impulse to turn and canter off into the trees with Matilda. He had regretted it even as he did it. But by then it had been too late to change his mind and join the Steeles' party.

Unwilling to dine alone in the formal dining-room, Harry

ordered his dinner served in the library, and he had barely finished his meal when the door opened and his sister walked in. He saw at once, by the tilt of her small chin, that she was in a rare pucker about something.

"Sophy, my love," he said soothingly. "Come to drink your tea with me, have you? I appreciate the company."

"When did Matilda arrive back from Bath?" Sophy demanded peremptorily, ignoring his attempt at a diversion.

"Matilda?"

"Yes, Matilda." She glared at him. "Surely you remember Matilda, your sister-in-law? *Nigel's widow?*" She placed special emphasis on the last two words, her voice filled with scorn.

"Why should I know—"

"Don't try to bamboozle me Harry," Sophy snapped angrily. "It won't fadge, you know. You were seen skulking around in the south woods with her this afternoon."

"I was not skulking around in the woods with anyone," Harry said hotly, annoyed that his sister had described his actions so accurately.

"Michael saw you, so it's no use denying it."

"If that young puppy is spreading malicious rumors about Matilda, I shall wring his neck for him."

"It was no rumor, Harry," Sophy snapped. "Angela saw you, too."

"And she came running to tattle to you, I suppose," Harry interrupted angrily, hating himself for the meanness of the remark as soon as it left his lips.

Sophy looked disgusted. "No, she did no such thing. And you haven't answered my question. When did Matilda return from Bath?"

"Yesterday."

"And she couldn't wait to set up an assignation with you, could she? How could you, Harry?"

"You are rushing your fences, my dear," Harry said wearily. "There was no assignation, as you call it. We met quite by accident. Matilda was out riding and—"

"On Castleton land?"

Harry regarded his little sister impatiently. "Of course, on Castleton land. How else would we have met?"

"That's exactly what I mean, Harry," Sophy pointed out. "You must be a shuttlehead if you cannot see what is as plain as the nose on your face. Unless I'm very much mistaken, our dear Matilda *planned* to meet you accidentally. Why else would she be on our land?"

"This used to be her home, too," Harry reminded her.

"Living at the Abbey for six years did not make it her home, Harry. Mama was always mistress here, as you must know. And Nigel didn't care who ran the household as long as the meals were on time and his own comfort assured. Matilda never had the gumption to say boo to a sparrow. I got so tired of trying to make her stand up to Mama, but she never would listen to me. Always the watering-pot Matilda was; when faced with a conflict, she would burst into tears. It was enough to make a cat sick."

Harry grimaced as he remembered Matilda's clear blue eyes brimming with tears that afternoon as she had attempted to explain just why she had been obliged to marry his brother instead of keeping her promise to her betrothed. Sophy was right, Matilda's beautiful eyes had often been filled with tears. But she had seemed so fragile and helpless that he had felt again the surge of protectiveness that had always characterized his relationship with her. She had evoked in him, once again, that old desire to save her from the rough edges of the world that he had thought dead forever in his heart.

Harry sighed. His encounter with Matilda yesterday had been a shock. Although he had been preparing himself for the inevitable meeting with his former betrothed ever since his return to the Abbey, he had not anticipated the effect her presence would have on him. She had been so achingly beautiful, seated on her mare Snowdrop, and dressed in the deep mourning which only accentuated her ethereal loveliness and fragility. Harry had come upon her unexpectedly in the south woods as he was on his way home from visiting an outlying farm. She had sat, motionless, waiting for him to approach, and his heart had jumped into his throat at the sight of her, a ghostly figure in the mist.

He shook his head to clear away these disturbing thoughts and brought his attention back to his sister, standing before the hearth and regarding him accusingly.

"I hope you are not filling Angela's head with a lot of nonsense about Matilda and me," he said stiffly. "That is all in the past now, Sophy, and there is no going back."

Long after Sophy had gone up to bed, Harry sat before the dying fire, hoping that he had spoken the truth, that his love for Matilda, intense and all consuming as it had been at the time, was indeed a thing of the past. He hoped so, fervently, for all their sakes.

Angela had passed a restless night, and the days that followed that clandestine meeting she had witnessed between her husband and Matilda in the south woods were filled with anxiety and secret pain. She had learned from a reluctant Sophy, who had obviously not been in raptures over her previous sister-in-law, that Matilda had returned to her father's house after spending the summer in Bath with a widowed aunt.

"I cannot imagine why Matilda did not stay on in Bath," Sophy remarked two days later, as she accompanied Angela and Jeremy on a brisk canter through the Park.

"She may have been homesick," Angela suggested calmly, unwilling to criticize her rival.

Sophy shook her head. "I know for a fact that she corresponded regularly with Mama, so she must have known that Harry brought a new bride back to the Abbey with him."

"She could still have been homesick, Sophy," Angela said. "I get that way sometimes myself."

"Oh, no. There is more to it than that, Angela. Mama tried to persuade her to return posthaste when we received news of Harry's arrival in London. She is much more biddable than you, Angela," she added with a grin. "You cast a rub in Mama's plans to leg-shackle poor Harry to someone like Matilda. You have no idea what a dust she kicked up when word came down from Mr. Hamilton that Harry had suddenly tied the knot with you. I thought that was just like something out of a novel, myself. Didn't it seem that way to you, Angela?"

Angela felt vaguely uncomfortable with Sophy's romantic perception of the events. "We all know that your brother only did what was necessary to save the estate from ruin," she said prosaically, determined to be circumspect about her marriage. "I hardly consider myself a likely character for one of Mrs. Radcliffe's romances."

"Oh, but you *are*, Angela," Sophy insisted.

"What are you talking about, Sophy?" Jeremy wanted to know as he rejoined them after a short gallop. "What is it that Angela is?"

"She and Harry are like two characters from a romantic novel," Sophy replied. "All the right elements are there. The returning hero wounded in the service of his country, the secret marriage, the dilapidated country estate, the mysterious rival, and the inevitable lost lady-love in the hero's murky past."

Both Angela and Jeremy gazed at Sophy in silent astonishment.

"Balderdash!" Jeremy exclaimed at last. "What a lot of fustian you do talk, Sophy. Their marriage was *not* secret because I was there. So were Mr. Walters and Julian. And the Abbey is *not* dilapidated; Angela has made countless repairs. Uncle Harry is certainly a hero, I agree with that, but he has no murky past that I know of. And who is this mysterious rival, I would like to know?"

"I had no idea you had such a fertile imagination, Sophy," Angela laughed.

"Trust you not to see the romantic side to things, Jeremy," Sophy grumbled. "And Harry's rival is Lord Medford, of course. The rejected suitor from the past, if I'm not mistaken." She glanced inquiringly at Angela.

"Nothing as romantic as that," Angela assured her quickly, wondering what other outrageous conclusions her sister-in-law would blurt out next.

"And I suppose you mean to tell me that this Matilda creature you were discussing is another rival from the past?" Jeremy said disgustedly. "I must say this whole affair is a hum,

Sophy. You had best not let Uncle Harry hear you talking such nonsense. He and Angela are married now, so I fail to see how rivals come into it at all."

Jeremy kicked his horse into a gallop and disappeared round a clump of rhododendrons, leaving Angela and Sophy to shrug their shoulders at such innocence and discreetly change the subject.

Angela was to remember Jeremy's naive assumption that marriage automatically eliminated rivals several days later when she was formally introduced to Matilda, the Countess of Castleton, at a lavish evening soirée offered by Lady Steele to welcome the former earl's widow back from a three-month sojourn in Bath.

If given a choice in the matter, the present Countess of Castleton would have preferred to avoid the encounter altogether, but Angela knew that her absence would give rise to any number of scurrilous rumors. Furthermore, she was determined that Harry, who had promised to accompany the Abbey ladies, should not be given free rein to dance attendance on his childhood inamorata.

So it was that she dressed with particular care that evening in a new ball gown of green Italian taffeta, cut daringly low across her shapely bosom, and worn with a diaphanous, spider-gauze overgown strewn with silver spangles. To offset such splendor Angela chose a simple diamond and emerald necklace and matching ear bobs, previous birthday gifts from her Papa. On impulse, she slipped on the exquisite jade rose ring Harry had given her on her last birthday. Perhaps, she thought ruefully as she allowed Clothilde to brush her dark curls up into an elegant sweep on top of her head, the ring will remind Harry where his duty lies.

If Angela had been previously apprehensive about her ability to compete with the beauty of her supposed rival, when she came face to face with the incomparable Matilda, she felt thoroughly outclassed and overshadowed. She had never thought of herself as a beautiful woman. Her complexion was, she knew, quite flawless, and her unusually colored eyes were her best feature. Other than these, she knew herself to be elegantly tall and impeccably gowned, but all this was no match for the ethereal blond loveliness of Harry's childhood love.

The blond beauty made her entrance fashionably late on the arm of her brother, Captain George Woodall, late of the 7th Hussars, Harry's old regiment. The commotion at the door caused Angela, who was dancing a quadrille with Lord Medford at the time, to glance surreptitiously around the room to see Harry's reaction. When she saw the eager look on his ruggedly handsome face as he made his way toward the newcomers, she wished she had pretended ignorance of the beauty's arrival. To her chagrin, when she turned her attention back to her partner, she saw that Roger had seen through her assumed indifference.

"The Incomparable Matilda has arrived." He grinned. "And all the besotted swains flock to pay homage to her fair beauty. But do not despair, my dear Angela, for I am not one of them. Matilda was never one of my favorites. Too insipid and vaporish for my taste. I prefer dark women with mysterious, smoky eyes and tempers to match. Fire is what I like in my women, Angela."

Medford gazed at her so suggestively that Angela felt herself blush, but she was saved from having to give him a setdown by Julia, who came up to carry her off as the set came to an end.

"I want you to meet Matilda, my dear," she explained. "You have to do it sooner or later, and I would rather introduce you myself than have someone else make a mull of it."

"I have been looking forward to meeting the countess, having heard so much about her," Angela said, telling herself that this was, at least, partially true.

Lady Steele looked sharply at her friend and smiled grimly. "Michael told me about the little rendezvous you witnessed last week, Angela, and I cannot but think that Harry's mother is behind it somehow. Matilda is too missish by far to have thought up something like that by herself. You must know by now that the dowager had definite plans for Harry's future which did not include you, my dear."

"Sophy has told me as much," Angela replied, somewhat discomforted by her friend's frankness.

"I cannot tell you how pleased I am that Harry had sense enough to make that decision on his own," Julia declared. "You are the best thing that has happened to that young man since he came out of short coats. But what I really wanted to say is this, Angela. Don't let Matilda overwhelm you, my dear. She has that effect on people, especially on the gentlemen. But there is no real substance there, dear, and Harry is older and wiser than he was six years ago. And if he cannot see that you are worth a dozen Matildas, he is not the man I think he is."

By this time they had come upon the group surrounding the new arrivals, and Angela was forcefully reminded of Julia's words when she found herself gazing into the most limpid blue eyes she had ever seen. One could search in vain for the real woman behind eyes like those, Angela thought. If Matilda had any feelings at all towards the wife of her former betrothed, she gave absolutely no sign of them. Her voice was soft to the point of being almost childish as she murmured her polite greetings. When Angela ventured to inquire about her recent stay in Bath, Matilda protested gently that since she was still in mourning for her poor Nigel, she had not gone about at all, nor had she participated in any of the summer amusements usually enjoyed by members of the *ton*.

Angela felt like a gauche outsider in the presence of this fairylike creature whose black silk gown, caught beneath the small bosom with a nosegay of dark purple rosebuds and adorned with yards of fluttering black lace, gave the impression of a ghostly apparition of some tragic queen from a Gothic churchyard.

"I would not be here at all this evening," the blond beauty was murmuring to Angela in her soft voice, "since I am but six months into my mourning. But the dowager assured me that if I did not dance—which I had no notion of doing anyway," she added hastily, "it would be quite unexceptionable for me to gather with a few close friends." She looked expectantly at Angela, as if seeking her approval.

"You are always above reproach, Matilda," Lady Steele cut in firmly, as if she wished to put an end to her guest's indecision. "And now, Angela, I wish to make you known to one of the most notorious flirts of the neighborhood. Yes, I mean you, George. Come over here and make your bow to Lady Castleton."

A tall young man of military bearing who had been standing behind Matilda, deep in conversation with the major, stepped forward, grinning sheepishly at Angela.

"George Woodall at your service, my lady," he said in a deep, pleasant voice, raising her hand to his lips. "I fear I am being grossly maligned by Julia here, who should know that my reputation with the ladies is spotless." He was not quite as tall as Harry, Angela noticed, or as broad, but his eyes twinkled with friendliness, and his blond hair, several shades darker than his sister's, fell about his ears in a riot of curls that most women would find irresistible, she thought. He was smiling at her engagingly, and Angela realized with a start that he was a truly attractive young man. While he lacked Roger's classical perfection, his charm was genuine, and he displayed none of the contrived boredom which Roger affected in company.

"And I am expected to take your word for that, am I?" Angela parried gracefully. She felt an immediate liking for the beauty's brother, who appeared to have inherited all the liveliness in the family.

"Harry will vouch for me, won't you, old man?" Woodall turned to the major, who was listening to something Matilda was saying and chose not to hear his friend's question.

"Nonsense, sir," Angela chided him. "If Harry is your friend, I can hardly expect him to enumerate your sins to me. You must think of another way of convincing me that you are a model of propriety."

"Perhaps if you honored me with this waltz which is just starting up, I might impress you with my sincerity, Lady Castleton," Woodall suggested, his blue eyes twinkling at his own audacity.

"I don't recall having saved this dance for you, Mr. Woodall, but you are in luck, for I am sure my husband will relinquish it to you. Won't you, Harry?" she added, catching her husband's eye.

"If you wish, my dear," he agreed, giving her a searching

look before turning back to respond to a comment by
Matilda.

Angela was glad of the excuse to get away from the group
around Matilda, especially when she noticed that Lord Medford had escorted Lady Steele onto the dance floor and that
Harry had somehow dispersed her other admirers and now
had Matilda all to himself. The sight of his dark head bent at-
tentively over her fair one made Angela's heart feel heavy in
her breast. It was all she could do to remember Julia's comforting belief that Harry was older and wiser than he had been
when he and Matilda were betrothed. Seeing them together,
sharing a past in which she played no part, Angela suspected
that her hostess might well prove to be wrong on her second
assumption.

In spite of never sitting out a single dance and giving the
appearance of enjoying herself hugely, Angela found it increasingly difficult to smile at her various partners. By the
time Roger came to claim the dinner dance, she was very
tired of watching Harry make a cake of himself over the pale
charms of his brother's widow. She had intercepted several
curious glances and raised eyebrows from their neighbors,
and Roger had not made matters any better by his marked attention to her, which often bordered on outright flirtation.

She wished she could plead a headache and go home, but it
seemed impolite to leave before the lavish cold supper Lady
Steele had gone to such pains to provide for her guests.

But even in the dining-room, where clusters of chairs and
small tables had been scattered about for the convenience of
the guests, Angela was not spared the sight of her wayward
husband paying what she could only consider unseemly attention to the beautiful young widow. On more than one occasion, Angela caught him observing her from across the room,
where he was seated with Matilda and Sir Joshua and Lady
Steele. Instead of feeling the bond which had previously been
established between them with that remembered kiss, Angela
now sensed censure in his gaze. Perhaps he is wishing that he
had not rushed into a marriage of convenience with a Cit's
daughter, she thought miserably. On impulse, Angela gave

him a direct snub the next time she caught him observing her and turned a glittering smile on Roger, who was just then proffering her a plate of food.

When the guests began to trickle back to the dance floor, Angela was claimed by Captain Woodall, who kept her amused during a country dance with his half-teasing accounts of his youthful escapades in the neighborhood.

"Harry and I were always up to our necks in one scrape or another," he confessed. "But we could never include Nigel in our adventures because he would invariably tell his father or mine, and that would earn us both a regular birching."

"How unsporting of him," Angela laughed.

"Nigel had a peculiar sense of humor," the young captain explained. "I believe he actually enjoyed reporting our misdeeds to his father. He was so different from Harry; they hardly seemed like brothers at all." He glanced over at Harry, sitting on the sidelines with Matilda, and Angela saw his brow crease into a frown. Could it be, she thought, that the lady's own brother found her monopoly of Harry's company objectionable?

Some time later, after having danced a boulanger with Sir Joshua Steele, Angela was standing with the baronet and Lady Steele, listening to Sophy recount an amusing story regarding the latest escapade of her mother's pug. Hercules, it appeared, had disgraced himself irredeemably by dragging a very dead rabbit into the morning room while the dowager was entertaining the vicar and his lady.

Angela, who had heard the story before, let her gaze wander around the room, and was surprised to notice that, for perhaps the first time that evening, Harry was not dancing attendance on Matilda. He stood with George Woodall across the room, near one of the French windows that opened out onto the garden. As Angela watched, she saw her husband glance in the widow's direction and then say something to Mr. Woodall before slipping out of the door into the darkness of the night.

Intrigued and vaguely uneasy, Angela looked at Matilda and found the Beauty's eyes riveted on the door through which Harry had disappeared. A cold feeling of apprehension spread through her. Had she witnessed the makings of another secret rendezvous? When she saw Matilda rise and make her way out of the room, Angela suddenly decided she had had enough of playing the complacent wife. She would not look the other way and allow this woman to make a fool of her husband.

Making excuses to her hostess, Angela slipped out of the room and hurried to collect her warm shawl from the retiring room set aside for the ladies. Then she ran down the back stairs, out the side door, and around the side of the house to the hedged pathway that gave access to the French windows. Stopping to look both ways, she saw that the pathway to the right was empty, though clearly lit by the light escaping from the windows. To her left, the path angled off towards an artificial lake and a summerhouse, much favored by Lady Steele in fair weather for informal tea parties.

Just then the moon, which was almost full, escaped from the low-lying clouds and allowed Angela to catch a glimpse of what she took to be a shadow disappearing round a rather untidy clump of shrubbery which lined the path. So, she thought with satisfaction, they are to meet in the summerhouse, is that it? She knew the way well, having taken tea there several times during the past month. As she turned in that direction, she thought she heard the sound of a door closing softly behind her. She must act quickly, she thought, picking up her skirts to hurry down the path. It was essential that she arrive before Matilda.

Her satin slippers made no sound as she reached the summerhouse and trod up the shallow steps. It was darker inside, but at the farther end she spied the silhouette of a male figure lounging against the lintel and gazing out over the lake. What a romantic setting, she thought, watching the patterns made by the moonlight shining through the trellis of honeysuckle. Her heart hammered in her breast. Softly she approached the tall figure outlined against the moonlit expanse of the lake. A sudden, alarming thought occurred to her, causing a frisson of fear to run through her body. What if this was not Harry?

But it was. When she was close enough to catch the faint, familiar smell of his Holland lotion, he must have sensed her

presence, for he turned and opened his arms. Angela stepped
into them and felt him suddenly tense.

"Angela? What are you doing out here?" he asked in a
husky voice, holding her loosely against him.

"Looking for you, Harry," she whispered before she could
lose her nerve. Thank goodness he had not called her Matilda,
she thought, relief flooding through her and making her knees
weak. Her palms were pressed flat against his chest, and she
could clearly feel the heavy beat of his heart.

"Is anything wrong, Angela?" he asked, his eyes dark in
the moonlight. "Has someone caused you distress, my dear?"

You have caused me enough distress to last a lifetime, my
love, she thought. But how can I make you see that you are
breaking my heart slowly, piece by painful piece, every time
you smile at Matilda? No, I am not supposed to feel that way
about you, am I? Ours is not that kind of a marriage. Oh, how
I wish I could talk to you, Harry. Really talk to you and tell
you how I feel. But she couldn't, of course, so she said what
she could.

"No, nothing is wrong," she said. "At least, nothing that
can't be mended. I merely thought it was time for me to return a favor you did for me recently. Do you remember,
Harry?" She leaned more intimately against him as she spoke
and felt his hands tighten on her waist.

"What favor is that, Angela?" His voice was low and
husky. He sounded perplexed but intrigued at the same time.

Angela smiled to herself. Foolish of her to imagine he
would remember the kiss he had given her to ward off the influence of the newly arrived Lord Medford. "Oh, Harry," she
chided, her voice deliberately light and teasing. "Surely you
remember how you protected me from that man in my past?
Don't tell me you have forgotten already. You kissed me,
Harry. Don't you remember? And you promised me that
every time I thought of that kiss, I would remember that I
must live in the present, not the past. You told me that I must
remember I belong to you now, and that the past is gone forever."

She felt him tense as she spoke, as if her words had made
him uncomfortable. But when she slid one hand up his chest

and cupped his cheek, she felt him relax again and pull her closer against him.

"Yes," he murmured. "Yes, I remember that quite clearly, my dear."

Angela took heart from the caressing tone of his voice and the way his hand was moving up and down her back, as though trying to find a place to rest. "Well," she said, a catch in her voice, "I merely wished to return the favor, Harry. I thought tonight would be the right moment." Standing on tiptoe, she leaned quite wantonly into his hard body, which suddenly arched over hers as if of its own accord. Her hand left his cheek and sought the thick hair at the nape of his neck. "I hope you will agree," she murmured against his mouth as she pulled his head down so that she could reach his lips with hers.

13

Summerhouse Scandal

Caught up in the magic of her husband's embrace, Angela lost all sense of time. The enclosed summerhouse provided a warm, secluded haven which seemed to isolate them from the rest of the world. The trellised roof, which Angela remembered as a dense riot of climbing roses and honeysuckle in the summer, now clearly thinned by autumn's ravages, let in sufficient checkered moonlight to lend the scene an air of unreality. Utterly seduced by such romantic surroundings, which seemed to have been purloined from one of the novels Sophy enjoyed so much, Angela abandoned herself to the sensuous enjoyment of Harry's embrace.

At first he had held her lightly, tracing teasing kisses across her mouth, over her face, and down to the tops of her breasts, which seemed to want to escape the confines of the green taffeta and press themselves into the warmth of his hand as it traced their fullness through the light covering. Angela found herself speculating, with immodest detail, what his hand might feel like against the bare skin of her breasts, her waist, her hips, her thighs. The vision these thoughts conjured up drove color to her cheeks, and she was glad that the latticed roof hid her confusion. She had not thought it possible for a gently bred lady, even if she were only a Cit's daughter, to entertain such wanton yearnings. A frisson of emotion ran through her.

"Cold, my love?" Harry whispered against her ear.

Mutely she shook her head. No, she was not cold. Quite the opposite was true, and now, as he pulled her closer against his hard body, Angela noticed, with a shock, that he was more aroused than she had realized. The sudden knowledge that her husband was not as invulnerable to her charms as she had

imagined made her heart leap wildly. Before she could stop to
consider the consequences, she found herself pressing against
Harry's tallness, her body shifting, reaching up of its own accord to find a more perfect fit. He wanted her, she thought
fleetingly, before his mouth found hers in a kiss more demanding, more revealing of his need than any he had yet
given her. Perhaps they could, she thought, as she surrendered
herself to Harry's increasingly ardent embrace, manage to
create a proper marriage between them after all. Angela knew
that she, for one, was ready and willing to attempt it.

Angela was jolted out of this blissful daydream by the in-
trusion of reality. The sound of a gasp from behind her broke
the spell of the moonlight and the romantic setting. She felt
Harry grow rigid and his grasp on her slacken. His head
snapped up, and his eyes probed the dimness of the summerhouse.

"Harry?" a soft voice, trembling with shock, interrupted the
sudden silence. "Is that you, Harry?" There was a suggestion
of reproach in Matilda's tone that raised Angela's hackles.
What right did this hussy have to follow *her* husband out into
the night? she thought furiously. The devil take the woman!
Did she have so little modesty that she would stoop to throw
herself at another woman's husband?

Angela kept her arm loosely around Harry's waist and, still
leaning suggestively against him, turned to stare at the in-
truder.

"Yes, it is," she replied. "Were you looking for him, my
lady?" Her question, deliberately cool and challenging,
seemed to inhibit her rival.

After an awkward silence, Matilda murmured in her soft,
childish voice, "Oh, no. That is . . . not really. You startled
me, that is all. I did not expect to find anyone here."

The last was so patently untrue that Angela could not hide
her amusement. "Well, you could not have chosen a better
place for a secret assignation, my lady," she said teasingly.
"Who is the lucky gentleman, or perhaps we should not ask?"

Matilda drew in a sharp breath. "There is no gentleman,"
she said, and Angela thought she sounded quite put out. "I
merely came out for a breath of air. It got so hot inside."

"Well, I do think it is a shame to waste such a romantic

spot," Angela laughed, wondering what Harry was thinking of his Matilda now. "I must confess that Harry and I were quite overcome by the spell of the moonlight. Isn't that right, my dear?" she said in a deliberately teasing voice, gazing up into his dark eyes.

Harry's face was expressionless, but Angela sensed that her husband was annoyed at being caught in a compromising scene with his wife. Well, she thought, it was time he stopped trying to rekindle the love of his youth and started accepting his responsibility as a married man. Before he could reply, however, they all heard the approach of footsteps on the path, and then the silhouette of a man appeared in the moonlit door-way.

After a pregnant pause, during which the newcomer sur-veyed the gathering leisurely through an ornate quizzing-glass, Angela let out the breath she had not known she was holding. The evening was turning into a Covent Garden com-edy of errors. Ruthlessly she fought down the urge to giggle as Roger's supercilious drawl cut through the dimness of the summerhouse.

"It appears that I am not the only one to be lured out into the night by the prospect of a stolen kiss under the full moon," he murmured, and Angela felt Harry immediately stiffen at the insinuation in Lord Medford's tone.

"I am afraid you have been caught out, my lady," Angela said lightly, although her heart was beating uncomfortably. Surprised as she was to see Roger, there was no doubt in her mind that he was there for her, not for the lovely Matilda. At all costs, she must avoid giving Harry the wrong impression. "Perhaps we should go, Harry," she said, slipping her arm through his. "There seems to be a surfeit of romance out here tonight."

After another awkward pause, during which Angela felt her lord's hesitation, Harry turned and strode to the door, fairly dragging her along with him. "Yes," he said shortly. "Besides, it's time we went home." Without a backward glance, he hurried her along the path towards the house, but Angela could feel anger radiating from him, and she began to fear that it was directed at her.

Behind them, in the ill-fated summerhouse, she distinctly heard Roger's mocking laugh.

It was nearly midnight when Harry helped his wife and sister out of the carriage in front of the Abbey's main entrance. Except for a few initial comments attempted by Sophy, who wanted to know why her brother had insisted on leaving the Steeles' party so early, the drive back to the Abbey was accomplished in an uncomfortable silence. When he merely grunted in response to his sister's questions, after Angela rather curtly suggested that Sophy apply to him for an answer, Harry felt a prick of regret at having acted so precipitously. He might well have waited another hour or two to allow his little Sophy the pleasure of dancing, which she enjoyed so much and did so little of.

But no, he thought, it was better this way. How could he have endured an extra two hours of watching his wife flirting with that cockscomb Adonis Medford? She had even evaded dancing that first waltz with him by expressing her preference for George Woodall. Damn George, anyway. Always so popular with the ladies, and such an elegant dancer that he was ever in demand at functions which included dancing. At times like these, Harry felt a great resentment for George and cursed himself immediately for the unkind thought.

As he stood there beside Matilda, his eyes fastened on the graceful figure of Angela twirling around the floor in his friend's arms, the unpleasant thought came to him that perhaps his wife had been anxious to avoid having to dance with a cripple. Although Angela had never, either by word or deed, revealed the slightest hint of revulsion for her husband's crippled condition, it stood to reason that a woman would prefer a man who was whole. And both Woodall and Medford were certainly that; and besides, both men were acknowledged favorites with the ladies.

Harry knew himself to have grown withdrawn and often morose as a result of his injured leg. If he were honest, he would have to admit that although it bothered him much less than it used to, it still throbbed painfully when he pushed himself too hard. And he had pushed himself unmercifully during the past months, trying to get his estate back on its feet again.

Or was he merely using his injury as an excuse for his strained relationship with Angela? he wondered. He had never been the charming flirt that George was, nor did he find pleasure in the careless chatter and flattery that women seemed to regard as an essential art in a gentleman. As a young man, he had never needed these arts to win the heart of the woman he had thought to spend his life with. And now, he thought bitterly, his wife had found a damned Park Saunterer from her past, who seemed only too willing to provide her with all the flattery and flirtation she could ask for.

Harry had glanced around the room and noticed that Lord Medford, although lending an attentive ear to the gushings of a simpering matron in a modishly extravagant puce gown, had his eyes riveted on Angela as she swept around the floor with George Woodall. Harry cursed softly under his breath.

"What did you say, Harry?" The soft voice broke into his reverie, and Harry glanced down at Matilda, who was gazing up at him reproachfully.

"Nothing," he replied shortly, wondering why he had spent so much of his time that evening talking about the past with his childhood inamorata instead of keeping a closer eye on his wife, who obviously needed watching. His ex-inamorata, he corrected himself quickly, noticing, as he had so often that evening, the deep mourning Matilda wore. The black color had a negative effect on him, for it reminded him that Matilda was in mourning for his brother. She was Nigel's widow. Matilda, the woman he had loved to distraction, the woman who had said she loved him but who had betrayed him so heartlessly the moment his back was turned. Try as he might, he could not forget the bitterness of this betrayal.

"She is very lovely, Harry," the soft voice continued. "You were indeed fortunate to find such a charming and elegant wife." After a small pause she added, "It's a pity she does not love you."

Harry felt his hackles rise at the pity he sensed behind this observation. "What makes you think Angela does not love me?" he demanded, more brusquely than he intended.

Matilda regarded him with a sad little smile. "Because I have loved you for years, Harry, or have you forgotten? So I know what it feels like. And believe me, I would never have

dreamed of allowing another gentleman to flirt with me as
Lady Castleton has been doing all evening."

For some reason Harry did not stop to examine, Matilda's
overt criticism of Angela made him both angry and uncomfortable. "I would prefer that you not make scurrilous remarks
about my wife," he said stiffly. It was one thing for him to
think such things himself, but he would be damned before he
would allow anyone else, even Matilda, to say a single word
against his wife.

He saw with a flicker of impatience that Matilda's beautiful blue eyes had filled with tears. "Oh, Harry. Please forgive
me, dearest. I did not mean to upset you. But it is no secret
that you made a marriage of convenience. It was something
you had to do. I can understand that. But it pains me to see
that she has come between us."

Harry sighed with exasperation. "Angela did not come between us, Matilda," he said gently. "Nigel did that long before
I ever thought of marrying Angela. Or have you forgotten
that?" he could not help adding, bitterness making his words
harsh to his own ears.

Tears threatened to spill down her pale cheeks, and Harry
cursed himself for a clumsy fool. The whole room would be
staring at them if he were not careful.

"Oh, Harry, please don't be so cruel to me. I have been so
desperately unhappy, you can have no idea." She made an attempt to control her agitation, which was beginning to attract
unwelcome attention. "We must talk," she whispered urgently. "I have so much I need to tell you."

"We talked the other day in the south woods, Matilda,"
Harry said ruthlessly. "And very unwise it was of you to be
riding around on my land all alone. Angela saw us, as you
well know."

"So what?" Matilda said, somewhat pettishly, he thought.
"We are old friends, are we not? Surely it is not wrong of us
to spend some time together? I must talk to you, Harry. Please
don't deny me this little comfort."

"Very well," Harry had agreed. "I will try to call at
Woodall House in the next day or two."

That had not been acceptable to Matilda, who had begged
him to meet her in the Steeles' summerhouse after the late

supper. Although this had appeared highly irregular and even
risky, Harry had finally agreed in order to avoid further argument. Later, he was to regret his weakness.

Yes, Harry remembered grimly as he followed Angela and
Sophy into the warmth of the Abbey front hall, he had been a
fool in more ways than one. How was he to have known that
the woman he would meet in that blasted summerhouse
would be his own wife?

The moonlit scene flashed vividly across his mind again,
and the memory of her passionate embrace made his blood
tingle anew. The sly hussy had deliberately set out to seduce
him, he thought. And the devil of it was that she had almost
succeeded. He remembered the silky perfection of her skin
beneath his lips, the tautness of her firm breasts under the soft
fabric of her gown. It had taken all his self-control not to pull
the gown down from her shoulders to taste more fully the
sweetness of her flesh. Her ardor had surprised and pleased
him greatly, and his response to the provocation of her body,
seeking to mold itself to his, had been charged with an ur-
gency that startled him. The violence of his arousal had been
such that, had it not been for the interruption, Harry might
well have ravished his wife then and there, on the cushioned
chaise longue in Lady Steele's summerhouse. And, by God,
she had been willing enough.

Luckily, he had been saved from making an utter idiot of
himself. Matilda's appearance had startled him; he had quite
forgotten that he had a rendezvous with her. Angela's presence had so rattled him that he had behaved like a veritable
flat, a moonling in the throes of his first infatuation. It had
taken Medford's sudden arrival and his indiscreet remark
about stolen kisses in the moonlight for Harry to realize how
he had been taken in. What a regular slow-top she must have
thought him, to be gulled by that Banbury tale. Looking for
him, was she? That scoundrel Medford was the man she had
come out to meet; any fool could see that.

Harry felt the bitterness at his wife's betrayal well up inside him. She was even worse than Matilda, who had at least
waited until his back was turned. Angela seemed determined
to flaunt her lover before his very eyes. Damn the wench, he
thought. For a moment there in the moonlit summerhouse,

Harry had felt that perhaps, once again, happiness might be possible, that perhaps with this woman he might become whole again. He should have known better, of course. If he had not agreed to meet Matilda there, he would not have been out in the summerhouse at all tonight. And then what would have happened? Harry did not want to face the answer to this question, but it hammered itself into his brain unbidden. Roger Hyland would have been there, and there was no doubt in Harry's mind that Hyland would not have hesitated to finish what Angela had begun.

Harry had been on his way to the library for a brandy, but this unpleasant thought stopped him short in his tracks. And it was followed by one that was even more unpleasant. If he were not careful, he would be saddled with a Hyland for an heir. The notion appalled him.

He swung around so sharply that a startled Jaspers, who was following his master with the brandy and glasses, nearly dropped the tray.

"Send up to tell her ladyship that I will be up shortly, Jaspers," he said harshly. "We have something of vital importance to discuss."

By the time Angela reached the safety of her chamber after that silent, uncomfortable ride back from Steele Hall, she knew, without a doubt, that Harry was furious with her. Did he resent the fact that she had interrupted his secret assignation with Matilda? He could hardly deny that they had arranged to meet in the summerhouse. Matilda's excuses had been transparent, and her surprise at finding Angela there genuine. What had they planned to do out there? She wondered, as Clothilde unbuttoned the green taffeta gown and slipped it off her shoulders. This was a question Angela had shied away from asking ever since Harry had escorted her from the summerhouse after that disastrous confrontation. It had festered in her mind all the way home, and now it clamored to be answered. Angela shuddered.

"Cold, my lady?" Clothilde inquired solicitously. "I shall call the footman to tend the fire as soon as I have you out of these underthings and into your nightrail."

Angela did not bother to protest, but allowed Clothilde to

help her into the pale blue silk confection the dresser had chosen for her mistress to wear to bed that evening. She wondered why Clothilde bothered to go through this nightly ritual of decking her out in these extravagantly lacy shifts when she must know that his lordship never came to his wife's bed. That he never had, she thought. The whole household must know that, except perhaps Sophy, who was an innocent romantic.

She sighed and slid her arms into the warm velvet robe her abigail was holding out for her.The memory of Harry's most recent kiss flooded back to her mind, and Angela shuddered again, this time with the remembered pressure of her husband's hands and lips on her body. She had been quite sure for those few blissful moments that he had wanted *her*, that he had been carried away with passion for *her*, for Angela Walters, the Cit's daughter he had once rejected as a fit mother for a Davenport heir. She had known, without any doubt, that the exquisite Matilda had been banished from his mind. But then that soft voice had come out of the shadows, and the magic had evaporated; she had lost him again.

Had Matilda reclaimed him so easily? she wondered. Or had Harry merely come to his senses and realized that he was kissing the wrong woman? Had he intended to kiss his ex-betrothed out there in the moonlit summerhouse? The thought was so painful that Angela brushed it away hurriedly. No, she told herself firmly. She would not think such negative thoughts.

But then she remembered Roger's unexpected appearance, and her heart sank. He must have seen her leave and followed her. Of course, he could also have seen Matilda leave, but Angela immediately discarded the idea. Matilda was not his style at all, he had said. Too insipid and vaporish? Yes, Angela had to agree that her rival had a lack of vivacity that might not appeal to some gentlemen; but that did not make her any the less beautiful. And it did not seem to bother Harry at all.

Angela tried to put the whole confusing incident out of her mind as she closed her eyes and relaxed under Clothilde's expert ministrations. The abigail had taken down Angela's elaborate hair arrangement and was now brushing the long black mass of curls vigorously. The effect was so soothing that Angela did not even open her eyes when she heard a discreet knock at the door. After a moment's whispered consultation, the door closed and Clothilde resumed the rhythmic strokes that were making Angela drowsy.

"Who was that?" she asked after a moment, not really wanting to know, at this late hour, if a new crisis had arisen below stairs.

"Only Jaspers, my lady," the abigail replied shortly. "He was sent to inform you that his lordship will be up shortly."

Angela sat up with a jolt. "What did you say?"

Clothilde regarded her speculatively before replying with her customary directness, "His lordship will be up to see you *bientôt*, my lady. That is what Jaspers tells me. It must have been the new gown, my lady," she added, her lips twitching into a satisfied, secretive smile that made Angela distinctly uneasy. "I told you it was very, how you say . . . *séduisante* on you. *Certainement*, his lordship thought so, too. Perhaps he has finally come to his senses and realizes that he has a wife who is, how you say . . . *ravissante*. Forgive me, my lady, if I say, *Il était grand temps*.

"It's about time?" Angela repeated without thinking. "About time for what?" she added before the implications of Clothilde's rather frank remark penetrated her confused brain and caused her to blush furiously. "No!" she said sharply, as Clothilde opened her mouth to explain. "I do not wish to hear any more impertinence from you tonight, Clothilde. You may go."

Clothilde gave her mistress's hair one last sweeping stroke and laid the brush down on the dresser. *"Bien sûr*, madame," she replied softly, with what Angela was convinced was an outright smirk. "I trust you sleep well tonight," she added with a saucy grin as she whisked herself out of the room.

Angela was left in a state of nervous consternation. What did Harry mean by such a message? *He would be up shortly?* Up where? Not to her room, surely? He had never, since the day of her arrival at the Abbey, so much as set foot in her room. After the first few agonizing nights of waiting for him to take possession of her bed, she had come to the unwelcome conclusion that he had no intention of consummating their marriage. The realization that she was unwanted was a severe blow to her self-esteem, but Angela had quickly suppressed the humiliation she felt and determined not to be missish about it. He had, after all, made no secret of the fact that he wanted no heir from her; he had told her so before the wedding, and although it had hurt at the time to know that she was not to have children of her own, she had not refused the alliance, as she might well have done.

No, she thought sadly, this was not to be the amorous midnight encounter Clothilde imagined. Harry was indoubtedly furious with her and couldn't wait till morning to ring a peal over her head. While this explanation sounded plausible and considerably reduced the agitation caused by Harry's message, Angela was acutely conscious of a feeling of disappointment. Could it be that she would have welcomed a midnight visit from a Harry bent on seduction? She had never put this question to herself quite so bluntly before, but now that she had, she felt the unmistakable weight of desire move within her. That was her answer, she thought. Her body was telling her that it was ready for the intimacies, whatever they might be, of the marriage bed. Perhaps she had been wrong about Harry's purpose. Perhaps he was not angry with her after all. Perhaps . . .

But no, she thought crossly, getting up from the dressing table and pulling her sash more tightly around her slender waist. The likelihood of Harry coming to her room with seduction on his mind was as remote as ever. What a ninnyhammer she was, to be sure. That kiss in the summerhouse had been a mistake; Harry had been primed for Matilda, not his wife. The harsh reality of this conclusion made her heart cringe, but Angela prided herself on being practical, and no amount of daydreaming, she told herself firmly, could obscure the fact that Harry had done everything but grind his teeth during that dreadful journey home tonight.

And even now, she thought with a sudden start, he must be waiting for her in the sitting room. Why hadn't she thought of that sooner? Hadn't he said he would be up shortly? And that must have been nearly half an hour ago. Nervously she tightened her sash again and pulled the robe more closely around her. She might as well get this interview over with, she thought, taking a deep breath and walking over to the communicating door.

Brushing a stray curl back from her face, Angela reached for the doorknob. Before she could grasp it, however, the door was jerked open, and Harry stood there, his face set in cold, harsh lines, his eyes a furious sapphire blue that bespoke anger and something else that made Angela's heart flutter with alarm.

14

The Dare

Harry stepped into the bedchamber and kicked the door shut behind him. The movement brought him so close to Angela that she took a nervous step backwards. There was something about his threatening presence and the violence of his entrance that unnerved her. She could not recall ever having seen him look so fierce and unapproachable. Yet something flickered in the depths of his eyes, regarding her so relentlessly, that made her catch her breath. There was something else besides anger there, she thought, with a surge of excitement. And if only she could get past the anger, which seemed about to explode in a shower of sparks over her vulnerable head, she felt that she might discover a softer emotion hidden in her husband's heart. The thought made her blood tingle and gave her courage.

"What is it, my lord?" she asked in what she hoped was a calm voice. "I was about to meet you in the sitting room, as you requested. I asked Jaspers to see that the fire was lit there so we could be comfortable."

"I said nothing about the sitting room, my lady," he said softly, and the smile that relaxed his mouth briefly had no humor in it.

Angela felt herself sinking into a sea of conflicting emotions. "I assumed that you meant . . ."

"You assumed wrong, then. What I have to say to you, my lady, is best said here in this room." He had not taken his eyes from her face since he entered her bedchamber, but now he let them wander brazenly over her, deliberately allowing them to linger on the swell of her breasts and the gentle curve of her hips provocatively emphasized below the tightly fas-

tened sash. "Which is also more appropriate for what I have
to do."

Angela felt herself shrink before the repressed rage of this
man who was suddenly a stranger to her. This was not the
Harry who had so often invaded her dreams with sensuous
yet tender caresses, with intimacies so daring that she had
awakened in the middle of the night to find her cheeks blazing with color and her body tingling with strange longings.
No, she thought, despair welling up inside her, a black, threatening cloud on the calm surface of her life as Harry's wife.
No, this man was not the Harry she knew, the man she had
grown to admire, and yes, she thought in a rush of emotion,
even to love.

The admission surprised her. Surfacing as it had in her
troubled thoughts, unbidden but entirely natural, as if it had
been there all this time waiting to be acknowledged, it calmed
her. Angela felt her strength return and resolutely suppressed
the despair which had momentarily weakened her spirit. If
Harry had turned into a stranger, a menacing force which
seemed about to destroy her, it should be possible to turn him
back into the other Harry, the real Harry she knew and loved.

Tentatively, Angela smiled at him and made a gesture toward the gold brocade settee and wing chairs clustered cozily
before the now blazing fire. "In that case, shall we sit down
here and be comfortable?" she murmured, hoping that if she
refused to be intimidated by his fury, it would dissipate of its
own accord.

Instead, her attempt at conciliation seemed to provoke him
still further. He took an abrupt step forward and, grasping her
wrist in a grip of iron, jerked her towards him so brusquely
that she instinctively placed a hand on his chest to prevent
herself from falling against him. It was then that Angela made
an unsettling discovery. Her fingers came into contact, not
with the crisp black superfine of his evening coat, but with the
plush, vaguely sensuous texture of warm velvet. The effect of
this tactile revelation on her overwrought emotions was elec-
tric. Her eyes, till that moment mesmerized by her husband's
stare, quickly lowered, and what she saw confirmed what her
fingers had told her. Harry was dressed for bed. Her fingers

nestled—almost indecorously, she noticed—in the thick bottle-green nap of his dressing gown.

How had she not noticed this before? she wondered, her gaze flying to the grim face that glowered down at her. Never before had Angela seen her husband in this intimate state of undress. She had seen him several times in his shirtsleeves, of course. In the seclusion of their sitting room during those first few weeks of relative harmony between them, Harry had relaxed enough to remove his coat. Occasionally, when they had pored over the proposed alterations to the Abbey together, he had rolled up his sleeves. And once, she remembered vividly, she had caught him without his shirt as he worked with a recalcitrant horse in the stable yard. She had been unable to look at her husband's rippling, bronzed muscles without a vague feeling of longing she had not identified at the time.

Now she knew, she thought. It was an emotion that well-bred females never harbored in their chaste hearts, or if they did, they never gave a name to it. Her fingers were transmitting electrical currents of it up her arm at this very moment. Her heart was full of it, she realized. Her body trembled with it. And her eyes must surely betray her wanton thoughts to this man who had provoked them.

In sudden confusion at her own immodesty, Angela lowered her lashes and made a deliberate effort to control her trembling. She was rewarded by a crack of laughter devoid of all humor.

"No use playing off your hoyden's tricks with me," Harry growled. "I caught you red-handed tonight, didn't I? So I know what you are."

This harsh, unexpected accusation chilled Angela's overheated blood as nothing else could. Her eyes, round with astonishment, flew to his face. "What exactly are you implying, my lord?" she demanded incredulously.

"I'm not implying anything. I'm *saying* it," he replied savagely. "You went out to the summerhouse tonight to meet that cockscomb Medford. Can you deny it?"

Before Angela could get over her astonishment, he continued to berate her in a voice so full of torment that it tore at her heart. "Very rash and indiscreet of you, of course. There must be a hundred better sites for clandestine lovers to meet right here on Castleton land without having to choose so public a place as an open summerhouse. Have you no shame at all? Or couldn't you wait to throw yourself at him?"

Angela felt as though the world were falling in upon her. "None of this is true, Harry," she cried, struggling vainly to free herself from his grasp.

"You forget that I was there," he snapped. "I saw him. And heard him boast of stealing kisses from you. How clever of you to fob me off with your feminine wiles. But it won't fadge, my dear. Do you take me for a complete flat? I dare you to deny that Medford came to meet you."

"I made no assignation with anyone," Angela replied truthfully. "I saw you leave the house and—"

"Don't lie to me, Angela," he interrupted sharply. "I am not likely to swallow that Banbury tale. It's as plain as a pikestaff that you are encouraging that Town Beau to dangle after you right under my nose." He glared at her for a moment, and then his eyes narrowed dangerously. "Or are you already lovers?" he rasped, and Angela felt him stiffen.

"You are mad to suggest such a thing," she cried, but he seemed not to hear her. He had gripped both her arms and shook her impatiently, his eyes blazing so intensely that Angela felt a frisson of fear ripple through her.

"Not as mad as you are to think you could get away with this deception, my lady." The last two words were uttered with such contempt that Angela cringed. "How long has this liaison of yours been going on?" he fairly spat at her from between clenched teeth.

Angela was so outraged and distressed at the tone and tenor of these monstrous accusations that she could not trust herself to speak. When she did not answer, Harry shook her again, and then crushed her up against his chest and glared down into her agonized face. "So? You do not deny it?" he hissed, his features contorted with rage.

"I do," Angela whispered against his chest. "Oh, I do, I do." But he could not have heard her, for he thrust her away to arm's length and regarded her with loathing.

"I despise women like you," he said finally, with such obvious bitterness that Angela wanted to reach out to comfort him. "You have no regard for a man's honor and can only think of your own frivolous gratification. I suppose you were already his mistress three years ago, and all that self-righteous indignation you displayed for my benefit was meant to mislead me into thinking you innocent." He laughed cynically and withdrew his hands from her as if he couldn't bear the contact.

"I *am* innocent," Angela said, but her voice seemed to falter. "I am innocent," she repeated, trying to infuse more strength into the denial of his ugly accusations.

"You set out to make a fool of me," he continued, as if she had not spoken. "And you almost succeeded, my dear. You certainly had me bamboozled with your performance when Medford visited the Abbey. A performance worthy of the great Mrs. Siddons herself," he sneered. "Was it your idea, Angela, to pretend that you couldn't bring yourself to face him again? Or did you plan it together?"

His anger seemed to have subsided, Angela was glad to see, but his eyes were bleak and the fire was gone out of them. Forgetting her own pain for a moment, she was overcome with the urge to soothe her husband's obvious distress, to cradle his dark head on her bosom and erase that lost look from his eyes.

"Harry," she began, stepping towards him. "I swear to you, by everything that is sacred to me, that these suspicions are unfounded. I am innocent of any wrongdoing."

Impatiently he waved her away. "Matilda, too, swore she was innocent of betraying me. And in her eyes, I suppose, she was. Her father made her marry Nigel, she insists. Is that going to be your excuse, too? Did Medford force you that first time? Did he?" His voice sounded rough with emotion. "I could have accepted that if only you had told me, Angela" he said, and his voice sounded tired. "But what I cannot and will not accept is my wife's lover running tame in my house."

Angela blenched at the picture her husband was painting, and her flagging spirits revived. "If you are determined to brand me a harlot without any real evidence, there is nothing more to be said," she snapped. "But let me tell you one last thing. You wrong me, Harry. You wrong me most grievously. And one day you will be sorry for it."

"Don't threaten me, Angela. I am past caring who you take into your bed. But let me tell *you* that if you ever present me with one of Medford's bastards as my heir, I shall kill the pair of you."

Angela felt herself reel under this new assault on her integrity. The blood rushed from her face, and she stood, pale and trembling, and would have fallen had she not grasped a nearby chair for support. Slowly she regained her composure, and with it came a renewed sense of outrage at this man who could so casually and callously denigrate her character. She raised her eyes and looked at him with all the courage she could muster.

"I repeat," she said clearly, her voice rising above the loud beating of her heart, "I am innocent. No man can say otherwise. Do you hear me? No man at all."

"If you say so, my dear," Harry replied with a cynical laugh which stung Angela to the quick.

"There is one sure way of finding out," she snapped angrily, before she stopped to think.

"Indeed?" Harry again allowed his eyes to wander insolently over her body. "And what makes you so sure I would want to be the one to fall into that trap?"

Angela felt the color wash over her face as the implications of her suggestion dawned on her. "I meant no such thing, my lord," she said stiffly. "I merely suggest that, if you truly doubt my innocence, a quick examination by any doctor would confirm it."

"Or deny it?" He laughed without mirth.

"No," she said firmly. "I would be vindicated. Of course," she added with a faint smile, "it might be rather embarrassing for you to have my innocence proclaimed by a local physician." The germ of an idea had begun to take shape in her mind, an idea put there by Harry's initial reaction to her suggestion. Perhaps she could turn this ugly misunderstanding that had arisen between them into something positive after all. It was worth a try, she thought, hoping that her nerve would not fail her. If she could force her husband's hand he would have to believe in her innocence.

Harry regarded her speculatively. "You are suggesting that

I should take you up to a London physician to confirm what I already know is true?"

Angela grasped the back of the brocade chair more tightly, appalled at the temerity of what she was about to attempt. "No," she said firmly, meeting Harry's cynical gaze without flinching. "You do not *know* any such thing, my lord. You merely jumped to certain conclusions about my behavior, perhaps because your own has not been entirely blameless." She paused when she saw the muscles harden along the length of his jaw, and a telltale flush stain his cheeks.

"I resent your insinuation that I have treated you with anything less than respect," he snapped, taking a menacing step towards her.

Angela stood her ground and forced herself to smile up into his dark face. After a long moment of staring searchingly into his eyes, she plunged on. "I resent it, too, Harry," she said softly. "I especially resent being slandered by the man who vowed to protect and cherish me when he took me out of my father's house."

Her husband put out a hand as if to comfort her, but quickly let it drop to his side again. "I apologize for my anger, Angela," he said stiffly. "That was unworthy and uncharacteristic of me. Please forgive me."

It would be so easy to forgive him, Angela thought, if only he would not look at her with that black frown on his face and suspicion in his eyes. But she could not afford to become maudlin now; she must press on if she hoped to break through to the Harry she had glimpsed behind that foreboding facade.

"I know that ours is only a marriage of convenience," she continued, reaching down into her reserve of strength to find the courage to say what had to be said. "And that you hold me in contempt for being who I am, a tradesman's daughter. I have enough town bronze to realize that, sooner or later, you will take a . . . a mistress." She put up a restraining hand when the major made as if to interrupt her. "That I can accept. I have accepted it and am resigned to playing the complaisant wife."

"I have never asked such a thing of you," Harry burst out angrily. "Wherever did you get that hen-witted notion?"

Angela merely smiled. From you, my dear, she thought.

From you and your neglect of me, and it is breaking my heart. But she could not say so. Instead, she strove to keep her voice expressionless. "Your actions have been clear enough, my lord. You hardly needed to say anything. Besides, I am not some schoolroom chit with a head full of romantical notions." A rueful little laugh escaped her. "I can accept that your desire to see the Abbey restored was much greater than your desire for a wife. And that had you been able to choose, you would not have chosen me." She paused, afraid that her voice would break with emotion. "That I can accept," she went on, suddenly anxious to have it all over and done with. "But when doubts are cast on my honor . . . yes," she added defensively, "tradesmen's daughters have honor, too, strange as that may seem to you. Then I have every right to expect you to believe me when I deny any impropriety."

"And if I don't?"

The question was spoken so softly and with such intensity that Angela felt her heart leap into her throat. Did he guess what she was about? she wondered. Was it possible that he had come to her room with just such an intention in mind? Involuntarily she shuddered, and her eyes probed the deep sapphire depths of his gaze, searching for some sign of tenderness. When she found none, she sighed. He was obviously not going to make this easy for either of them. As the silence stretched out between them, Angela was tempted to draw back from the edge of the abyss opening before her. But she was so close, only a step away from the Harry she yearned for.

"Then I dare you to find out for yourself, my lord," she said finally, and her voice sounded clear and cool in spite of her wildly pounding blood. Her hands dropped, as if of their own accord, to the knot of her sash and rested there in mute invitation.

Harry's face lost its scowl, and he took another step towards her, bringing him close enough for Angela to catch a whiff of his Holland water and the brandy on his breath when he spoke.

"Here and now?"

Angela tilted her chin to meet his gaze and noticed that his eyes were dark with suppressed emotion, and that his mouth, relaxed for the first time since he had entered her room, was softened by a faintly ironic smile.

"Yes, my lord," she replied, firmly stepping out into the abyss from which there was no return. "Here and now."

Flustered by the sudden heat of his gaze, Angela dropped her eyes to her hands, which were tugging ineffectually at the knot at her waist. Before she could untie the sash, she felt Harry's hands brush hers aside, make short work of the knot, and slide the dressing gown from her shoulders. She heard his breath expel as the velvet robe slid from her arms and fell in a bright pool around her bare feet.

The major rang for Jimmy Dunn at an exceptionally early hour the following morning, and when his batman appeared with his master's shaving water, it was to find the major standing in his small clothes staring moodily out of the window. If Jimmy wondered what could possibly have attracted the major's attention in the inky darkness of pre-dawn, he did not say, nor did he inquire. He had known the major long enough to recognize when his master was in one of his rare black moods.

Harry admitted that he was blue-deviled almost as soon as he returned from his wife's room and threw himself into his own bed. Sleep evaded him tenaciously, and after two hours of tossing and turning, he got up and sat before the dwindling fire, cursing his own foolhardiness. As soon as he dared, he rang for Jimmy. A half hour later, dressed for riding, he gulped a scalding cup of coffee served by a startled Jaspers, and then strode down to the stables, slashing fretfully at his booted leg with his riding crop.

He had thought to escape—at least momentarily—the memory of his infamous behavior of the night before, but he soon discovered that no amount of racing along deserted country lanes could blot this iniquity from his mind. All he achieved, Harry soon realized, was to tire old Duke unnecessarily, and frighten an ancient shepherd half out of his wits when he put Duke over a bramble hedge into a narrow lane filled with sheep on their way to pasture. After this near disaster, Harry drew Duke down to a sedate, mile-eating canter and gave himself up to the memories he had been unable to banish from his mind.

No sooner did Harry stop fighting back the memories of last night which had been fluttering around the periphery of his brain like so many Furies bent on vengeance, than they swarmed in to overwhelm his senses. They carried him instantly back to that tense moment when he had burst into his wife's bedchamber to confront her with her betrayal. His motives for being there had been crystal clear in his mind and drove him with a fury he had not experienced since that day, so long ago now, when he had received news of Matilda's marriage to Nigel. Bitterness had welled up inside him then, as it had last night, until he thought he would choke on it. Last night the Furies had been on his side, flailing his emotions to fever pitch in his quest for vindication. It was not until later, after he had behaved like a complete cad, that they turned their talons on him.

As well they should, he thought morosely. He should have followed his first instinct when he had found his wife in such a delightful state of dishabille, her bright red dressing gown clasped just tightly enough to emphasize all the femininity of her form, her dark curls falling in sweet disarray around her shoulders and down her back, her bare toes briefly glimpsed beneath the red hem. Unexpectedly, it had been his wife's bare toes which had almost undone him, he remembered. They were so small and delicate, and suggested such an unsuspected vulnerability in her that he had been paralyzed for several heartbeats and sorely tempted to kiss them.

Yes, he thought grimly, guiding Duke round a hay wagon that took up most of the narrow lane, he had been a fool from the very start in last night's encounter. Instead of complimenting his wife on her radiant looks—for she had been nothing less than radiant in the soft candlelight—he had scowled at her. What would have happened, he wondered, if he had told her how bewitching she looked in red velvet? Perhaps her glorious smoky eyes, filled as they had been with startled alarm, might have become soft and yielding. Granted, he had never been much of a hand with flowery phrases, but even the most callow moonling might well have acquitted himself creditably if he had seen Angela by candlelight in her night clothes.

The thought of another man seeing his wife in such intimate surroundings brought Harry's meditations abruptly back to his purpose in visiting her last night and made him groan aloud. Duke's ears flicked back at the sound, as if attentive to his master's moods. Harry kneed the horse encouragingly, and Duke continued to canter along the dirt road, his stride unbroken. The rhythm was relaxing, and Harry had often found solace in this silent communion between horse and rider. But this morning there was no comfort in it for him. The Furies rode with him and gave him no quarter.

He had purposely chosen the most outlying of his farms as his destination that morning, hoping that a visit with taciturn old Ned Turner, a tenant whose family had occupied the same Davenport land since before Black Harry's time, might help to get his mind off his troubles. Before he was even halfway there, however, he felt an urge to return to the Abbey. The autumn sun had barely tinged the eastern horizon with streaks of light before Harry was wishing he had stayed at home. He should not have run away, he thought restlessly. Because that was exactly what he had done. He had run away. Instead of going back to her and confessing how wrong he had been to suspect her, he had taken the coward's way out. He had run away.

Abruptly he pulled Duke to a halt and swung his head toward home. But as the horse stood, his inquisitive ears pointed forward, then flicking back as if waiting for his master to make up his mind which way they were going, Harry vacillated. No, he thought, swinging Duke full circle and pointing him once again in the direction of the Turner farm, he could not do it. Not yet, at any rate. He needed more time to compose his chaotic emotions, to allow the enormity of what he had done to his wife to become less vivid and corrosive in his mind.

If the old local folk belief were true, Harry thought, and the punishment for sinners against the innocent was indeed to be condemned to relive eternally the anguish their sins have caused, then surely his punishment had already begun to run its course. For his wife had, without a doubt, been innocent of the crime he had laid so implacably at her door. Yes, to his eternal shame, he had found out for himself that she was the innocent she had claimed to be.

It was the manner of that discovery which had later filled his soul with self-disgust. If he had not been so consumed with his own wrongheaded assumptions, if he had only listened to her, given her denials some credit, he would have avoided making a complete jackass of himself. No, he corrected himself, it was much more serious than that. Lord, how he wished it were only a jackass he had made of himself. He groaned again, but this time Duke ignored him and cantered on between the overgrown hedgerows.

He should have known. He should have known. The implacable voices of the Furies gave his conscience no respite. And how could he deny it? What kind of insensitive sapskull was he that he had failed to recognize the obvious signs of innocence? Her eyes should have warned him as soon as he had slipped the dressing gown off her shoulders and let it drop to the floor at her feet. The perfection of her body, enhanced rather than hidden by the cloud of blue silk, had taken his breath away and reminded him forcefully that he had been celibate for too long. After his wounded leg had healed enough to allow him to walk, Harry had stayed away from women, plagued by a sense of incompleteness, and since returning to England, his energies had been channeled elsewhere. As he stared at his wife's full breasts, pointing at him provocatively through the gossamer silk, he had felt a rush of desire in his loins.

Inevitably, this arousal reminded him of the scene played out the previous evening in Lady Steele's summerhouse. He had been aroused then, too, he recalled, aroused by the wiles of this same wanton woman standing before him. The vividness of the false seduction—for he had been certain of this at the time—had rekindled not only his desire but also his anger. The mocking laughter of Roger Hyland had echoed again in his ears, and he had reached out instinctively to rip the flimsy garment off her.

Something in her eyes had stopped him. A gasp had escaped her when she realized his intent, but she did not back away. He had paused, his right hand grasping the soft silk, his fingers resting lightly against her skin, in the warm valley of her breasts. He had clearly felt her wildly beating heart, and this alone should have told him how frightened she was, how unprepared for the violence he was about to unleash upon her.

But he had not listened. Damned, obstinate fool that he was, Harry thought. He had not listened, had not heard, had not seen how it was with her. Perhaps he had not wanted to recognize her fright for what it was. That would have entailed admitting that he was in the wrong, when he was so sure he was right. *Had been sure,* he corrected himself quickly. Because now he knew, irrevocably, that he had been wrong. Her eyes had tried to tell him so last night, but he had not heeded the plea he had seen in their smoky depths. Harry cursed himself, long and pungently.

It was small consolation that he had not, after all, ripped the nightshift from bodice to hem as he had intended. They had stood for several endless moments, staring into each other's eyes, until he had slowly withdrawn his hand. Something in her expression must have penetrated his obdurate brain, he thought, grateful for not having to claim this barbaric act among the others he had committed last night.

But, then, neither had he kissed her, he remembered with chagrin. If he had, perhaps he would have come to his senses; perhaps the sweet innocence of her would have communicated itself to him sooner, in time to deflect the rage that had built up in his heart and hardened it against yet another betrayal. But he had deliberately avoided the sweetness of this intimacy. Damned fool that he was, Harry thought angrily. So much might have been different had he allowed himself to be seduced by the warmth of her lips as he had been in that infernal summerhouse. And she had wanted him to kiss her. Instinctively, she must have known her power to turn his rage into something she could share with him. But he had needed that rage to bolster his pride, to fortify himself against her wiles. And, yes, he admitted reluctantly, he had wanted to punish her.

Punish her! Harry let out a snort of mirthless laughter which caused Duke to prick up his ears nervously. He was too well mannered to shy, but his ears communicated his unease at his master's moodiness.

"Steady, old boy," the major said softly, and the horse tossed his head in response.

Of all the blockheaded reasons for doing what he had done, that was the most senseless. He was the one who should be boiled in oil, he thought, touching his crop to the brim of his tall beaver as an open carriage, packed with giggling young ladies barely removed from the schoolroom, passed him at a spanking trot. A kiss from his wife might have saved him from a lifetime of knowing that he behaved no better than a half-drunken stable hand tossing up the skirts of a young housemaid in a thoughtless coupling in the corner of a barn. He shuddered at the brutishness of his own comparison, but he could find no excuse for softening the bluntness of it. He had rejected that chance she had offered him to shed his anger and behave like a gentleman. As he had touched her, running his hands, almost insultingly, down her body, and then up again to cradle her breasts in his palms, she had reached up to bring his head down to her proffered kiss. But he had brushed the gesture aside, and she had remained unkissed.

Instead, he had picked her up, surprised at the lightness of her, and carried her to the bed, And it was then that she had said the only words she had uttered during the entire ordeal. *Don't do this in anger, Harry,* she had whispered against his ear. *Please, not in anger.*

Harry grimaced at the memory of that plea for tenderness which went unheeded. The sound of it would ring in his ears for the rest of his days; of that he was perfectly certain. He had, if not exactly thrown her, at least placed her roughly on the bed and tossed his own dressing gown on the back of a chair. Resolutely, Harry closed his mind to what happened next, but try as he might, visions of blue silk, its softness indistinguishable from the softness of her skin, intruded into the chaos and confusion of his brain. And the cry. Never in a thousand years would he forget the sharp cry she had uttered, nor the absolute silence which followed it. It was as if she had shut him out at the very moment he had entered her.

Harry wondered if his wife would ever speak to him again.

15

Runaway Wife

If anyone had told Angela that one day she would actually experience that state of abysmal despair which seemed to be the permanent condition of so many lovelorn heroines in the innumerable romantic novels she had purchased from Hatchard's Book Shop, she would have laughed outright. Although she had often indulged herself on rainy afternoons in following the harrowing adventures of the young ladies who populated these novels, Angela had always been skeptical of the depths of anguish such damsels had professed to experience. She was skeptical no longer, however. After Harry left her room that disastrous night of Lady Steele's ball, Angela discovered that the maelstrom of emotions described by the heroine in Mrs. Radcliff's latest novel fit her own feelings exactly.

She slept hardly at all that night, and when she did finally slip into a fitful slumber, her dreams were filled with tall shadows of vaguely threatening, faceless men who stood at the foot of her bed and accused her of unspeakable crimes before disappearing through the sitting room door and closing it behind them with a finality that chilled her heart. It was not surprising that when Rosie came in with hot chocolate at her usual early hour, Angela was wide awake and feverish.

Clothilde came bustling in when she heard that her mistress had decided to lie abed that morning, her shrewd Gallic face alight with speculation.

"*Bonjour, ma petite,*" she cried with genuine affection. "*Alors,* what is this I hear? It is not like you my lady, to become, how you say . . . a slugabed, *n'est-ce pas?*" Her teasing tone disappeared abruptly when she saw the listless expression on her ladyship's face.

"*Qu'est-ce que c'est ça, madame?*" she cried in alarm, placing her palm on Angela's brow.

Overcome by this kind gesture, Angela fought the tears which threatened to mist her eyes. "Oh, it is nothing Clothilde," she said. "A slight headache, that is all. I did not sleep well last night." The sharp, knowing glance that her dresser gave her at this confession made Angela wish she had held her tongue.

"*Ah! ma pauvre petite,*" Clothilde said softly, brushing back a stray curl from Angela's forehead. "That is the way it is, my lady. Men can be such unfeeling *bêtes,* but where would we be without them, eh? They think they know everything but are fools when it comes to love. And believe me," she added with a flicker of amusement, "tonight will be better for you, I can promise it."

"I have a headache," Angela protested weakly, turning away from the all-too-knowing eyes of her abigail. Whatever was she thinking of to allow Clothilde to rattle on like this? And what was she suggesting about tonight? Angela gave a shudder at the thought of another night like last night. How could she bear it? she wondered. It was not as if she had asked for or expected protestations of undying love, as Mrs. Radcliffe's heroines always did. But Harry's cold detachment and complete lack of tenderness had appalled her and left her with a sense of shame and worthlessness quite foreign to her nature. So Clothilde was wrong. Tonight, or any other night, would not be better for her. If anything, it would be worse. Last night she had been made to feel like a lightskirt, a woman to be used for a moment of passing pleasure. It seemed incongruous to Angela that her own husband could make her feel so unmarried. But then he had not been her husband last night, she told herself. He had been a total stranger. One who looked like Harry, even smelled like Harry, but who had neither sounded nor acted like her Harry, the one who had kissed her so passionately in Lady Steele's summerhouse last evening.

If only he had kissed her with the same abandon when he came to her room, she thought, she might have been able to chase that black scowl from his face and the anger and faint contempt from the depths of his sapphire eyes. She might even have been able to convey to him how ready she was, ready and willing to be a real wife to him. But he had not kissed her, and when she had reached up to him, he had brushed her arms aside, as if rejecting the warmth and tenderness she had craved. After that, she had shriveled a little inside and turned her face away, passive and dry-eyed and silent, except for that one cry that had suddenly escaped her.

Angela signed and felt a tear inch a warm path down her cold cheek. She needed to cry, to purge some of the unhappiness which had built up in her heart until her throat hurt with the strain of it. She had hoped to do so alone, but after the first tear broke through, she could no longer hold back. She felt Clothilde's strong arms go round her as she broke into a series of jerky sobs and a torrent of tears. She was intensely grateful when the abigail said nothing, but merely rocked her gently until her grief wore itself out.

"*Allons*," Clothilde said at last, reaching into the pocket of her voluminous pinafore for a large white handkerchief smelling of summer lavender. "*Ça suffit!* Enough! No more tears, my lady. You will make yourself sick, and no man is worth that." She proceeded to wipe Angela's ravaged face. "I will order a nice hot bath for you, *ma petite*. And while you bathe, I will put fresh sheets on the bed and then have Rosie bring up your breakfast."

"I am not hungry," Angela mumbled between hiccups.

"*Quelle sottise!*" Clothilde replied cheerfully. "A good meal will take your mind off your discomfort." And before Angela could think up a good excuse to be left completely alone to cry herself to sleep again, her abigail had issued crisp orders for bath and breakfast, and Angela found herself caught up in a whirl of activity that did indeed take her mind momentarily off last night's debacle.

When Sophy joined her for a light nuncheon later that morning, Angela learned that Harry had taken himself off at an unreasonably early hour and was not expected back until after dinner.

"Jimmy Dunn told me that Harry has gone to call on old Ned Turner, over near Bromley Green," Sophy informed her, munching on a cold capon leg with considerable relish. "Though why he would want to see old Ned at this time of year, I cannot for the life of me imagine. He has arthritis in his knees, poor old man, and gets very crotchety as soon as the weather turns cold. In the village, the rumor has it that it wasn't pneumonia that carried Mrs. Turner off ten years ago but a strong desire to be rid of old Ned's bad humor."

"That sounds like a hum to me," Angela said, drawn into the discussion in spite of herself. "I cannot believe that a wife would prefer death to a few scolds from her husband."

"Then you don't know Ned Turner, my dear," Sophy laughed. "He is the most ill-tempered, nasty-minded old man I know. Harry says he remembers our grandfather, Black Harry, having the most flaming rows with old Ned. I can't understand why Harry didn't send his bailiff instead."

Angela understood only too well why Harry had not sent his bailiff over to Turner's farm. It had given him an excuse to avoid her for a whole day. Well, he needn't have worried, she thought, for she intended to stay out of his way permanently. When she could no longer find excuses to stay in her room, she would think of something else, but she was determined to show him the same kind of indifference he had shown her last night, even if it meant being a recluse for the remainder of her life.

A week later Angela had begun to regret her decision. She was heartily sick of being cooped up in her room, playing the role of invalid to all visitors, most of whom were fobbed off with the story that her ladyship was still suffering from a mild fever and persistent megrims. Clothilde was the only one who knew the real nature of Angela's malaise. Nothing had been said directly, but Angela was sure that the sharp-eyed Frenchwoman had guessed her secret sorrow.

Harry did not come near her. Angela had been fearful that second night that her husband might suddenly appear in the doorway to the sitting room as he had the night before. As the hour grew later, however, and he did not come, she began to relax. When he did not come the third night either, she felt a sense of relief and no longer dreamed of faceless men invading her room. By the end of the week, her relief was tempered by a feeling of emptiness. If she had not known differently, she would have identified this heaviness in her heart as disappointment. But that, of course, was nonsensical, she told herself.

At the end of that first week, when Angela still refused to come down to dinner, Sophy began to suspect that her sister-in-law was not telling her the truth about her prolonged indisposition.

"Have you had a tiff with Harry?" she asked one day, as she sat by the fire in Angela's room, embroidering the family crest on one of the six handkerchiefs she was making for Harry's Christmas present.

"A tiff?" Angela looked at Sophy curiously, her gray eyes revealing none of her true feelings. A tiff indeed, she thought, not without irony. That was hardly the word she would have used to describe what had happened between herself and Harry.

"Yes, a tiff," Sophy repeated impatiently. "You know, a quarrel of some sort. Happens all the time with married couples, I'm told."

Angela smiled faintly, wishing her falling-out with Harry had been that simple. "No, of course not, silly. Whatever would we have to quarrel about?"

Sophy gave her a look which made it clear that she would not be fobbed off by this bland diversion. "Then it is something more serious, Angela? Please tell me. I want to help you. If that brother of mine has done anything to hurt you, I shall—" She stopped short, an arrested look on her lovely face. After a moment she continued in an awed voice. "You're increasing, is that it? Oh, Angela," she whispered, her eyes sparkling with sudden understanding. "I'm so very glad. But why didn't you tell me, dearest? Don't you think an aunt should be informed of these events? Oh!" She paused for breath and looked at Angela searchingly. "Does Harry know?"

For a moment Angela's heart seemed to stand still. For some reason she could not understand, the notion of conceiving Harry's child during that humiliating encounter had never occurred to her. Now that Sophy had mentioned the possibility, Angela paled at the thought. Harry had made it abundantly clear that he wanted no heir from his wife, a mere commoner. Jeremy was his heir, he had said. Jeremy was a true Davenport; no tainted blood ran in *his* veins. Harry had not actually said that, of course, but it was obvious he had been thinking it. Angela remembered all too well the arrogant tone of his voice, as he stood there in her father's morning room and harshly rejected the notion of setting up his own nursery.

He had meant it, too, she thought, for he had made no attempt to claim his marital rights. It was all her fault that he had finally done so, prompted by that stupid dare she had thrown in his face. How could he have avoided it? she wondered. And now, what if Sophy were right, and she was carrying Harry's child? No, it simply couldn't be true, she argued. She refused to believe it, because if it was true, Harry would be utterly furious with her, and she couldn't bear it. She shuddered at the thought of Harry's anger.

"Well?"

Angela realized that Sophy was regarding her quizzically, waiting for confirmation of her suspicion. "No, of course not," she stammered. "How absurd you are, Sophy."

"Harry does not know? Why haven't you told him?"

Angela stared at her in astonishment. "I meant that you are wrong, Sophy. I am not increasing. And I do wish you would not upset me with your freakish starts. Remember, I have a headache."

"Fustian!" Sophy exclaimed. "I don't believe a word of it. I shall have to ask Harry if you will not tell me the truth, Angela."

Angela's mind raced wildly, searching for a way out of this impasse. "If you do anything so foolish," she replied after a brief pause, "Then I will not invite you to come up to London with me next week."

Having made the spur-of-the moment decision to go up to London to seek refuge with her father again, Angela wondered why she had not thought of it before. The truth was, she admitted to herself as she supervised the packing of the single trunk she intended to take with her, that she felt at home here, at Castleton Abbey. At least, she had felt at home until that night when her illusions about her marriage to the Earl of Castleton had fallen in shards about her feet.

The Earl of Castleton, she mused, adamantly rejecting the dress she had worn to the Steeles' ball, which Clothilde was holding up for her inspection. She had never thought of Harry as the Earl of Castleton, but always as Major Davenport, the dark soldier with the slight limp who had at first repelled her and then—she could not precisely put a finger on the reason—made her change her mind and accept his suit.

"No, Clothilde, not that one," she said firmly as her dresser hesitated, the green Italian taffeta ball gown still in her hand. That was one gown she never wanted to see again. Angela realized, since it reminded her too painfully of that evening in the summerhouse. She would cut it up and make cushions with it, or put it up in a trunk in the attic to be used by future Davenport generations for fancy-dress balls. Jeremy's grandchildren, perhaps. Certainly not hers. The notion that Harry had deliberately excluded her from the future generations of his family depressed her and gave her a feeling of being deprived of something vital, something that mattered to her. Her poor Papa would be deprived, too, she thought. The memory of his disappointment that Harry's arbitrary announcement of her interesting condition had been premature was still fresh in her mind.

Perhaps if she had seen him for the titled aristocrat he really was back then, she would not be in this uncomfortable predicament now, she reasoned. Because that was exactly what had happened; she saw it all clearly now. The man who had come to her room that night had been the arrogant Earl of Castleton, a man she would never have married had she not been blinded by the sight of a soldier and a young boy who had—or so she had thought at the time—actually needed her.

She sighed at the unsuspected complications that rash decision had engendered. One would think that she might have learned her lesson from Roger's perfidy, but the distress she had suffered at his hands paled in comparison to the distress Harry was putting her through. Perhaps in London, back in the safety of her father's house, among those who loved her for what she was and not merely tolerated her for what she could give them, she might find an answer to this terrible sense of worthlessness which had invaded her.

In spite of this eagerness to find relief for her aching heart,

Angela found little pleasure in the journey up to London, and had it not been for the presence of Sophy, bubbling with enthusiasm over her second visit to the metropolis in less than six months, Angela might have entertained second thoughts about leaving the Abbey.

When John Coachman finally drew up before the house in St. James's Square, dusk was falling, and Angela felt a surge of nostalgia for the carefree days of her girlhood. This feeling was intensified by the warm reception she received, first from Higgins, whose craggy face broke into a wide smile at the sight of her, and then from her father, who came out of his study to discover what all the commotion in the front hall was about.

"Angela, my pet!" he exclaimed, enveloping his daughter in a bear hug that set her elegant fur bonnet askew and brought a warm flush of happiness to her pale cheeks. "Why didn't you let us know you were coming, sweetheart? Mrs. Higgins will be all atwitter when she hears we have two extra plates at the dinner table."

"Nonsense, Papa," Angela smiled. "You know what Mrs. Higgins's idea of a small family dinner is. She could probably feed twenty of us without running short of anything." She gazed up at her father lovingly, warmed by his unrestrained show of welcome. She had sorely missed this demonstration of feeling which had been the rule rather than the exception in the Walters' household. "Oh, Papa. I have missed you so," she murmured, her voice breaking.

"Now, now, my lass. None of this missishness if you please," he exclaimed, his eyes suspiciously bright. "I must welcome our dear Sophy, here," he added, advancing on that young lady, who had been observing them quietly. "I know Julian will be disappointed that he was not here to receive you, my dear."

"Oh," Sophy murmured from the depths of her host's welcoming hug. "Mr. Scarborough is not here?"

Mr. Walters chuckled at the disappointment in Sophy's voice. "Never you fear, my dear. Julian will be home in time for dinner. But I know he would rather have been here to welcome you back to London."

Angela did not fail to notice that Sophy blushed rosily at

these words, and it occurred to her, not for the first time, that perhaps her young sister-in-law was developing a *tendre* for Julian. The suspicion increased when Sophy slipped into her room while she was dressing for dinner to beg Angela to help her fix her blond ringlets into a more sophisticated arrangement.

"Why, Sophy," Angela could not resist the urge to tease. "Your hair looks so beautiful in those loose ringlets fastened with a bow."

"But it is so childish to wear one's hair loose," Sophy pouted. "I want to put it up in a more stylish chignon."

"That's too old for you, dear. Ask Clothilde if you don't believe me."

"I am no longer in the schoolroom, Angela. And what is the use of having a modish new gown," she cried, gesturing at the pale blue figured silk she wore, "if I'm am not allowed to put my hair up?"

"There will be plenty of time for that when you have your come-out next spring, my love," Angela said soothingly. "By then you will be eighteen and a proper young lady."

"I'll be eighteen in December," Sophy replied stubbornly. "And that's barely a month away. So why do I have to wait until spring to wear my hair up? I want it up now. *Please*, Angela."

"Why this sudden interest in growing up, dear?"

Sophy blushed and twirled around in front of Angela's cheval mirror. "To show off my new gown, of course, silly."

Clothilde caught her mistress's eye in the dressing room mirror and smiled knowingly. "I think Mam'selle is correct, my lady. This gown is too lovely to wear with her hair hanging down her back like some ragamuffin. I will fix it for you, Miss Sophy, if you wish."

Angela had to admit that when Clothilde had finished with her, Sophy looked every inch the fairy princess in her pale blue gown over a darker underskirt, a light shawl of gossamer blue wool over her shoulders, and her hair caught on top of her small head with a sapphire clip and falling in a halo of pale gold ringlets about her face. She was, Angela thought, the epitome of the fashionably fair lady of quality, and she wondered if Julian would be suitably impressed.

She did not need to worry. After a crushing hug and a brotherly kiss on his sister's cheek, Julian turned to greet their guest, and Angela could see that, much as he tried to hide it, he was not only impressed; he was enchanted. It was only later, after the gentlemen joined the ladies in the drawing room, that Julian came and sat beside Angela and said, quite pointedly, that he found her pale and not her usual radiant self. And although Angela tried to fob him off with innocuous excuses, she caught her brother's speculative gaze on her several times during the evening.

Angela wondered how long she could keep up this masquerade of happily married wife when it became evident to Julian and her father that she had run away from her husband again.

A fortnight later, when a severe rainstorm had forced the ladies to postpone a shopping expedition in Bond Street planned for that morning, Angela was sitting with an unopened book in her lap, gazing vacantly at the stream of raindrops sluicing their way down the window of the library. In the billiard room across the hall, amid much laughter and teasing, Julian was initiating their guest into the intricacies of the game. Angela could clearly hear their murmured voices from where she sat in the window embrasure. She knew that she should, for the sake of propriety, be sitting with Sophy and her brother in the billiard room, and every time a burst of Sophy's laughter floated across the hall, Angela told herself that she simply must make the effort to be more sociable. But each time her limbs refused to budge, and the tartan rug wrapped warmly about her knees to keep out the raw November chill seemed to contribute to her inertia with its soft weight.

The sound of the library door closing behind her jerked her out of her semi-somnolent state, and she turned her head to see her father advancing across the room towards her.

"Papa?" she greeted him in surprise. "I thought you had gone down to the warehouse early this morning. Julian tells me you are expecting a ship in from India this month. I am so looking forward to showing Sophy all the treasures once they are unloaded." Angela suddenly realized that she was babbling nervously and that her father was looking at her keenly, a worried frown on his face. "Is anything wrong, Papa?"

"Yes, my love," he replied, a slight smile belying the severity of his tone. "There is something wrong with my dearest daughter, and I want to know what it is. Julian has noticed it, too, in spite of your protestations to the contrary. I refuse to be fobbed off with another Banbury story, my dear. So you may resign yourself to telling me exactly what has you blue-deviled, Angela, for I will not leave until you do."

As Angela stared at her father, she felt a wave of tenderness constrict her throat. If she were not careful, she would become a veritable watering-pot, and that would never do. She forced herself to smile and saw instantly that her father was not to be fooled so easily. But she tried, anyway.

"It's nothing, Papa. Really."

"Balderdash! You cannot deceive your old father, child. Remember, I know you too well, my dear. Now, stop this nonsense and tell me what is bothering you. Is it the dowager again?" When Angela shook her head, he continued. "Then it must be Harry, my love. You can tell your father, you know. What has he done this time?"

Angela lowered her eyes and shook her head. She did not trust herself to speak.

Mr. Walters cleared his throat. "Remember that men are not perfect, my love. Even the best of us often appears clumsy and unfeeling. Your dear mother, bless her soul, made me realize that before we had been married a month. But we can learn, if you will only be patient with us. I know Harry holds you in very high regard, sweetheart, because he told me so himself last time he was here. And he was so happy at the prospect of starting his nursery—almost as much as I was, for that matter. And I do realize what a great disappointment it was to both of you when that didn't happen."

Angela's eyes flew to her father's face at this reminder of Harry's glib but deceptive explanation of her previous flight to London. She barely managed to choke back a sob, and tears threatened to blur her vision. Part of her longed to unburden herself on her father's willing shoulders; she knew that his plain common sense would ultimately find a way out of her dilemma. On the other hand, she knew that she could never reveal, even to her dearest Papa, the true nature of Harry's accusations and subsequent behavior. No, she told herself firmly, this was a burden she must bear alone. The thought caused a tear to spill over onto her clasped hands.

"So that's it, is it, my love?" her father said, sitting down beside her on the window seat and putting an arm around her. "I thought it might be. Another false alarm, is that it? Well, you must be patient, my pet. What has it been, now? Barely four months since you were married. These things sometimes take time, Angela. And you must not blame yourself, dear. You will only make yourself sick, if you have not done so already."

"Oh, Papa," Angela wailed, suddenly unable to resist letting some of the pain out. "I feel so awful!" She buried her face in her father's smoking-jacket and was subtly comforted by the familiar smell of his favorite tobacco. What harm would it do, she thought recklessly, if he misinterpreted the reason for her unhappiness? Right now she desperately needed the comfort her father could give her. His misunderstanding had made this possible.

He patted her shoulder reassuringly. "There, there, my pet. It's not the end of the world, you know. I will ask Sir William Burton to come in and take a look at you, sweetheart. At the very least, he can corroborate what I have just told you, that these things take time."

Angela raised her head at her father's words. "Oh! No, Papa," she insisted, trying to compose herself. "There is nothing the matter with me that a few days of rest here in London cannot cure. There is no need to call in a physician."

"A few days of rest in London?" Mr. Walters laughed. "You have already been here over a fortnight, Angela, and you have shown no signs of improving. In fact, you seem to be more blue-deviled now than when you arrived, which is not like you at all. No, my girl. You will see Sir William as soon as I can engage his services. Humor me in this, love."

More than willing to please her father, Angela finally agreed to a visit from the eminent Harley Street physician, although privately she considered it a waste of time. Better than anyone, she knew what was wrong with her. It was not her body at all, she thought impatiently, but her heart that needed repair. And how could any doctor, even one as prominent as Sir William, cure the aches and pains of love? Only one man could do that for her, Angela knew, and now he seemed to have cut himself off from her irrevocably. Nothing remained between them except the bittersweet memories of an impossible love.

Three days later, Angela discovered that she was entirely wrong; there was much more between herself and Harry than she had imagined. Sir William's bluff, good-humored confirmation of this fact caught her so unprepared that she refused to believe her ears.

"I beg your pardon?" she said, staring up at the doctor in alarm.

"Yes, you heard correctly, Lady Castleton. Your condition is entirely normal for a young married lady." He snorted with merriment at his own witticism. "There is absolutely nothing wrong with you that nature will not take care of in due course. Approximately eight months from now, if I'm not mistaken." Again his braying laugh burst on Angela's astonished ears.

"I am delighted to be the first to congratulate you, my lady," he added with boisterous good humor. "So glad to be able to give you these good tidings."

Angela listened to the good doctor's hearty laughter fade as he wished her good day and disappeared into the hall, closing the door sharply behind him.

16

Harry's Angel

For the entire first week after Angela's departure for London, Harry tried to pretend that his wife's absence made no difference at all to him. When the weather permitted, he went about the estate with Crofts, his tireless bailiff, making seemingly endless lists of repairs that still needed attending to, herds that should be replenished, and farm machinery needing replacement or repair after the recent harvest activities. He was also drawn into making plans for crop rotation and seed purchases for the spring planting. While none of these activities absorbed him as they had during the first four months of his return to Castleton Abbey, at least they kept his memories of Angela at bay.

In the evenings, however, as he sat over his solitary meals in the silent dining room, those memories returned to plague him. As he stared down the long table at her empty chair, he could visualize her sitting there in one or another of her elegant evening gowns, her black hair curled about her shoulders, her expressive gray eyes regarding him quizzically, her mouth curved in a gentle half-smile.

Impatiently he pushed his plate aside and took up the letter from Sophy which had been waiting for him on the hall table when he returned that afternoon. It was the second he had received since she had gone up to London with Angela, and her cheerful news of the entertainment the two ladies were enjoying in the metropolis did nothing to relieve his morose mood. Although the Little Season was in full swing, Sophy pointed out, with all the nonchalance of a seasoned member of the *ton*, they had attended very few soirées and only two musicales given by Angela's distant relatives, which turned out to be dreadfully boring. They had, on the other hand, she informed him, cut a swath through the fashionable modistes on Bond Street, whose contributions to her wardrobe she proceeded to list in elaborate detail. The name of Julian Scarborough figured prominently in his sister's recital of their activities, and for the first time Harry envied the younger man the opportunity of escorting Angela around London.

At the bottom of the letter, almost as an afterthought, Sophy mentioned that Angela was still feeling poorly and that Mr. Walters had decided to call in the famous Sir William Burton to examine his daughter. When was Harry coming up to London? his sister wanted to know. Didn't he miss them at all?

Harry carried the letter into the library with him, where he had taken to retiring with a bottle of brandy after dinner. Miss them? Of course he missed them—more than he cared to admit. And the news of Angela's ill health disturbed him. Of course, she had claimed ill health for days after that fateful night he had tried so hard to forget, but he had always thought it merely a ruse to avoid him.

By the end of the second week of this bachelor existence, Harry was seriously considering admitting defeat. Even the company of Jeremy, whom he had taken to inviting down from the nursery to share his evening meals, failed to lift his spirits. As the days dragged relentlessly by, he began to wonder how he had ever been such a fool as to imagine that he was indifferent to Angela's absence. Not only was he definitely lonely without her, but he missed the deft manner which she had adopted with the dowager when that lady took it into her head to dine at the Abbey.

The dowager had taken Angela's absence as an excuse to visit the Abbey more frequently than usual. After the fourth evening of coming home to find his mother waiting to vent a torrent of venomous gossip into his ears, Harry gave instructions to Jaspers to inform her ladyship that he would not be dining at home. As a result of this evasive action, Harry received a blistering missive from the dowager, informing him that she considered his behavior unnatural in the extreme. She summoned him, in a tone that brooked no argument, to dine with her the following Sunday evening and hinted that she had a pleasant surprise in store for him. He should have known better, of course, than to believe that his mother's idea of a pleasant surprise would be pleasant to anyone but herself. And he realized his mistake as soon as he strode into her drawing room to find that the Woodalls had been invited to make up a cozy party, as the dowager insisted on calling it.

George he was glad enough to see, but Matilda's presence angered him. His former betrothed's blond perfection and limpid blue eyes, which regarded him reproachfully, seemed suddenly cloying rather than charming. With something of a start, Harry realized that his taste in women had changed radically since those days, which now seemed so long ago, when fair Matilda had been his ideal. As the two men sat over their port after a prolonged meal during which the dowager kept up a steady flow of cutting comments about all her acquaintances, and the fair Matilda said little or nothing, Harry chided his friend for not warning him.

"Matilda insisted that, as your friends, we should support you during this trying period, old boy," George explained.

"What trying period are you referring to?" Harry snapped, an uneasy suspicion that his mother's hand had been at work here crossing his mind.

George coughed nervously and looked uncomfortable. "The rumor is that . . . I mean, your mother assured us . . . oh, the devil take it, Harry. We thought that Angela had left you. Run away, you know. Done a bunk, as they say. The dowager told us that you needed a little cheering up, lad, and that Matilda might help you. For old time's sake, you know."

Harry felt his face grow rigid with fury. After a long pause, during which George grew increasingly uneasy, Harry spoke through lips that were taut with anger. "Well, you are mistaken," he said softly, fighting a rising urge to wring his mother's neck. Abruptly he stood up. "The past is over, my friend, and your sister, of all people, should know that. You may make my apologies to the ladies for not joining them tonight."

He had left after that, riding back to the Abbey at break-neck speed, anxious to distance himself from those false ru-mors that his mother had made it her business to spread. And, of course, they were false, he told himself repeatedly. Angela had not left him; she would be back as soon as she had tired of London. She would bring back her smile, her sense of humor, her vital energy and enthusiasm that had begun to turn this stodgy old ancestral pile into a home.

The thought of Castleton Abbey becoming a real home was suddenly immensely appealing to Harry. It had never been a home to him, in the true sense, when his father was alive. But with Angela it would be possible. The realization of what he had almost destroyed with his unfounded suspi-cions and stiff-necked pride alarmed him. On impulse he told Jaspers, as the butler helped him out of his greatcoat in the front hall, that he would take his brandy upstairs in his private sitting room tonight. He would make it up to her in every possible way, he thought, taking the stairs two at a time and leaving Jaspers gaping after him in amazement. He would erase the painful memory of that dreadful night and show her what love and tenderness he was capable of. He no longer doubted that he was capable of it. Four short months ago, if anyone had suggested to him that he would experience such excitement at the thought of his own wife, he would have laughed them to scorn. But now, as he opened the door to their sitting room, the faint scent of her perfume which lingered there made his pulse race.

He stood for several minutes staring at his wife's closed bedroom door. Before he realized what he was doing, he strode forward and flung it open. Her perfume was stronger here, but the wave of cold air from the unheated room daunted him. His euphoria subsided. What had he ex-pected? he asked himself bleakly, suddenly conscious of the old ache in his thigh, unused to such boyish exuberance. For a brief moment, the kind of scene Harry wished he had played out with his wife that night flooded through his mind with all its tantalizing nuances. But he was too late, he thought. Angela was gone. A sudden fear gripped him and caused him to stride over to his wife's wardrobe and fling it open. A sigh of relief escaped him, and he felt himself relax. She would not have left all these clothes behind if she were not coming back, he reasoned.

A gleam of red in the candlelight caught his attention, and he reached out to touch the velvet softness of Angela's dressing gown. The sensuous warmth of the material triggered a longing so intense that Harry groaned aloud. As he stood there, enveloped in bittersweet memories of his wife's presence and the dawning awareness of what her absence meant to him, Harry heard Jaspers stoking the fire in the sitting room behind him.

Without fully considering the ramifications of his sudden decision, Harry knew what he must do. "Jaspers," he called out, softly closing his wife's wardrobe. "Send a message to the stables that I will be needing the curricle and four at first light tomorrow. I'm going to London."

Angela had not particularly wished to attend the theatre that evening, but Sophy had so wanted to see the famous Mr. Kean playing Shylock at Drury Lane that she allowed herself to be convinced that she would enjoy the outing. No sooner was she ensconced in her seat, however, than she regretted her decision. Before the lights were dimmed and the curtain raised, she had caught a glimpse of Roger Hyland sitting at his ease beside the opulent Lady Cullen in a box directly across from her father's. A sardonic smile slowly curled his well-shaped lips as their eyes met.

The play, which Angela had begun to look forward to, lost much of its attraction for her. She found herself questioning, as she never had during her many readings of Mr. Shakespeare's work, the intolerable arrogance of a father who would dare to risk his daughter's happiness on what was essentially a guessing game. Who cared if the candidate for her hand made the right choice of caskets if his love were true? she wondered. What if some quite impossible mushroom, or miserable squeeze-crab, or even a shocking libertine and rakehell like Roger were to choose the lead casket and win the prize? She shuddered at the thought, although she could hardly imagine Roger choosing anything but the golden casket and being reminded, as the Prince of Morocco was even at that moment on stage, that:

> All that glisters is not gold;
> Often have you heard that told:
> Many a man his life hath sold
> But my outside to behold.

The reference to a man selling his life for gold reminded her inevitably of Harry, and Angela wondered if her husband's black moods had anything to do with the fact that he had been forced into accepting a marriage of convenience to a tradesman's daughter. And what else was that, she thought sadly, but selling his name for the gold he needed to restore his beloved estate? She had not been as lucky as Shakespeare's heroine, Angela had to admit. The man who came to win her hand and fortune, as the bankrupt Bassanio had come to win Portia's, had not loved her. Nor had she loved him, at least not at first. But now Angela felt her heart swell with grief and longing as she listened to Portia's second suitor, the Prince of Arragon, chastised for choosing the illusory bliss in the silver casket:

> Some there be that shadows kiss;
> Such have but a shadow's bliss.

Yes, she realized with sudden clarity, that was all she had enjoyed as Harry's wife. *A shadow's bliss.* Was that all she was destined to have with the man she loved? Or perhaps not even that much, if Harry reacted as she fully expected to the news that she was carrying his child. As Portia's third and only true love came forward to make what everyone knew would be the right choice, Angela felt the tears well in her eyes and cursed herself for her weakness. She wished that she had her own choice to make over again; she would be wiser, she thought, oh, how much wiser she would be if only she could push back the clock to that summer morning when the taciturn Major Harry Dav-

enport had walked into her life. She would send him packing, wouldn't she? Of course, she would.

Her attention returned to the stage, where the lovers were
finally confessing their love for each other. As Portia
spoke, her passionate words seemed to take on a special
significance for Angela, as the distraught young woman
sought to express the inexpressible anguish of loving:

> *One half of me is yours, the other half yours,*
> *Mine own, I would say; but if mine, then yours,*
> *And so all yours. O! these naughty times*
> *Put bars between the owners and their rights;*
> *And so, though yours, not yours. Prove it so,*
> *Let fortune go to hell for it, not I.*

Angela felt as if those impassioned words were coming
straight out of her own heart. How incredibly true, she
thought. And what a ninnyhammer she was to imagine that,
given a second chance, she would reject her Harry. She was
his, as Portia was Bassanio's, body and soul. There was no
going back. She must never give up trying to tear down the
bars between them instead of helping to build them. Angela
saw it all clearly now; she never should have left the
Abbey, never left her husband to the mercy of the beautiful
Matilda. After all, Harry's accusations were false, weren't
they? She was innocent, and he knew that now beyond any
doubt. Why, oh why, had she run away? There was only
one thing to do now, she saw that clearly. She must return
to the Abbey, to Harry, and confess, as Portia had done, her
true feelings and trust that she could find the Harry she
knew to exist beneath the callous exterior of the Earl of
Castleton.

The rest of the evening went by on leaden feet. Angela
thought she would shriek with frustration during the inter-
minable trial scene, and Portia's clever arguments were
quite lost on her. Even during the intermission, when Roger
had the temerity to wander nonchalantly into her box to pay
his respects to his beloved Angela, as he called her in low
tones, bending mockingly over her hand, she remained

aloof from the boisterous chatter around her. All she could
think of was her return to the Abbey. She would leave tomorrow, she thought, dismissing a disgruntled Roger more
curtly than she was wont to do. She would start packing
tonight, she decided later, as Julian handed the two ladies
into their carriage and jumped in to sit beside a radiant
Sophy.

By the time they drew up before the house in St. James's
Square and were ushered into the warmth of the hall by
Higgins, Angela was quite determined to take whatever
steps were necessary to achieve a measure of stability and
contentment in her marriage. With any luck, she thought
optimistically, the child she carried would be a girl, and
Harry would be saved the embarrassment of having a Cit's
grandson for his heir. And she could have a little daughter
of her own, Harry's daughter. The thought gladdened her
heart and made her cheeks glow radiantly.

"Motherhood seems to agree with you, my love," Julian
remarked affectionately, as he helped her remove her fur-
lined cloak. "I disremember the last time I saw you in such
good looks. Wouldn't you agree with me, Sophy?"

"Why, yes indeed," Sophy responded, giving Angela an
impulsive hug. "I am quite in ault about it myself, if you
must know the truth. I can't think of anything more excit-
ing. I do so envy you, Angela."

Angela laughed at this naive and quite inappropriate enthusiasm from a young unmarried lady. "Your turn will
come, dearest. Just be patient," she could not resist teasing,
and was surprised to see the intensely proprietary gleam in
Julian's eyes as he gazed at their guest.

A stab of something very close to envy pierced her heart.
This is how it should be, she thought. If only Harry could
be brought to countenance this match between his sister
and her brother. She sighed, unwilling to speculate on the
happy outcome of such an unlikely event, and turned toward the stairs, more than ever determined to seek a prompt
encounter with the major.

"My lady," Higgins addressed her as she set her foot on
the first step. "The master would like to see you before you

retire, my lady. He instructed me to ask you to join him in the library if you are not too tired."

Angela was far from tired. Her decision to return posthaste to the Abbey had made her previous lethargy evaporate. She had intended to let her father know of her plans at the breakfast table tomorrow morning, but she could do it now just as well. She thanked Higgins, who preceded her along the hall to the library, tapped discreetly, and opened the door.

The library had always been Angela's favorite room, and now, as Higgins ushered her in and closed the door softly behind her, memories of all the happy hours she had spent with her dearest Papa in their private sanctum came crowding back into her mind. The familiar smells of well-worn leather, old books, and her father's pipe tobacco assailed her nostrils and made her nostalgic for those carefree days of her youth.

Her father had risen when she entered, and she advanced towards him across the dimly lit room, her hands out in welcome. "Whatever are you doing sitting here alone in the dark, Papa?" she exclaimed teasingly. "Let me ring for Higgins to bring in some more candles."

"No, daughter," he replied, bending his tall frame to kiss her cheek. "There is no need for more light, and I am not alone, my dear."

"Of course, you're not, silly. For I am here with you." She regarded her father anxiously. "What were you thinking about while you sat here by the fire, Papa?"

Mr. Walters looked amused. "I was thinking about you, Angela. About you and Harry. And my grandchild, too, of course. Granddaughter, I should say," he corrected himself with a chuckle. "Because I have that same feeling I had before you were born, my dear. I knew your mother would have a baby girl."

"Speaking of Harry, Papa," Angela began, anxious to have her father's approval for her plan, "I have come to a decision tonight. It came to me while I was listening to Portia's suitors play that silly game with the caskets. I know exactly what I want to do about Harry."

Did she imagine it, Angela thought, or did the laughter fade from her father's eyes, to be replaced by an unaccustomed somberness? In the dimly lit room, she could not be certain.

He cleared his throat and took both her hands in his. "I know you will not act rashly, my dear. And that any decision you make will be fair. Now, tell me what you have decided to do about Harry."

Angela smiled up at him, perturbed by the gloomy tones of his voice. "Nothing to be so blue-deviled about, Papa," she laughed. "I have decided to go home tomorrow. Home to Harry, that is. He has much to answer for, that's true, but in spite of everything, that's where I belong."

She saw his face break into a happy grin. "That's my girl," he said, his voice charged with emotion. "I am heartily pleased to hear it, love. And I can tell you now that Harry is pleased to hear it, too.'"

Angela looked at him in surprise. "How can you possibly know that?"

"Why, by the grin on his face, for one thing, lass," he replied, glancing over her head and giving a broad wink. "What do you say, Harry? Am I right or not?"

With a gasp Angela spun around. She blinked. Harry was indeed here in the library with them, leaning against the sideboard, a glass of brandy in one hand. Even as she stared at him, unable to utter a word, he put the glass down, strode purposefully across the Axminster carpet, and took both her hands, suddenly as cold as her heart, in his strong grasp.

He looked down into her startled eyes for a long moment before a smile flickered across his face. "What? No word of welcome for your husband, Angela?"

Angela let out a small sigh and lowered her eyes to their joined hands. This couldn't be happening, she thought, and felt her heart palpitating unevenly. "Welcome, my lord," she heard herself say in a stiff little voice she hardly recognized as her own.

"My lord?" he repeated. "Whatever happened to Harry?"

"I would like to know that, too," she blurted out before stopping to think.

After a brief pause, during which she felt his fingers tighten on her own, he said in a strange, almost faltering voice, "I need to talk to you, Angela. There are so many things I need to say to you, my angel."

Angela felt the room sway around her. Here it comes, she thought miserably. *My angel,* he called her. But she, better than anyone, knew that he didn't love her, that Matilda was his true love. He was only being so polite to her because Papa was here, but he really wanted to ring a peal over her head. She could feel the tension building in him; his fingers trembled with it, and before much longer it would all explode around her head. As if in a dream, Angela heard her father's voice.

"In that case, I'll leave you with Harry, my dear, and join Julian and Sophy in the drawing room," Mr. Walters said happily. "If I know anything about these matters, as indeed I do,"—he winked at her—"they must be in need of a level head right about now to restrain their youthful impetuosity."

A wave of panic swept over her. "Oh, no! Papa, please don't leave on my account," she exclaimed, trying not to sound as desperate as she felt.

"Nonsense, girl," he laughed. "I can tell when I'm *de trop,* as your Clothilde would say. Have your talk with Harry, child. Wasn't that your purpose in going back to Kent tomorrow? He has saved you that long journey, my love, so the least you can do is let your husband have his say."

As she watched her father leave the room and heard the door close behind him, Angela wondered if he had any notion of the real nature of the "talk" her husband wanted to have with her. No, of course not, she thought, or he would not sound so cheerful. Her reverie was broken by the warm pressure of Harry's lips on her fingers. He had bent to kiss them lingeringly, and the sight of his dark head so close to her exposed bosom caused a frisson of erotic delight to run through her. Quickly she jerked her thoughts away from this dangerous ground. The warmth of his lips was intoxicating and somehow reassuring. This was the first kiss he had given her since that night in the summerhouse when she had unwittingly kindled that intensely passionate response in her husband and discovered, to her dismay, that her own desires were far less ladylike than she had imagined.

Resolutely, Angela tried to put the memory of that night—both the good and the bad—out of her mind, but something nagged at her. She knew now that she could forgive Harry almost anything; she wanted to forgive him—indeed, in her own heart, she already had. But for the sake of her own peace of mind—and yes, her pride, too—she needed to know that their erotic encounter, that precious moment of shared passion in Lady Steele's summerhouse, had not been intended for another woman. She had to know. For some obscure, irrational reason, her whole future as Harry's wife hung on this tenuous thread. Angela knew, as surely as she knew that she loved him, that if she were to find contentment for herself in Harry's house, if not in Harry's heart, she would have to put the strength of that thread to the test.

Harry had raised his head and was looking down at her with a strange gleam in his eyes. He seemed unable to say whatever it was he had wanted to say to her. "Is anything wrong, Angela?" he said unexpectedly.

"Why, yes," she burst out before her courage failed her. "I was wondering if you would have kissed Matilda in the summerhouse that night." There, she thought, it is out in the open now, and she held her breath, half wishing it had remained unsaid.

Harry looked startled and then he grinned. "Your father is right, my love, you *are* an angel. But he was also right to warn me that you would stand for no roundaboutation, so my answer to your question is a definite *no*. I would not have kissed Matilda then or at any other time, nor have I done so since I went into the army six or seven years ago. Even when I came home for my father's funeral two years ago, she was in no danger of being kissed by me. And still less now that I have you, my sweet."

Harry was looking at her with such warmth in his sapphire eyes that Angela felt the color flood into her cheeks. This was not the answer she had expected. Even in her wildest fantasies, she had never imagined such a confession from her husband's lips. For the second time that evening, she wondered if she were dreaming.

"Now you, my love," he continued in a voice that had deepened noticeably, "are a different matter altogether." He raised her fingers again and regarded her intently as he held them against his lips. "Offhand, my dear, I would say you are in imminent danger of being kissed. I have a secret weakness for angels."

Angela's gaze, which had been fixed in fascination on her husband's lips moving lazily over her fingers, flew up to meet his.

"That is," she heard him add softly, "if you can ever bring yourself to forgive this old gudgeon of a husband of yours for behaving like an utterly contemptible sapskull. There is no excuse for what I did, Angela, and Lord knows, I've tried to find one. It must have been the thought of that rogue Medford following you out there—"

"But I didn't know he—"

"Hush, my love. I know you didn't. I was a brute to doubt you, and I don't deserve to be forgiven, but your father advised me not to retreat just yet. The field was not lost, he assured me. He's quite a man, your father, my love. I only hope he was right in thinking you might be willing to forgive me." He paused for a moment, regarding her with such tenderness that she lowered her eyes in confusion. "Can you, Angela?"

A lump had begun to form in Angela's throat during this unexpected speech, and it occurred to her that Harry and her father seemed to have formed a new alliance destined to undo her. An affirmative answer to Harry's question trembled on her lips when she suddenly recalled the other matter that had to be resolved before she could be comfortable as Harry's wife.

"Can you forgive *me*, Harry?" she murmured.

The major looked at her in surprise. "Forgive you, my sweet? I have nothing to forgive you for, you silly goose. Whatever gave you that idea?"

"But you're forgetting the child, Harry. I know you never wanted . . . You told me that . . . well, that Jeremy was your heir. I'm so sorry to disappoint you like this, but—"

"Disappoint me?" he exclaimed so sharply that Angela jumped. "Now you are being a goose, sweetheart."

"But you said—"

"I know what I said, Angela. But please believe me when I confess that I have said and done some dashed addle-pated things in the last four months, dearest. I should have known when I first met you—" He stopped short and gazed at her, a dawning comprehension in his eyes. "Even back then, I should have known how it would be. And fool that I was, I thought I could fight it."

Angela was thoroughly puzzled. Nothing about this interview was going the way she had imagined. "What should you have known?" she demanded.

Harry laughed, and the sound made Angela's heart skip a beat. "I should have known that you, my sweet innocent, would be my final defeat, my Waterloo, so to speak. As a seasoned soldier, I should have seen that I was outmaneuvered right from that first skirmish. Do you remember it? You accused me of being uncouth, and indeed I was. But I just refused to admit it until . . ." He paused and drew a deep breath before continuing, his eyes never wavering from hers. "Until that night I was so sure I was the victor but turned out to be vanquished by your innocence, Angela. Can you ever forgive me, love?"

"Tell me why you are not angry about the child, Harry. My father told you, didn't he?"

"Yes. He wrote me as soon as he knew, but I must have left Kent before his letter arrived." He reached out to cup her chin in his hand. "I wish you had told me, Angela."

"I thought you would be angry with me."

"I shall be extremely angry with you if I'm not the first

to know about our second child, Angela. I can promise you
that right now."

Angela gasped and turned a bright pink, quickly lowering her lashes to hide the surge of joy that she knew must
be reflected in her eyes.

"I have promised your father to call this one Sylvia after
your mother. I certainly can't imagine calling her Augusta
after mine, poor thing. We have decided, your father and I,
to call the next one after him if it's a boy, George Harold.
How does that appeal to you, my love?"

"Oh, you have, have you?" Indignation at this high-hand-
edness from her two most favorite gentlemen made Angela's gaze snap up, gray eyes sparkling dangerously. "Was
I not to be consulted at all, my lord?"

Harry looked at her in surprise, his fingers still in firm
possession of her chin. "But you are being consulted, my
dear. I was under the impression that I just asked you how
George Harold sounded to you. George Harold Davenport,"
he repeated, apparently savoring the sound of his unborn
son's name. He brushed a feathery kiss on the tip of her
nose. "What do you say to that, my lady?"

"Are you quite sure this is what you want, Harry?" Angela murmured breathlessly, acutely conscious that her husband's left hand had somehow come to rest lightly on her
hip, then meandered up her tingling back and down again
to encircle her waist. As if of its own accord, her body
swayed against his, and she felt his arm tighten to hold her
in the curve of his tall frame.

"Oh, absolutely, my sweet. This is exactly what I want."
His breath was warm against her hair, and the masculine
smell of him was doing odd things to the muscles in her
knees. "At least, we might say it is *one* of the three things I
want at this moment," she heard him whisper close to her
ear, the rich quaver of amusement in his voice causing her
to tremble with excitement.

"And the second thing?" she murmured, her nose inches
from his simply tied cravat. His right hand, she suddenly
realized, had released her chin and was now tracing a tingling path down her cheek, stopping a moment to explore

her ear, then making its leisurely way down her neck and across her bare shoulder. The effect was mesmerizing, and Angela wished the caress would go on forever.

He cupped her chin again and raised her head so that she had to look directly into his eyes. "I want you to forgive me, Angela. If you can't forgive me, nothing else matters." His voice was low and intense, and Angela noticed that his expression was serious and vaguely apprehensive, as if he feared her rejection. Her heart went out to him, and she knew, before she had time to consider the consequences, what her answer would be. Portia's words came back to her: *One half of me is yours, the other half yours.* There was her answer. *And so all yours.* How could she not forgive the man she loved? she thought, lowering her lashes to hide the truth she was not quite ready to confess.

"Tell me you will, sweetheart," she heard him whisper, his lips now hovering inches from her own. Angela wondered at the new note of triumph in his voice. She had wanted to draw out this delicious moment of suspense for as long as possible, but he seemed to have already guessed what was in her heart. Then she noticed, with something of a shock, that her arms were entwined about Harry's neck in the most immodest manner imaginable. He must think her a wanton creature indeed, she thought, not at all troubled by this possibility. She raised her eyes and smiled at him, feeling an answering chuckle from deep inside his chest, pressed so intimately against her.

"If I do, would I be in that imminent danger you mentioned?" she ventured to ask with a daring she had not known she possessed.

Harry's smile broadened into a devilish grin. "No doubt about it, my love." She felt his arm tighten about her waist. "Care to put me to the test?"

As Angela gazed up into her husband's brilliant blue eyes, she knew that whatever invisible barrier had separated them had crumbled. Harry loved her. He had not said so, as Mrs. Radcliffe's dashing heroes invariably did, with improbable outpourings of violent passion, at the close of her novels. But Angela did not want an artificially romantic ending to her own love story; she wanted it to be real. And the woman in her knew, without having to be told, that Harry's love was real, and that before the night was out, he would give her all the proof she needed. She smiled at the thought of the delicious intimacies she would set in motion with her answer to his question. Yet she hesitated, savoring this moment of feminine power over the man she loved.

"Well?" Harry's mouth had descended again, and she could feel the warmth of his breath on her eager lips. "Do you or don't you want to be kissed, minx?"

"Yes," she said, savoring the moment of surrender much more than the teasing suspense. "I certainly do."